GLITTERATI

Also by Oliver K. Langmead
and available from Titan Books

Birds of Paradise

GLITTERATI

OLIVER K. LANGMEAD

TITAN BOOKS

Glitterati

Print edition ISBN: 9781789097962
E-book edition ISBN: 9781789097979

Published by Titan Books
A division of Titan Publishing Group Ltd
144 Southwark Street, London SE1 0UP
www.titanbooks.com

First edition: May 2022
10 9 8 7 6 5 4 3 2 1

This is a work of fiction. All of the characters, organizations, and events portrayed in this novel are either products of the author's imagination or are used fictitiously. Any resemblance to actual persons, living or dead (except for satirical purposes), is entirely coincidental.

A CIP catalogue record for this title is available from the British Library.

Printed and bound by CPI Group (UK) Ltd, Croydon, CR0 4YY.

For Ross

Wednesday. Or was it Tuesday?

"Georgie, darling?"

"What is it, dear Simone?"

"Is it Wednesday, or Tuesday?"

"It's Tuesday today."

"Did we not have a Tuesday yesterday?"

Georgie paused, to consider. Then, she said, "No, dearest. We had a Monday yesterday. I recall it being Monday quite clearly, in fact, because Gabriel was wearing a beaded Savinchay dress, and as you well know, it would be outrageous to wear beads on any other day of the week."

That settled it, then.

Simone unpeeled his face from the pink leather chaise-longue. Last night had been a rainbow of cocktails, resulting in the headache now threatening to impinge on his usually immaculate poise. He went across to the gold-plated Manchodroi dresser, which he only ever used on Tuesdays, and was astonished to find that his usual dose of painkillers was gone.

"Georgie!" he cried.

"What is it, Simone?"

"My medicine is missing!"

"Have you checked the Manchodroi dresser?"

"I have opened the very drawer in which my Tuesday dose is stored, and that drawer is quite empty. Might you have accidentally taken them?"

"Certainly not."

"And you're absolutely sure today is Tuesday?"

"I'm positive, dearest Simone. I was just reminiscing about Galvin's outfit at the gala last night – he wore that beaded Crostay gown of his, and it quite took my breath away. I am absolutely, one hundred per cent certain today is Tuesday. Could it be you've misplaced your medication?"

"Well," said Simone, uncertainly. "It could be. I remember very little of last night."

"Use the supply we set aside in the upper left cupboard of the wardrobe in the guest bedroom. And do get ready. You have work in two hours, and it would be simply awful were you to arrive too late."

This was true. It being a Tuesday, it would be the talk of the office were Simone to arrive at work anything more than twenty minutes late. Simone quickly rushed through to the guest bedroom and rooted around in the wardrobe, locating the spare painkillers. He went into the guest bathroom and spread the white powder across the shining surface beside the mirrored sink, which was inlaid with diamonds, and then proceeded to snort it all up in one go. The drugs fizzed in his brain, and his headache began to recede.

"Superb," he said to his ruffled reflection. "Most delightful."

Tuesday, then, which meant wearing white to work. Simone returned to his own bedroom and searched through his walk-in wardrobes for his white suits: the first, a close-fitting number from Messr Messr; the second, a looser but tastefully trimmed alternative from Karrat; and lastly, his brand-new white suit, made with a freshly invented meta-material infused with light-emitting micro-LEDs from Karpa Fishh, which was at the very forefront of fashion technology. Still not feeling quite himself, Simone settled on the understated Messr Messr suit, and laid it out while he got to work on his face.

Tuesday was a pale day, so he decided to use his collection of Flaystay cosmetics, which were designed to really bring out one's bone structure. He began with a three-point washing formula followed by some moisturiser, and cleared it away with some body-temperature water. Then, he moved on to his foundation, applied with his silky-soft Karrat brush set, and finished up with a layer of ivory-white powder. The powdering done, he blended some of his grey blushers together and began to highlight the shape of his skull, applying liberal shadows to the space beneath his cheekbones. Then, once his face was perfectly skull-like, he began to draw out his eyes with his eyeliners and eye shadows, until they were quite the centrepiece of his face. Running his fingers along his collection of Dramaskil false eyelashes, he selected a white pair speckled with a dusting of black powder, and proceeded to affix them to his eyelids. These, he finished off with a little mascara, just to really bring them out. Finally, he settled on a light grey lipstick, applying it carefully to avoid staining his vividly white teeth.

Pouting to make certain all was in place, Simone sealed his face with some Grantis Granto makeup fixer – spraying it liberally to make certain nothing would slide off during his busy day ahead.

Face affixed, Simone pulled on his Messr Messr suit and tightened his tie.

Two forty-five already? Simone hastened through his home and air-kissed his wife. She was still wearing her pyjamas and sat at her own dresser, gently rubbing moisturiser into her skin; Tuesday was her day off, and she would be spending the majority of it maintaining her complexion. Admiring himself in the hallway mirror, which was framed with bulbs bright enough to reveal every single possible flaw in the beholder, Simone felt satisfied. He left for work.

* * *

Unfortunately, Simone's route to work took him above the streets of the city suburbs, where the poor unfashionables lived.

The windows of the pristine vibro-rail carriage revealed the depths below, where the houses were made for practicality instead of design. They looked, to Simone, like terrible parodies of the packaging some of his least fabulous items of clothing came in.

The uglies. The unwashed, unmanicured masses. The unfashionables.

It pained him to see them down there, milling around without the first idea of how dreadful they appeared. Their untrained aesthetic senses were so underdeveloped they could barely comprehend their own hideousness. To think that they did actual labour! To think they used things like shovels and wrenches and drills! Simone shuddered, but found himself unable to look away. The horror of it drew him in completely.

It was unfathomable that people existed like that.

The vibro-rail carriage slipped through a tunnel, and suddenly he was there, at the heart of the horror, where beyond the unornamented fences the unfashionables lumbered around. If only Simone's tear ducts hadn't been removed – why, he would have wept for them. Feeling his gut squirm around inside him, he watched them go by, bumping into each other, smiling their unpainted smiles, staring open-mouthed and lustily at the vibro-rail train as it swept past: at its contents – the beautiful glitterati.

To think that they were the same species. It boggled the mind.

Simone secretly hoped the unfashionables would all catch a disease and die. Of course, it wasn't fashionable to think such thoughts. The fashion was that the uglies were to be pitied, and charity in the form of discarded past-season wardrobes was a sign of good character. But Simone only said he sent his old wardrobes down to the unfashionables. In reality, he burned his clothes when he was done with them. The mere thought of his discarded clothes touching the skin of any of those aesthetically impaired creatures made him feel ill.

So caught up in horror was he that Simone barely noticed the vibro-rail gliding to a halt. As he stood, he realised he had been alone in his carriage, and was the only one leaving the train.

The vast and crystalline Tremptor Tower rose ahead, and Simone felt his heart lift. It was like working in heaven – those fluted glass cylinders, which made the whole building look like an enormous celestial organ, always made him smile. He was careful with his smile, of course. It simply wouldn't do to affect his face before making his entrance.

He checked his watch. Precisely twenty minutes late. Perfect.

There was a queue at the front entrance, and the instant Simone set his eyes upon it he felt his heart stop. Every single man and woman in the queue was wearing purple.

What could it mean? Had he missed an issue of one of the one hundred and sixteen different fashion magazines he was subscribed to? Holding a hand delicately to his chest, Simone felt as if he should flee. But it was too late. He was already caught up in the queue. And those behind him…

Simone risked a glance backwards. Open mouths and wide eyes. Horror.

Maybe it was a joke. Maybe everyone in Tremptor Tower was in on it. Maybe he would make his entrance and everyone would applaud and laugh, and he would laugh with them, and they would all drink champagne and reminisce for years to come about how delightful the jest had been.

The queue moved forwards. Then, it was Simone's turn.

Throwing his shoulders back, Simone sashayed inside.

Absolute silence. The hands poised mid-clap to receive him were completely still. The long red runway felt endless, but still he sashayed on – eyes on the horizon, lips pursed. Not a single camera flashed. But there, at last, his salvation: the steps leading off the entrance runway and over to the lifts. He would have run the last few metres, but not a single drop of sweat had been shed in Tremptor Tower since its construction, and he certainly wouldn't be the first to desecrate the hallowed ground.

Inside the lift, Simone pressed the button for the fifty-sixth floor with one shaking finger. Everyone around him was wearing purple. They kept glancing at him, but he kept his eyes down, studying the elevator's intricately designed carpet.

What could have happened? What had gone wrong? Unless… Simone's eyes grew wide.

What if it wasn't Tuesday after all? What if it was actually *Wednesday*?

The implications were unbearable. Was he to spend the entire day unfashionable? Wearing all white when it was a complete faux pas to be in white on a Wednesday? But what could he do? Possibly, he could phone his wife and get her to bring a spare outfit. But then – what about his face? The Grantis Granto makeup fixer would be solid for at least the next eight hours.

Eventually, the elevator arrived at the fifty-sixth floor.

Simone power-walked the final few steps into his office and shut the door behind himself. Using the glass misters, he crystallised the walls so that they were opaque, and sat down behind his three-tier desk. He would simply have to hide in his office all day. If anybody came knocking, he would claim to be in a meeting. It was the done thing, after all. An actual meeting had not occurred in Tremptor Tower since its creation, but to use being in a meeting as an excuse to not meet people was polite.

He would have to get creative in order to bide his time. Nobody in Tremptor Tower actually did any work, after all. It would have been a dreadful waste of the mind. Work was for the unfashionables, who could afford the brainpower.

Simone took a deep breath. It would be all right. He would simply read magazines all day. Selecting the latest *Gentlemen's Art* from his desk, he flicked between the pages and eventually began to relax. It would be fine. Only a few people had seen him, after all. He would laugh it off tomorrow. They would all laugh it off, and drink champagne, and it would be a funny anecdote.

It was good to catch up on the newest fashions, anyway. They tended to move quite quickly, and magazines were the most efficient means of keeping track.

There came a knock at the door. "Simone?" It was Darlington.

"I'm in a meeting!" he cried, hiding behind his magazine.

"But, Simone, you simply must come out. It's Trevor Tremptor! He's come to see us."

How dreadful! Simone had still been operating under the assumption that it was Tuesday, when it was in fact Wednesday, and on Wednesdays Trevor Tremptor, fashion icon and head of the Tremptor Company, liked to mingle with those on the fifty-sixth floor of his tower. Simone was mortified. This could mean embarrassment before the whole company. Worse – this could mean demotion.

Trembling, Simone stepped out into the corridor and stood before his door.

Everyone else was lined up, all dressed in purple. As soon as they set eyes on him, there were gasps. White? On a Wednesday? It was outrageous.

There was Trevor Tremptor now, air-kissing each of his

employees in turn, and offering little compliments. Everyone blushed the correct amount, and blinked in deference. Trevor himself was so incredible to look upon that it hurt Simone's eyes. Had ever a more fashionable being existed? Simone wanted to disappear into the carpet.

At last, Trevor Tremptor arrived before Simone. There was a long silence. Everyone was holding their breath.

"Simone…" said Trevor carefully, but Simone couldn't meet his gaze. He kept his head down, so ashamed of what he was wearing. "Simone…" said Trevor again, and Simone closed his eyes, waiting for the guillotine to drop. "That… is… *fabulous*."

* * *

Simone was invited to luncheon up on the ninety-ninth floor of Tremptor Tower, where the company's most highly regarded fashionistas worked.

The offices he passed were bursting with poised statues and intricate pieces of useless electronic equipment, and even the stacks of blank paper were of top quality – a creamy white watermarked with this month's Tremptor logo. Simone kept his chin high, doing his best to pretend he was not in awe of the people he passed.

The luncheon was set up on tiered silver trays with leafy greenery dripping from the edges, making them seem like waterfalls of food. The tiny sandwiches balanced upon the trays were identical triangles, and each slice of cucumber glinted with precisely the correct amount of moisture, so as to suggest a crispness of texture without compromising on juiciness. The slices down on the fifty-sixth floor never looked quite so artfully arranged. Beneath the trays were small white porcelain plates, also marked with this month's Tremptor logo, and beside them was an array of silver forks so well polished that Simone could see himself reflected in them. For a brief moment, Simone was horrified by his reflection – his pale face looked so *bloated* – before realising it was the shape of the fork distorting the image.

Of course, nobody was eating anything; there were too many perils involved. Simone imagined finding a crumb on his suit, or a smear of butter on his cheek, or, worst of all, a piece of lettuce stuck between his teeth, and shuddered.

"White on a Wednesday?" said a voice. "It's simply incredible! Unheard of. It's so subversive. The irony of it, and the precision of it."

A woman in purple was posing beside a portrait of Trevor Tremptor. It was a well-chosen spot because she was being complemented by the sunlight currently cascading across the portrait (which was lending Trevor a celestial mystique).

"Thank you, darling," said Simone, as was customary, and he shared an air-kiss with the woman. He caught a little of her scent during the kiss, and it lit up the corners of his mind.

"You smell like a garden on fire," he said.

"Very perceptive," she said, with a wink that rained purple glitter down her cheek from her dusted lashes. "It's an exclusive Karpa Fishh blend. He cultivated a floral greenhouse over a period of twenty years, then burned it all in one go and bottled the scent. Beauty and destruction. Only a hundred bottles exist."

"Simply marvellous."

"You must be Simone," she said, running her purple talons across the collar of her dress. The dress shimmered with the movement, the sequins acting like the scales of a fish, and Simone found himself staring at the colours, absorbed in their aesthetic finery. "The office is simply *abuzz* about you. I," she said, gently running those same talons across the back of Simone's hand, "am Justine."

"It is splendid to meet you," said Simone. He was suddenly very aware of the place he was standing – an awkward, unaesthetic place somewhere between the table and the portrait, with one of his shoes in the gush of daylight that illuminated Justine so ethereally. Glancing around, he attempted to quickly locate a better place in which to pose.

The room was full of fashionistas, all of whom seemed to have found perfect places. There was a man holding a plate of uneaten sandwiches, staring wistfully out of the broad windows, his face positioned to cast intricate shadows across his jaw from his extraordinarily sharp cheekbones, and there was a woman perched at the edge of a stool beside the door, her face arranged to make it seem as if she were amused by a private joke, and there was another man at the head of the table, where the overhead lights converged, with the back of his palm against his forehead, as if in an agony of indecision about where to eat his luncheon, and all of them were so brilliantly posed that Simone felt the panic rising inside him. If he did not find somewhere to stand, he would embarrass himself when Trevor Tremptor arrived.

As if sensing his panic, Justine gracefully stepped aside. "Here," she whispered, her purple lips close to his ear. "You take the light. It will complement your paleness."

With tremendous relief, Simone stepped into the daylight beside the portrait, feeling its warmth wash over him. Justine was right; the sun made his suit and his skin glow, and Simone instantly felt radiant, as if the light was coming from somewhere inside him. He quickly relaxed into a casual pose, arching his brows and pouting to make himself look thoughtful.

Without hesitation, Justine swept across to one of the potted plants nearby, which was tall and currently flowering pink. The flowers served to complement the purples of her dress, and she arranged herself to make it appear as if she were deeply absorbed in the scent of the plant, but Simone knew she had given up a superior place for him.

Trevor arrived in another gust of aesthetic superiority that made Simone feel unworthy, as if his very bones were arranged in unpleasing, ugly shapes. Trevor went from fashionista to fashionista, this time shaking hands and even smiling a little – an extraordinary expression that did nothing to crack his cosmetics, which said a lot for his skill. Simone only ever allowed himself at most three smiles a day; any more might compromise the integrity of his face. Eventually, Trevor made his way over to Simone and shook his hand, enveloping it in a grip so soft yet firm that Simone felt as if Trevor's hand might be that of God himself. Then, in a rush of empty words that Simone barely registered, Trevor was gone. Everybody in the room seemed to relax.

"There," said Justine, gliding across. "I think you pleased him."

"Do you think?" Simone straightened his collar. Of course, his collar was already straight, but the gesture was considered a polite way of expressing nervousness without risking such dreadful things as wrinkling one's brow.

"Yes," she said. "I think you are extraordinary, Simone. Tell me – if I were to invite you to a little soirée this evening, would you say yes? I simply must show you off to my friends. There may even be a few magazines present – searching, as they do, for the latest in fashion news. I dare say your outfit may make some headlines."

An invite to a party from one of the company's most prolific fashionistas? "Of course!" he cried, perhaps a little too loud. Recovering himself, he tried again. "Of course, Justine. I would be delighted to attend. May I bring my wife?"

Justine parted her lips in a smile that did not reach her eyes, which was probably wise because it might have affected the eyeshadow darkening them like purple bruises. From between her painted lips, pearly teeth emerged. "Of course. I would be honoured to meet the spouse of such an innovative fashion icon," she said.

* * *

The interior of the stretch limousine yawned out before Simone. He had tried to put as much distance between himself and its unfashionable driver as possible, but there was no escaping the fact it was still there, sat beyond the darkened partition. It was a wonder that the limousine, its every curve harmonious, its very length ostentatious, did not just open its driver-side door and vomit out its hideous chauffeur like a half-eaten meal. In fact, Simone imagined he would much rather see a vomited-up meal than endure the sight of the person sat behind the wheel of his car.

Of course, Simone was aware that the uglies were everywhere in his life. All the food had to come from somewhere, after all – and from time to time rooms did need a little redecoration in order to keep up with the latest trends. The uglies were usually very good at remaining out of sight, however, hiding away in their little alcoves and cupboards and such until everybody worth anything was gone and they could emerge, oozing into the light in order to maintain the lives of their betters. Simone enjoyed never having to think about them. The problem with the limousine was that he knew precisely where the wretched creature was, and what it was doing.

"Simone, darling?" Georgie was lounging across the dark leather seats nearby, a fluted crystal glass of something bubbly and golden fizzing between her fingers. She had cleverly opted to wear a pale suit of her own – a Messr Messr number that was just at the very edge of purple and might, at a stretch, be described as pink – in an effort to maintain the Wednesday fashion but also complement Simone's own radically white attire. She had also slightly shadowed the underside of her slender jaw (a feature that Simone was most proud of in her) to make it as sharp as a knife, and thinned her lips to make them appear almost as deadly. Her hair was swept up above her, the same shade of light purple as her suit, and to Simone it looked like a swirl of blue candyfloss with a drop of blood mixed into it.

"Yes, dear heart?" he replied.

"You seem distracted."

Simone realised he was slouching, and quickly straightened himself, snatching a fizzing glass of his own from the counter, inhaling deeply of it and letting the bubbles tickle the insides of his nostrils. "Did we remember to alter the limousine's exterior?"

"Of course we did, darling." The limousine's chassis was equipped with colour-changing panels, allowing the owner to accessorise their car. For tonight's event, Georgie had arranged the vehicle to be pearlescent, swirling between pearly white and glittering pink, so that when she and Simone stepped out it would complement their outfits. Simone breathed a sigh of relief, rippling his fizzy drink.

"Truth be told, dear heart, I am a tad nervous."

"You do seem…" Georgie shifted her pose, leaning towards him. "…a little frayed."

"Frayed?" Simone almost choked.

"Not to worry. I have something to help." Opening her Vladstang leather clutch, which was studded with tiny pink gemstones that flashed in the limousine's interior lighting, Georgie retrieved a small pink tin and unscrewed it, revealing a mound of white powder. "An electric blend, or so I'm told."

"Oh, marvellous. I do love you so, Georgie."

"And I love you, Simone."

From his inner jacket pocket, Simone retrieved his straw, which was made of ivory to match his outfit. Carefully twisting it up one nostril (so as to leave his face undisturbed), Simone lowered the other end into the powder and began to inhale. He inhaled for a long time, until almost half of the powder was gone, and the limousine's interior shone with a new light, as if all the tinted windows had been rolled down to let the sunset in. Only then did he unscrew the straw from his nose and sit back, sniffling slightly while the powder did its work. "It is, indeed, electric," he said breathlessly.

Georgie inhaled the rest of the powder herself, in delicate little snorts.

At last, the limousine came to a halt, and Simone and Georgie emerged into the light. It proved to be an opportune moment, because the sunset was blushing a soft pink that really set off Georgie's attire and the limousine's panelling, and even served to soften Simone's suit. If anybody had been around to behold their exit from the limousine, Simone imagined they would have applauded and taken pictures, but, as luck would have it, the driveway outside Justine's house was filled with cars instead of people. Of course, there were the drivers of all the cars, hidden in their seats and no doubt admiring the illustrious arrival of Simone and Georgie, but Simone did not count them because they were all ugly.

Simone beheld the other cars. Of course there were a fair few limousines, each with its own set of adjustable panels, today set to varying shades of purple, but there were other cars as well – sleek sports cars, heavy muscle cars, and even faux-vintage vehicles, featuring not colour-changing panels but chrome so polished there seemed to be a whole other sunset taking place across them. Simone and Georgie spent a while standing before a particularly shiny example, admiring themselves together, and Simone felt a strong surge of affection for her; the way she complemented him with her every movement. Why, together they were more striking than the sky.

Another sunset was taking place across the house itself, which was not mirrored but set to mimic the magnificent view behind it, rendering its façade transparent. Disembodied windows hung on the horizon, and the front doorway stood at the precipice of the sharp cliff overlooking the city, as if one might step through and plummet down to the streetlights below (which were only now emerging in tandem with the stars in the sky). Simone felt a rush of vertigo as he approached the doors, which stood open to reveal the house's interior – a palatial space brighter than the blushing sunset.

This was the most fabulous party Simone had ever been invited to.

The mirrored entrance hall hosted a thousand Simones and a thousand Georgies moving in perfect synchronicity, making their advance a dance, all of their mirror selves dancing along with them. Through an open side door was the cloakroom, and Simone slipped his jacket from his shoulders, attempting to find a vacant hanger along the racks. Everywhere he tried, a magnificent coat was already hanging; there were so many extraordinary designs crammed together that by the time he found a place, he was feeling giddy.

Triumphant, Simone turned to see Georgie, who was weeping.

Georgie was stood beneath one of the overhead lights so that the brightness of it splashed over her, making the parts of her capable of glinting glint. From her clutch she had taken a tiny bottle of tears (sourced, no doubt, from only the cleanest unfashionables) and had dripped several into her eyes to make them fill and glisten. Currently, there was a single droplet running down her face, rolling from the precise centre of her left eye. Georgie was a well-practised weeper, and Simone felt another rush of pride. Nobody else wept quite as beautifully as Georgie. "The furs!" she cried.

Simone turned and took stock of the racks hosting the furs, and they were so outrageously thick that they bulged outwards, as if they were competing with each other for the spotlight. There were a great many creatures he recognised – pink zebras, and purple cheetahs, and scarlet mink, each bred using the finest of fashion technology to bear the most luxurious coats imaginable – but there were some he did not. One particular specimen caught his eye, and he approached it warily, running his fingers down the pink-tinged fur.

"The hide of a polar bear," Georgie whispered, as if she was afraid of disturbing the fur by speaking too noisily in its presence.

Simone was aghast. "This looks new! I thought they were extinct?"

"Very nearly, darling."

Simone brushed the soft fur against his face. "I have never seen it in pink before."

"I read about it in *Fur and Fury*. The bear is very carefully exsanguinated over a period of weeks so that its own blood gently dyes its coat."

"Such suffering!"

"Isn't it just *exquisite*?"

It was indeed exquisite. In fact, there were so many exquisite coats on the racks that Simone once again found himself feeling a wobble of nervousness. "Georgie, darling?"

"Yes, dearest?"

"Do you have any more of your electric powder?"

"A touch." She presented the remains of the tin to him, and he rubbed his finger around the rim, massaging every last particle into his gums. The powder gave him a little buzz that made him feel as if someone had switched on a spotlight in his brain, and he spent a moment inhaling and exhaling deeply, feeling his nervous wobble subside.

"Are you ready, dear heart?" enquired Georgie, her eyes sparkling with the remainder of her tears. There was still a trail of moisture down her cheek from the tear that fell, and she had placed a purple rhinestone at its point of termination beside her lip.

"I am, Georgie. Will you hold my hand?"

"Always."

Hand in hand, they entered the party.

The runway was a rich purple carpet so brightly lit that it felt as if several suns shone upon it. At the head of the runway, Simone struck his finest pose: splaying his fingers at his neck, and turning his chin up and slightly to the right, to cast a complex series of shadows across himself with his fingers. A spotlight burned into his retinas, but he ignored the pain and continued glaring up at it, assured that the brightness was doing some rather marvellous things to bring out the whites of his eyeballs.

Simone felt the catwalk music tremble up through the base of his feet and into his veins, arteries and heart. This month, it was fashionable to play catwalk music at precisely one hundred and twenty beats per minute, which suited Simone very well because he was comfortable synchronising his heart rate to it. There had been a fashion, a few months ago, for music played at one hundred and eighty beats per minute, which had always left him breathless at parties. In fact, a great many of his friends had suffered heart attacks that month, which was very unfashionable indeed. Focusing on the burning white spotlight, Simone felt a small thrill as his heart synchronised with the beat. He was ready to make his entrance.

Justine had been kind enough to arrange for Simone to arrive last of all. It was an honoured position, especially at such a fabulous gathering as this, so Simone delivered his very best poses as he sashayed down the runway to the beat; all those special stances he had been saving up for an event as esteemed as this. Beside him, Georgie synchronised her movements to his, so that both of them moved in a gorgeous, flowing dance of beauty, their heart beats matching the beat and each other. Together, they moved from spotlight to spotlight, caught up in the splendid rhythm of the catwalk.

The applause was almost loud enough to be heard over the music. Simone, temporarily blinded, could not see beyond the drop at the edge of the runway, but no doubt beyond stood all manner of remarkable fashionistas, rapt at the display. This was his moment, he knew, and he felt electric in his radical white attire, as if he was brighter than any of the spotlights gushing over him. Why, were he to simply keel over and die at the end of the runway, Simone would consider his life a success, having culminated in such a moment as this.

Then there was the end of the catwalk, and the steps leading down to the party.

The music continued unabated, so loud that nobody could hear anybody else, but that didn't matter. Simone moved among the glitterati and understood them better by their outfits, gestures and the particularities of their poses than any words might ever be able to convey, and right now they were telling him he was *fabulous*. It was in the way they arched their brows and angled their heads to look at him; it was in the way they tugged their cufflinks in his direction, and held their hands over their hearts, and regarded him through the lengths of their eyelashes; and it was in the way they had accessorised, choosing small pale touches for their outfits – perhaps a ring with a pink stone, or a small pink flower looped into a lapel – to honour his choice of white for the day.

The ballroom was mirrored, making the party appear endless. There were chandeliers above, composed of twists of crystal that cast complementary light over the entire room, making it so that anyone might strike a pose anywhere without worry of their immediate environment clashing with their outfits. Small tables stood everywhere, upon which pyramids of fizzing champagne glasses gleamed, untouched by all, and at the feet of those delicate pyramids were silver trays laden with piles of white powder, heaped so lavishly that a little haze rose above each powder mountain. Every now and then, a fashionista would delicately huff up a considerable amount, and yet there was so much of it that it seemed as if none of the mountains would ever be reduced to hills.

Taking his straw and carefully rolling it up one nostril, Simone leaned over and took in a steady stream of powder himself. The spotlights still burned in his eyes, so he snorted more than he was usually comfortable with, until every part of him tingled and the spotlights began to fade. Thus electrified, he spent a few moments admiring Georgie as she, in turn, inhaled a sizeable quantity of powder, turning her eyes slightly upwards so that she would appear in a state of elegant rapture while imbibing her fill. When she was sated, Simone took her by the hand again, and the two of them sauntered through the party, exchanging pleasantries with all they passed by offering appreciative glances and eyebrow raises.

There were a few photographers present, fashionable in their own peculiar ways. Simone always liked to see them – the way they crowded their heads with lenses that gleamed wonderfully no matter the lighting – but he was always a little afraid of them as well. There were some magazines that took delight in ridiculing the unfashionables, and from time to time one of Simone's friends would be implicated in a dreadful scandal by one of them: exposed wearing the wrong kind of cravat, or captured standing in an ill-lit corridor, or, worst of all, caught wearing something out of season. *Flash flash flash* went their cameras, immortalising the illustrious glitterati, and Simone did his best to look as if he were paying them no attention at all.

Through the party Simone strutted, searching for its host.

After a while wandering the tables, and enjoying copious amount of white powder, it became apparent to Simone that Justine was not present. This was most peculiar, and it was reflected across the poses of the party. People tilted their heads, and held themselves at angles that denoted curiosity and anticipation, and Simone felt himself falling into the same arrangement, keeping his chin close to his shoulder as if glancing over it, in case she might somehow appear behind him, and walking in slow loops around tables, as if she might always be hiding somewhere along its far edge. Perhaps, Simone thought, she had left already? It was plausible that someone as fabulous as Justine might have left her own party early, in order to attend an even more exclusive event elsewhere.

Suddenly, the music stopped and the room was plunged into darkness.

There were ripples of little gasps, and the gentle tinkle of crystals. A single spotlight snapped on, highlighting the far end of the room with dazzling white light, where a tall, white staircase met a mirrored wall. New music began, but this was not the precise one hundred and twenty beats per minute that Simone had synchronised his heart to – no, this music was orchestral, and flowed from the staircase, as if making an announcement. Without the rhythm of the beat, Simone felt his heart jostle in his chest, leaping about inside him with all manner of nervousness. It was most unbecoming.

At the head of the staircase, the mirrored wall slid open and Justine emerged.

She looked like a perfect corpse.

Justine was wearing a white cotton dress designed with a mastery that utterly defied its unadorned simplicity; though the dress was undecorated, and made of an apparently inferior material, it drew the eye across its subject in a way that lent it a poetic rhythm, flattering her wonderfully. So too was her face decorated: intricately designed to make it look as if she wore no powders, or creams, or liners, or lipsticks at all. This, combined with the way she had rendered the pallor of her skin a ghastly ivory, had the effect of making her look dead. Why, the shadows under her eyes – she might have passed away mere moments ago!

The response from the party was ecstatic. The applause was loud enough to drown out the orchestral music, which Simone only now realised was a dirge. Hundreds of exquisitely manicured hands met, serenading her descent to the party below, the spotlight following each step. And she wasn't even wearing any shoes! She padded down on bare feet, her manicured toenails exposed for all the world to see, and her audience began to cheer, convinced, just as Simone was, that she might have just stood up from a mortuary slab.

Cameras flashed everywhere.

Simone realised his fists were clenched at his sides, and was hasty to correct his mistake. Were he to not applaud Justine, he would be seen to be ungrateful for the honoured arrival time she had given him. So, clenching his teeth together, he began to clap, trying to slow his heart, which was beating furiously against his ribcage.

Sensing Simone's discomfort, Georgie took him by the arm and whispered in his ear, "Simply marvellous, isn't she?"

Retaining his composure, Simone hissed back through his teeth, "She *upstaged* me."

"Yes, darling. But this is her party."

"She *upstaged me*, by using *my look*, and *doing it better than me*."

With Justine's descent complete, the lights came back on and the thumping one-hundred-and-twenty beats per minute music resumed. Georgie gently towed Simone to one of the quieter corners of the room, where there was a long bar at which all manner of fabulous people were mixing rainbow cocktails. Simone usually enjoyed cocktails – he liked the way the colours of them ran together, no doubt rendering his interior just as fabulous as his exterior when he drank them, staining his stomach with all their vividness – but he was finding it difficult to concentrate on anything. Nobody was paying him any attention, he noticed; all eyes were turned instead to the party's host. Simone had been forgotten.

Taking a cocktail in each hand – after making certain their colours complemented his and Georgie's attire – Simone strolled out beyond the doors at the end of the bar and on to the veranda. The veranda was open to the sky and constructed with the same panelling as the rest of the house, making it look as if the swimming pool was floating in mid-air. So too did it seem as if Simone strolled, god-like, high above the city; the hideous masses crawled in the dirt below, while the glorious glitterati walked on air. At the edge of the veranda Simone sipped at his cocktails and felt his heart flutter.

Above, the stars glittered, and below, the city glittered.

There was a full moon tonight, and while it was fashionable to admire the moon, Simone secretly hated it because of the way it was pock-marked and asymmetrical, resembling the faces of the dreadful uglies who never bothered to correct any of their natural deformities. Indeed, the veranda was lit by a selection of superior pale globes, suspended above the swimming pool, and they had no such scars and craters inflicted upon them. Simone glared up at the moon, draining his cocktails and imagining, in delicious detail, throwing Justine off the edge of her own veranda.

Georgie emerged from the shadows with a silver tray, heaped so high with white powder that a little drifted from the edges. "Here, darling," she said gently. "A little something to raise your spirits. You were wonderful tonight. I promise."

"Was I?"

"The applause for your entrance still rings in my ears."

Simone placed his empty glasses upon the edge of the tray and retrieved his straw from his inner pocket, using it to inhale powder until it began to sting his throat. Then, he continued to inhale, gulping so much powder that the world turned bright and swirled around him. Only when his vision began to wheel did he stop, almost choking when he took a step back. Georgie steadied him with an arm. "Darling?"

"Wonderful," said Simone. "Simply wonderful."

There was something about the way the light of the globes suspended above the pool refracted through the gently rippling water that attracted Simone, and he wandered across, delighted at the glowing patterns. Standing at the very edge, so that the tips of his shoes almost, but not quite, touched the water, Simone began to feel better.

A drop of something dark fell into the water.

The black liquid, whatever it was, began to spread out like ink, and Simone watched it in horror, unable to draw his eyes from the tentacle-like extremities of it, spreading like an infection. There was a small splash as a second droplet fell, and then a third, mingling and intertwining and staining the pool with darkness. Watching those dreadful droplets dissipate, Simone began to feel dizzy, as if he might topple over and into the pool himself, dissolving like one of them.

"*Simone!*" It was Georgie. She sounded panicked. Dragging his eyes from the horror of the pool, Simone turned to see her aghast, eyes wide, hands raised in horror, as if she might have to hide herself from the sight of him.

It was then that Simone felt the wetness on his upper lip. Dabbing a finger experimentally at it produced the same black liquid that had fallen into the pool. Hardly daring to breathe, Simone glanced down at his suit, and saw there were droplets of it everywhere, smearing it with darkness. "Georgie?" Simone was suddenly terribly afraid.

"Your nose." Her voice trembled. "It's *bleeding*."

Being foolish enough to wear something unfashionable could result in the subject being ostracised and mocked almost indefinitely. Accidentally wearing a past-season wardrobe was enough to warrant exile from polite society. But having an actual *bodily fluid* drip out of your nose and stain your suit? Why, it was worse than unheard of. It was mortifying! Simone knew he would never be able to show his face again.

He glanced about, splattering his shoulders with more of his own blood. Luckily, it didn't look as if there was anybody else out on the veranda; only he and Georgie were visible. Georgie herself was breathing heavily and doing everything in her power to avoid looking at him, turning her eyes to the moon, the stars, the pool, the city. "Georgie," said Simone. "We must leave. Quickly. Before I am noticed."

"Yes. Yes!" She raised one trembling finger to the darkest corner of the veranda. "There is a back gate! Perhaps we might be able to reach the limousine unseen?"

Quickly, they hastened across. Clear glass steps descended to the dark driveway ahead, where all the cars idled. More droplets of blood oozed down Simone's suit, and he paused momentarily, trying to stop the flow from his nose by pressing his fingers to it. The gesture only served to increase the blood pouring from him, so he removed his hand and flicked his fingers, spraying droplets over the edge of the cliff.

There was a sudden bright flash, and the whir of a camera from somewhere across the veranda. Someone had taken a picture.

Georgie hurtled down the staircase, almost tripping with every step, and Simone followed, trying desperately to maintain his balance through his panic. Then, they were back in the car park, and hastening between all the exquisite vehicles. No doubt the ugly drivers at the wheel of each had witnessed Simone's undignified escape, but it didn't matter if they saw; if they tried to tell anyone about it, they would be summarily dismissed due to their ugliness.

At last, there was the limousine, glowing pearlescent white and pink in the dark, and there was Georgie, swinging the rear door open. Simone dived into the safety of its interior.

There was a stack of serviettes on the drinks cabinet, and even though they were only meant for aesthetic purposes, Simone grabbed all of them and used them to wad his nose. Still too delirious to think properly, Simone laid back against the cool leather of the limousine and let his vision whirl. "Home," he whispered, beneath the tissues. "Take us home."

* * *

Simone ran himself a bath. If there was one part of his apartment he was particularly proud of, it was the bath. Built into the floor of the bathroom, and approximately the length of a small swimming pool, it was his pleasure to pour every manner of cleansing chemical into its considerable depths, until it swirled with bubbles and colours and perfumes so luxurious that Simone would bathe for hours at a time, until he felt as if he were truly clean.

The bath gently filled behind him as he removed his face.

The wipes he used were as gentle as whispers as they worked to reveal his skin. Slowly, and in patches, Simone's own features began to emerge. Nearby, his beloved white Messr Messr suit burned on the open fireplace, turning the flames all kinds of unusual colours with its intricate blend of meta-materials. Every now and then, there would be a little flare of crimson, which Simone assumed was his blood catching light. He had never seen burning blood before, and he found that he was delighted by the little bursts of red – each one heralding another stage of Simone's cleanse.

Makeup removed, Simone moisturised his face. Then, he applied a face mask, taking his time to run it smoothly over every angle of his features, with no tears or bubbles or misalignments, so that once again he was hidden from himself. Finally, he approached the bath, and descended into its depths, feeling the heat of it rise through his feet and legs and up to his heart, and then to his arms and all the way to the tips of his fingers, which tingled with pleasure at the warmth. The red droplets of blood still clinging to his neck and chest were swift to dissipate, dissolving and mingling with all the colours of the water and leaving Simone feeling free, at last, of the dreadful evening. He lounged against the edge of the enormous tub and let himself soak.

Eventually, Georgie slipped in at the other end.

The bath was long enough that they had to shout at each other across it, and Georgie's features, which were also currently hidden behind a face mask, wavered in the heat rising from the waters. "How are you feeling, darling?" she called.

"Much recovered, dear heart."

"I am glad to hear it. You gave me such a fright."

"Thank you for your help. I don't know what I would have done without you."

Georgie did not smile, because smiling might disrupt the placement of her mask, so she swirled at the waters with the tips of her fingers instead. "It was very lucky that nobody saw you."

Simone ran his hands over his skin, as if smoothing down any possible deficiencies in the same way that he smoothed his face mask. "There may…" he began.

"Pardon? Do speak up."

"There may…" Simone tried again, "…have been a photographer."

There was silence from the far end of the bath. Bubbles rose in the air between them, drifted and popped against the tiles. "Darling?" said Georgie, eventually.

"Yes, dear heart?"

"Did the photographer take a picture?"

Simone felt as if he would like to sink into the bath and never emerge again. "I believe so."

Once again, silence from the far end.

"Georgie?" tried Simone.

"I'm thinking, Simone. Be quiet for a moment."

"Of course."

There was a faint splashing. The drip of the taps.

"There's nothing else for it," said Georgie, at last. "You simply must return to Justine's house this instant, and demand to speak to her. She may be able to help you prevent the picture from reaching print."

"Do you think so?"

"I can see no other way."

Simone did not want to return to Justine's house, so he stayed put, hoping the problem might just dissipate like so much of the steam rising from the bath.

"Simone? Did you hear what I said?"

"I did."

"Quickly now."

Reluctantly, Simone stood up. "Very well," he said.

Dragging one foot after the other, Simone returned to the sink and peeled his face mask off. It felt rather like removing a disgusting, cloying layer of old skin to emerge fresh from beneath it. While doing so, he considered what to wear. The fashion when it came to clandestine late-night meetings was for black clothing, which made a lot of sense because it did wonderful things for a figure trying to remain conspicuous but also fabulous.

Right now, there was also a rather interesting fashion for faux-military face paint, which Simone was fond of. He was aware, in an off-hand way, that the uglies did things like form armies to kill each other, which seemed to him like a rather efficient means of culling their numbers, and he liked the way fashionistas had taken an aesthetic element of war and developed it into something far more pleasing to the eye. It was symbolic, he thought, of the way he secretly hoped that the hideous masses would find a way to kill each other off for good.

Wandering through to his walk-in wardrobes, Simone fetched a slim-fitting black turtleneck and trousers by Romain Romain – which were deeply uncomfortable to wear but did some excellent things to the calves of a figure crouched in hiding – and, after some deep consideration, settled on a pair of black military-style boots to accompany them. Outfit ready, he headed to his dresser and applied another layer of moisturiser, then a layer of Flaystay concealer and powder to act as a foundation for his faux-military face paint. Sliding aside his substantial collection of mascaras, he selected a midnight black shade of face paint (from Stephan Kite's Subterfuge collection), and carefully, with the use of a fine brush, applied jagged black patches of camouflage paint, making certain that the distance between each dark shard complemented the others and also the shape of his face. When he was satisfied with the way the face paint broke his features into small, uneven islands of beauty, he sprayed on some makeup fixer, to make sure that none of it would be affected by his clandestine night ahead.

Simone paused to air-kiss Georgie from the doorway of the bathroom, and then snuck down to the garage.

* * *

Simone had the limousine set to stealth mode. This meant that the coloured panels, much like his face, were camouflaged, the limousine made to look sleek and dark and dangerous as it prowled the streets at night. Of course, the limousine remained prominent – the point of the camouflage was not to not be seen, but rather to be seen seeming to want to not be seen. Any observant fashionista happening to glance out of their windows might catch sight of the mirror-dark limousine, and perhaps remark to their significant other about its clandestine aesthetic, praising Simone's choice of chrome and black and dimmed headlights.

Somewhere between the engine and the rear compartment was the limousine's ugly chauffeur, but Simone did his best to ignore that fact, concentrating instead on his cuticles. They were little white arcs, slivers that resembled the waxing moon, and he was going to great lengths to ensure that each of them was smooth using a special little tool developed by Stringham. It had been a long day, of the kind where he had found himself using his hands for more than aesthetic purposes on multiple occasions, and it simply would not do to be anything less than perfectly manicured.

Simone resolved to spend a few days using his hands for little else other than posing. He was rather good at using his fingers to cast aesthetic shadows across himself, after all.

The limousine smoothly came to a halt, and Simone slid from the rear door.

Justine's driveway was completely empty except for her own car, which idled near the gateway. A series of softly glowing white lamps cast pools of light all the way up the rise to the house, and Simone shifted from one to the other, making certain to pause beneath each so that any observer watching him sneak up the driveway would be able to properly appreciate his look. In the shadows between each lamp, Simone moved gracefully, composing himself before stepping into the next pool of light, until, at last, he came to the house proper. Glancing about, he was disappointed to see that the driveway remained empty; it was possible that nobody had seen him sneak up to the house. Still, he supposed, sometimes being seen was not about being seen by others, but about being seen by one's self.

The house was gone.

Rather, the windows and doors that had seemed to hang in mid-air had vanished, revealing instead the open sky with its millions of stars and hideous moon. And it would have been easy to believe that there was no house at all on top of the hill, were it not for the single window still there, suspended alone in the rich, cloudless night. The tall window had a balcony with a black railing, white curtains billowing either side of it, and the light inside was a pleasant, soft white. Simone circled the grounds, in search of the door by which he had entered, but the house's video panelling was too perfect, and he refused to debase his freshly manicured hands by doing something as crude as fumbling around in the dark with them. Imagine!

Instead, Simone stood beneath the single window and cleared his throat.

Time passed, with no response.

Simone cleared his throat a little louder.

A figure emerged from between the billowing curtains. Simone was relieved to see that it was Justine, wrapped in a white dressing gown that looked as if it was made of the fur of the soft inner ears of several hundred snow hares. She had her hair curled up in an intricate knot on the side of her head and she wore a face mask with a particularly pleasing sheen to it, as if she had peeled off the face of a prominent fashionista and placed it temporarily over her own. Behind her mask, Justine's eyes gleamed, just as they had back at luncheon. "Simone?" she called down. "Is that you?"

"It is indeed I, Justine."

"Splendid to see you again. Did you enjoy the party?"

"I had such a marvellous time. Thank you once again for the invite."

"Of course, darling."

There was a brief pause between them. Then, Simone said, "I was wondering…"

"What were you wondering?"

"Were there any pictures taken of me this evening?"

"Pictures? Why, of course! You were quite the talk of the party. I should imagine that your innovative look will be taken up by at least a handful of magazines."

"Quite!" said Simone. "I'm sure. However…"

"What is it?"

"I was wondering. Might you be aware, by any chance, whether there were any… ah… compromising pictures taken of me?"

Justine's face remained poised beneath her mask. "Why, whatever do you mean?"

"I may have… that is to say… there may have been something of a small incident."

"What kind of incident?"

"My…" Simone felt his heart flutter against his ribs. "My nose may have bled, a little."

"I see."

"Could you… I was wondering… could you perhaps, with all of your contacts, find out whether a picture was taken?"

"I could certainly do that." Justine stepped up to the very edge of her balcony. "But what would you have me do were I to determine that such a picture did exist?"

"Well. If it's not too much to ask…"

"Ask away."

"Would you be so kind as to have it destroyed?"

Justine's smile was so slow that it did nothing at all to wrinkle her face mask. "Of course," she said, revealing her lengthy incisors. "Anything for a friend such as yourself."

* * *

The problem with Simone's bed was that it was full of fish.

It was fashionable to sleep on a waterbed composed of a mattress with a clear membrane and filled with all manner of aesthetic aquatic life. There were even quaint little lights along the base of the mattress, to lend the walls of one's bedroom an underwater look, as beams refracted through the mattress's ever-shifting contents. The fish themselves were remarkable specimens, Simone had to admit; all kinds of vivid, exotic creatures, with shimmering scales that would have made him blush with envy were it fashionable to blush (which it currently was not). In fact, for the first few days he had slept quite soundly upon the mattress, lulled to sleep by its gentle wave-like sloshing, and entertained by the flitting of the pretty fishes upon awakening. Once, he even saw a large yellow fish devour a small red fish whole, and was delighted by the way its belly turned orange.

A couple of weeks ago, however, Simone had awoken to witness horror. He had rolled over, taking special care to keep his silken pyjamas immaculately unwrinkled, and set his eyes upon a bulbous pink fish, which looked to Simone like a collection of pink balloons with fins and bulging eyes. The pink fish had made him giggle – it was the way it jiggled about in the water like blancmange. But then, something strange had happened. As it was swimming along, a string of something brown had emerged from somewhere beneath its tail. Simone watched the brown string, watched the way it detached itself from the fish, and then watched as it slowly sank down to the very base of the mattress, where it settled among small glass pebbles. And it was there, among those pebbles, that Simone saw yet more pieces of brown string, slowly disintegrating in the mattress's aquatic movements.

It took him the best part of the day to realise what the brown string was.

Of course, Simone was aware that other people defecated, but it wasn't something he really thought about. Defecation was for the privacy of the bathroom; a simple matter of the aesthetic body ridding itself of unaesthetic waste (except, of course, for those mornings after he had consumed a considerable amount of cocktails, rendering his stools all kinds of interesting colours). Yet, he had never considered that lesser creatures might also defecate. It made sense, of course – he supposed that such beautiful fish must have a means of ridding themselves of ugly bodily detritus – but to be confronted so brazenly by that fact in the comfort of his own bedroom, why, it was unfathomable! To think, all those weeks he had spent lounging upon his fishy mattress he had inadvertently been sleeping upon an aquatic lavatory! Worse, the fish just carried on swimming around in it, and breathing in it, as if they were entirely unaware of the hideousness of their existence, trapped in their private toilet.

Since that dreadful day, Simone had been unable to sleep on the mattress. Georgie still did, of course, and she was there now, curled up in her own set of luxurious pyjamas, which were striped pink and red and made her look like a beautiful prawn. Simone beheld her for a while, considering whether he could face the fishy mattress, but eventually decided against it. For all that it would be delightful to sleep beside Georgie again, he would prefer to wait for a new bedroom fashion to come in – one, he hoped, with considerably fewer fish. So, instead, Simone went to the pink leather chaise-longue, which had become his temporary place of sleep, and curled up on it, doing his best to strike a comfortable yet still aesthetically pleasing pose.

Gently, he drifted away to sleep.

There was a dreadful, but perfectly pitched wail.

Simone opened his eyes to see that it was morning. He knew it was morning because the sun was just starting to come in through the window at an angle that cast fingers of light across the room, as if the sun was brushing its hand across the plush carpet. Simone realised his own hand was currently buried in the carpet and gently removed it, flexing his fingers to get his blood circulating, and casting his bleary eyes about the room, in search of the source of the wail. Thankfully, it appeared to have come from Georgie, and not himself. Simone was proud of his vocal cords, which, he had been told, gave his voice a certain music, and he often worried about putting undue strain on them.

Georgie had flung herself across the wall beside the door, illuminated by the desk lamp up on the dresser beside her. She had taken the time to aim the lamp so that it cast its light vertically across her, elongating the shadows of her face and lending her eyes a gleam. Her mouth was open, aghast, and the jewelled bluebottles attached to her cheeks shimmered ethereally, like insectoid teardrops. It being Thursday, the day of the week when it was currently fashionable to accessorise with pieces of nature, she was also wearing a pair of butterfly-wing earrings, which fluttered as they swung, and each of the buttons of her crimson blazer was a varnished ladybird, red and dotted and shiny. "Oh, Simone!" she cried. "It's simply awful!"

Thursday also meant it was fashionable to turn up to work early, which explained why Georgie was already up and dressed, but Simone could see no immediate cause for alarm. Unpeeling himself from the chaise-longue, he sat up and stifled a yawn. "Georgie, darling," he said. "What is it?"

Closing her eyes, so that her false lashes, which were made from the legs of spiders, brushed up against each other, Georgie placed the back of her hand against her forehead and leant back, using the light of the lamp to enhance the drama of her pose. "It's almost too much to bear," she said. "As you well know, it being a Thursday, the day of the week when it is simply outrageous to do anything less than dress in your best natural styles, I decided that it would be appropriate to venture out into the garden to find the perfect flower to button through my lapel. I stepped out mere moments ago, and all was lovely and quaint and rich with all manner of perfumes, and even the bees seemed to have pulled on their most dazzling yellow and black jackets for the occasion, and I was leaning over a patch of violet orchids when… I heard a noise."

"What was it you heard, my dearest sweet?"

"It sounded like a kitten – a mewling that at first quite excited me, what with the fashion for kitten-fur mittens. So, I followed the noise, hoping for a litter – enough, perhaps, for my own pair of luxurious gloves."

"You do have lovely hands, Georgie."

Georgie fluttered her fingers, as if to emphasise the thought. "I drew closer to the sound, pursuing the mewling through the garden until I came to the source. But it wasn't a kitten at all!"

Simone gasped. "It wasn't a kitten?"

"No, Simone. It was… it was…"

"What was it?"

Georgie took a deep breath. "It looked like a person, but very small, and there were tears running from its eyes, and another clear liquid running from its nostrils, and it kept making that same kitten noise, but in slow, ebbing sobs that reminded me of waves, but not the good, gentle kind of waves – the kind of waves that splash erratically across the bathtub when you try to exit it too quickly. And oh, it was hideous! Its face was asymmetrical, and its hair was all tangled up, and its hands were filthy with dirt. And it was wearing denim, Simone. *Denim!*"

Simone felt his eyes widen. There had been a very short-lived fashion for denim a few years ago, which had died out when an exposé by a prominent magazine revealed that it was a material much favoured by the uglies. To think – that there was a very small ugly person wearing denim in Simone and Georgie's garden right now! "What did you do, darling?"

"Why, I ran! What else is one to do when confronted by such unexpected hideousness?"

Simone nodded. This was a wise course of action. "Do you think…" he began, but the thought was almost too dreadful to complete. "Do you think…" he tried again, "…that it might still be there? In the garden?"

Simone and Georgie shared a moment of horror, contemplating the idea of the unaesthetic creature waddling about, perhaps on bare muddy feet, and corrupting the carefully cultivated garden with its presence.

"Perhaps…" ventured Georgie "…it's gone away by now?"

"Yes." Simone breathed a sigh of relief. It was completely plausible that the horrible creature might have just flown away or something.

"Perhaps we should go and have a look?"

"Yes." Simone stood up and straightened his silken pyjamas, shuffling his toes into a pair of puppy-hide slippers that made his feet feel as if they were being hugged by clouds. "A marvellous idea, Georgie. We two will go out into the garden, and see that the ugly little person is gone, and then we'll return inside and have a glass of champagne to celebrate."

Georgie sighed a sigh of relief. "Wonderful," she said. "Simply wonderful."

Arm in arm, they ventured outside.

The sun was particularly hot today, and the cloudless sky was such a fetching shade of blue that Simone immediately decided that his outfit for the day would complement it. Perhaps he would break out one of his favourite cloud-pattern parasols, so that white tufts would follow him wherever he went. The garden itself, which Simone was particularly proud of, lay bathing in the sunshine, its every branch and leaf richly verdant in the bright morning light. Flowers bloomed in beds, arranged in patterns that simultaneously suggested careful placement and wild, untended growth, and there were a few trees dotted around the edges of the broad lawns, each as well-trimmed as the hair upon Simone's head.

The garden jutted out at the edge of the colossal silver skyscraper where Simone and Georgie lived, offering views of several similar silver skyscrapers nearby. The apartment had been quite the find – situated more than halfway up the considerable height of its particular tower, and featuring a balcony garden positioned at an opportune convergence, where no fewer than three other towers overlooked it. As such, Simone and Georgie always kept their garden in immaculate condition, according to the latest trends. Simone had become especially adept at ordering all the latest gardening magazines and making sure to leave them open at the appropriate pages so that the uglies who maintained the garden would have the best idea of how to go about doing so. That being said, Simone had never seen any of the gardeners who maintained his garden, and was quite sceptical of their very existence – it was plausible, he thought, that the garden maintained itself, growing with the latest fashions due to the proximity of its fashionable owners.

Simone took a deep breath. "Oh – what a wonderful morning!" he declared.

"Isn't it just?"

They meandered down the paths, taking care to make sure neither of them accidentally stepped on to any of the lawns. Despite the lavish grass, Simone was all too aware of the filthy soil underneath. Eventually, they came to the edge of the garden, where a railing overlooked the city below. Down there, Simone knew, the uglies tottered about in the dark between the skyscrapers. The sounds of cars and sirens and voices echoed upwards, and Simone recoiled, swiftly moving away from the railing.

"Where was it, darling?" he asked. "The tiny person?"

"Just ahead."

Simone felt Georgie's grip around his arm tighten. With any luck, the small person might have just fallen off the edge of the garden, or vanished in the way the uglies did when anybody fabulous was around. But there, beyond the leaves of a pair of tall, potted shrubs, was the thing itself, just as Georgie had described it, and so much worse. It sat on the lawn, bunching the grasses in its pudgy little fingers, and its face was drenched with all kinds of bodily fluids, and its open mouth revealed a selection of uneven teeth, gleaming like pearl tombstones between its cracked lips. The tiny person gurgled, and then emitted a piercing and discordant wailing when it noticed Simone and Georgie.

Simone shirked back from the screaming, but could not draw his eyes from the creature. Why, Georgie had been right – it *was* wearing denim! Clothed only in a set of denim overalls and tiny, mismatched socks, the soft rolls of its skin emerged haphazardly, as if the small person was oozing from its outfit. "Georgie?"

Georgie could only utter a little gasp.

"It looks…" Simone muttered to himself, feeling his waking mind starting to whir. Then, he realised. "I think it might be a child."

"A child?"

"Yes." Simone had never seen a child before, but he was aware of them as a concept. The idea, from what he understood, was that it took something close to eighteen years for a human to fully develop its aesthetic instincts, and that it was necessary for children to be hidden away from polite society until they were completely formed. In fact, from what Simone knew, a young person's memories were completely removed before they were allowed to become a member of the glitterati, so that none of the embarrassments of its formative failures might follow it into adulthood, leaving it an empty shell equipped with the finest aesthetic instincts. In fact, Simone's first memory was of exploring his father's walk-in wardrobes, and understanding, implicitly, the implications of each outfit therein.

"But why is it so small?" whispered Georgie, trying not to draw the child's attention.

"I believe..." said Simone carefully, trying to remember the few fragments of information he knew about children. "I believe that it might still be growing."

"Like a tree?"

"Yes, darling."

"How utterly grotesque."

Simone could only nod in agreement.

"Where do you think it came from?" asked Georgie.

The precise mechanics of human reproduction (beyond the exciting sexual elements) were largely unknown to Simone, but from what he understood it was a rather messy business. Fashionable parents routinely had their memories of the process removed, which resulted in some enormous gaps in memory. Choosing to have a child meant giving up more than nine months' worth of recollections. "I believe that there is a sort of expulsion."

"No, darling. I mean the garden. How did it get into the garden?"

It was true. The garden was very high up, and the child barely seemed capable of holding itself upright, let alone climbing a skyscraper. "I'm not sure."

For a while longer, they watched it wail. "Oh, Simone," said Georgie, eventually, "will you stop it making that dreadful sound?"

"But how?"

"Well, it sounds quite upset to me. Perhaps if you paid it a little compliment?"

This seemed like a most sensible idea to Simone. It always cheered him up to be complimented when he was feeling sad. Untangling his arm from Georgie, he ventured forth a little way (but not far enough to tread on the lawn), leant over slightly, and said, "Excuse me." The child did not cease wailing, but it did turn the full force of its bleary attention on Simone. Weathering its vile gaze, Simone sought something to compliment it on. After a few moments, he settled on, "I say. You have a marvellous complexion." The compliment was true; the child really did have wonderful skin – it looked very soft and clear – but Simone's words appeared to have no effect on the tiny creature's mood. It continued its horrible screaming unabated.

"Oh, Georgie," said Simone, dashing back across to her. "Whatever shall we do?"

Georgie raised her chin, bravely dispelling her horror with resolution. "I have an idea, darling. It might be dangerous, but it may prove an adequate solution."

"Do tell, dearest one."

"I believe we should attempt to lock the child in the greenhouse."

Of course! The greenhouse – a construction Simone did not

understand the purpose of, but did appreciate the aesthetic value of – stood nearby, its panes reflecting the blue sky. The door to the greenhouse was always open, revealing rows of things like vines and vegetables, and though Simone never ventured inside himself, due to the intolerable heat always wafting through the open doorway, it did seem like the perfect prison for a creature such as this child. But how to get it inside?

"Georgie," said Simone.

"Yes, darling?"

"I think I am going to do something very brave."

"I am here with you, my dearest."

"I love you, Georgie."

"And I love you, Simone."

Taking a deep breath to firm his resolve, Simone removed his slippers. The feel of the smooth marble beneath his feet was dreadful, but he steeled himself for the worse to come. Brandishing his slippers, one in each hand, and taking a few more deep breaths, he leapt on to the lawn before his nerves left him. The grasses crunched beneath Simone's feet, and the soil squelched between his toes. Clapping the slippers together and making shooing noises, Simone advanced on the child.

Startled by the racket, the child wobbled upright, clenching its pudgy fists even tighter, its wailing reaching a new crescendo. Simone clapped his slippers together even louder, and made a lengthier series of *shoo-shoo*s, which he was really rather embarrassed to emanate, until the child began to run, slipping on the grasses and staining its denim overalls with each clumsy stumble.

Trying his best to make sure not even a single stray blade of grass clung to his bright white pyjamas, Simone steered the child towards the greenhouse. The open door stood a mere few steps away, filled with tomatoes so ripe it made Simone's heart rise to see them there, dripping with moisture, like unblemished globes of flesh.

With one more clap of Simone's slippers, the child toddled inside.

Rushing across, and throwing his slippers aside, Simone quickly shut and bolted the glass door, which immediately stifled the child's screaming. Then, regaining his breath, he took stock of his feet. They were every bit as filthy as he had imagined: bits of grass clung to his skin, and there were grains of earth attached to the soles and edges, marring their usual soft paleness. Shaking, he turned to see Georgie, who was watching from nearby. "You did it, darling!" she cried.

Turning to examine the greenhouse once more, Simone was delighted to find he could no longer see or hear the child. There were only thick rows of sweltering foliage. "Yes," said Simone, relief washing through him.

"I'm so proud of you, Simone."

Pausing only to air-kiss his wife, Simone gathered his slippers and started to hobble back towards the veranda, trying his best to prevent any of the filth on his feet from affecting the veined marble slabs of the pathway. It was time for another bath.

Just beside the veranda, Georgie leaned down over a flower bed, plucking the head of a geranium with particularly frilly set of red petals. Then, she threaded the little flower through her lapel. "What do you think, darling?" she said, turning to and fro.

"Oh…" said Simone, his memories of the child fading already. "It's perfect."

* * *

Simone's weekend began on Thursday, so he decided to go to the beach.

There were all manner of fabulous people using the vibro-rail to get to the seafront, and Simone spent a while admiring them. Most folk, having observed the bright day occurring outside, had opted for sky blues and sunshine yellows. There was an entire row of people wearing yellow sandals beside the doors, their toenails painted the colours of the ocean (replete with artfully drawn white lines that resembled the foam of waves), and each of them posed beside the railing, which was painted such a splendid shade of yellow that it served to further enhance their respective outfits. There were a few fashionistas wearing suits, obviously on their way to their various seaside professions, but most people seemed destined for the same location as Simone, clothed in shorts that revealed their smooth legs, and thin shirts made of shimmering materials that appeared even thinner in direct sunlight. In fact, Simone could not see a single pair of eyes aboard his carriage: all were hidden behind large sunglasses rimmed in seashell white or sky-blush red.

Simone had taken hours agonising over the right outfit, and had settled on a deep-sea blue skirt by Stella Plush, featuring the latest in underwater aesthetic technology: when submerged, it would glow, undulate and develop little tassels, so that it would look as if Simone was wearing a living jellyfish. Of course, Simone would never dream of submerging himself, or so much as approaching the waves of the sea, but that wasn't the point; the point was that people would see him wearing his remarkable skirt and be in awe of the potential of it. Sometimes, as Simone knew all too well, the allure of transformation was even more powerful than the transformation itself.

The carriage slipped quietly through the city, and Simone idly considered what must have become of the incriminating photo taken of him at the party last night. He knew that someone as fabulous as Justine would absolutely stay true to their word, but part of him wondered whether she might have glanced at the picture before having it destroyed. Surely Justine was of a moral calibre that put her beyond such indulgences? Fabulousness was the foremost indicator of good character, after all.

Beyond the windows the uglies lurched, and Simone did his best to ignore them. The day being as bright and hot as it was, many of the uglies had decided to shed their clothing, and were slowly crisping in the sun, their unprotected and unmoisturised skin turning to bacon. There were altogether too many reddening bellies and arms and pates for Simone to handle, so he turned back to the row of yellow-sandal-wearing fashionites beside the door and focused with all his might on admiring them.

Eventually, the carriage pulled into the seafront.

There were gulls flying over the ocean today, which made Simone wary. He knew there was a discreet bird-repelling sonic barrier to make certain nothing avian could approach the beach, and he had to admit that their dark silhouettes and smooth arcs through the sky were rather fetching, but their presence still made him nervous – what if the barrier failed, and a gull were to sweep across, all hoarse croaking and strange webbed feet? What if one were to fly overhead and unload a measure of guano, splattering one of Simone's shoulders? Simone instinctively winced at the thought, glancing at the sky to make certain there were no feathered silhouettes circling above.

The promenade was busy today, which made sense considering the weather. The bright sunshine meant that anyone who was anyone would be finding a sliver of beach to be seen beside. Simone wandered over to the edge of the promenade, where there was a long wooden balustrade dividing the walkway from the beach, and admired the empty sands beyond it. The beach arced around the coast like a well-manicured fingernail, its sands soft and gleaming golden in the sunlight. To tread on those sands would be to invite aesthetic disaster (sand was known to be a clinging, grainy substance), so they remained untouched; a backdrop for beautiful people. In the near distance, the sea lapped at the shore, its rhythmic waves washing and sloshing so sweetly across the sands they almost hypnotised Simone with their motions.

Yes. It was a good day.

Unfurling his parasol, Simone strolled down the promenade. The parasol was made with special colour-shifting plastics that superimposed small white tufts of cloud across the sky beyond its clear membrane. Simone turned the parasol between his fingers, whirling the clouds above him slowly around, so that he felt as if he were the eye of a gentle storm. Ahead, there were rows of deckchairs set out to face the empty beach, most of which were filled with fashionistas.

And there was Darlington! Simone felt his heart flutter. It was always so good to see Darlington, and today he was perched daintily at the edge of a deckchair, wearing a sand-coloured bathing suit that did all kinds of wonderful things to enhance his muscular figure. He was sporting a bristling blonde moustache, which he had dusted with glitter that sparkled like the sun across the sea, and as Simone approached he was tweaking the ends of it, so that a little glitter sprinkled his chiselled lower jaw. "Simone!" he cried, arcing his blonde brows to accentuate his cheekbones. "How are you?"

"Very well, thank you." They air-kissed, and Simone kept his parasol turning, to cast interesting shifting shadows across his outfit.

"Is that a new skirt from Stella Plush?" asked Darlington.

"Why yes, it is! Astute of you to notice."

"Very fetching."

"Thank you. I like what you've done with your moustache."

"Oh." Darlington sighed, doing just enough to feign modesty without appearing too modest. "It's only a little glitter. Chiselled from nuggets of raw, unprocessed gold. Nothing special."

They exchanged a few more polite compliments with one another.

"I say," said Simone. "Would you mind if I joined you?"

"Of course not," said Darlington, removing his towel from the chair beside him.

"Marvellous. I'll just go fetch something to read."

Darlington tweaked the end of his moustache in assent.

There was a small magazine stand nearby, bedecked with all the latest magazines, and Simone wandered across. Only, as he approached, he noticed that most of the magazines had exactly the same cover, and felt his heart begin to race. This was a rare event, but not unheard of; from time to time an urgent fashion innovation would arrive, and every magazine worth its glossy sheets had to publish it immediately or face being labelled obsolete. Simone sped up, determined to discover the important new fashion before it became common knowledge.

Arriving before the magazine stand, Simone felt his heart stop.

On the cover of almost every single magazine was Justine, wearing what he had seen her in last night. She still looked like a corpse: her elegant white dress, her pale feet, her cold skin, all serving to make it look as if the photographer had slid open a drawer in a morgue and taken a picture of one of its most fabulous residents. Indeed, Justine's eyes were wide, as if she was surprised by her own death. Only… in the picture there was blood streaming from her nose. It ran in twin lines, one from each nostril, and dripped redly across her bloodless lips, and oozed down her chin, and splattered her chest, and the photographer had managed to take a picture that made it seem as if every droplet was a gleaming ruby, sparkling in the intense white lights of a morgue.

JUSTINE, read the headlines, FASHION GENIUS.

* * *

“Simone? Are you well?” It was Darlington.

Simone emerged from his momentary fugue to notice he was holding an ice-cream, which was, he thought, both a bad thing and a good thing. The ice-cream was bad because it filled him with a panic so terrible it threatened to shake his arm, which would dislodge chocolatey globules of melted dairy and send them splashing all over his pristine chest, but the ice-cream was good because the panic it was invoking in him was serving to override his feelings about Justine. Indeed, as he observed the creamy brown balls resting so perilously upon the cone, he noticed that a single droplet of melted ice-cream was making its way to the base of one of the balls, and, were he to neglect its descent any longer, it would fall and splatter onto his wrist. With as much elegance as he could muster, Simone dashed his tongue across the droplet, capturing it before it could cause any harm. This, however, simply worsened Simone’s predicament: by licking up the one droplet, he had loosened two more.

The ice-cream parlour was busy; it was fashionable to eat ice-cream when it was sunny. Worse, it was fashionable to heap one’s cone with altogether too much ice-cream, to suggest delight in the decadence of the sweet treat. This made for a very pleasing summertime aesthetic, but had the drawback of forcing dedicated fashionites to consume their ice-creams as quickly and carefully as possible, to prevent the messy food from affecting anyone’s articles of clothing or, indeed, anyone’s skin. As such, while the ice-cream parlour was busy, it was also completely silent but for the gentle lapping of tongues across cones.

Darlington had opted for butterscotch and caramel, which matched his outfit, and was doing an expert job of consuming his heaped confection without getting so much as a tiny droplet of it in his moustache. Simone was impressed, and would have taken the time to compliment Darlington, were he not so absorbed in desperately trying to finish his own ice-cream before it could drip on him. Today was an especially warm day, which was doing nothing to help the speed at which it was melting.

Between licks, Simone noticed Darlington raise a single brow, as if to punctuate the question he had posed mere moments ago.

"Apologies," said Simone, finding a moment between mouthfuls. "I seem to be rather distracted today. But this is delicious."

This appeared to satisfy Darlington, and the two of them went back to devouring their mountainous treats. Beyond the doors of the colourful parlour the horizon was an unbroken blue line, and Simone tried to focus on it, calming himself with its simplicity and falling into a rhythm of licking that was doing wonders to diminish his ice-cream while retaining his poise. After all, it simply wouldn't do to appear as if one were desperate to finish one's ice-cream – one must appear relaxed, and happy, as if one were taking absolute delight in one's confectionery marvel.

Something red caught Simone's eye, and he turned to see a woman wearing a sky-blue bathing suit holding a cone heaped high with cherry ice-cream and strawberry sorbet. Simone did not recognise the woman, and was drawn to her not because of her aesthetic but because of her pose, which was somewhat unusual. The woman was holding her cone between both hands, tilted slightly so that the heaped red and pink balls atop it jutted perilously over her chest, and she licked ever so delicately at the top in a manner that suggested she was deliberately melting it as quickly as possible. As Simone watched, he noticed several red droplets drip down the heap of ice-cream and sorbet, until, at last, they began to fall. The first droplet hit the woman squarely across her chest, making her shiver. This was followed in turn by several more red drips, each adding to the mess slowly accumulating across her exposed skin and staining her pale bathing suit purple. Then, the woman began to lick harder at her ice-cream sorbet combo, until it was running from her lips and down her chin in red streaks.

Everybody was watching, now.

Nearby, someone began to copy the woman. This man's ice-cream was not red, but blue, but the effect was much the same; droplets ran down his chin and spattered his chest, worsening with each expertly measured lick of the ice-cream. Then, even more fashionistas began to join in, staining themselves with the sticky sugars they had been consuming so carefully mere moments before. By the time Simone finally managed to finish his own ice-cream, everybody was following suit, including Darlington, whose bathing suit and chin were now muddied caramel. "Wonderful," he commented. "That Justine. Such an innovator."

Simone tried to offer polite agreement, but when he opened his mouth, no sound came out.

"Are you sure you're well, Simone?" asked Darlington, concerned.

"Yes," he managed. "Yes. Simply in need of some air."

"Of course," said Darlington, smiling with his butterscotch-stained lips. "As it so happens, I have been invited to a little get-together aboard Gabriel's yacht. Would you care to join me?"

"I would be delighted, Darlington."

"Marvellous. Just along the bay."

The walk along the promenade did wonders to clear Simone's head. Here and there, fashionistas were flying kites, because it was currently fashionable to fly kites, and the way the kites bobbed up there in the air, suspended on the warm breeze rolling luxuriously across the bay, made Simone's thoughts feel just as light and free as they were. He idly considered bringing his own kite the next time he came to the beach, perhaps made out of the same materials as his parasol, so that it would look as if all the clouds in the sky had been confined to a small, floating diamond, shimmering in the bright blue expanse.

Ahead lay the docks, where bobbed all manner of yachts. They gleamed white and gold in the sunshine, and even from this distance Simone could hear the rhythms of several competing sound systems, intermingled with the clinking of glasses (which Simone recognised as champagne glasses by their particular timbre) and the soft murmur of gentle laughter. There upon the decks of the yachts mingled the glitterati, all enrobed in the most fashionable beach attire imaginable, and between their fingers they held the skinny stems of their flutes, raising them so the contents glittered, their pale throats bobbing rhythmically with each supple sip. Simone found himself licking his lips.

"Just ahead," said Darlington, and there was Gabriel's yacht.

"Goodness!" exclaimed Simone. The yacht was new, he knew, because it was flaunting some of the latest in fashion technology, which Simone had only read about last week in *Boating Monthly*. The yacht's hull was built out of a special meta-material that repelled water with such tremendous force that the entire boat floated above the sea. Its underside sliced through the waters that lay beneath it, as if the yacht were a knife so sharp that it did not need to touch its subject in order to cut it. Adding to the effect of the floating yacht was its mirror-panelled exterior, which reflected the sea beneath, and the horizon beyond, as if a second ocean were imprisoned within its curves. Not a single droplet of seawater touched the boat, and nor would they ever: the yacht would remain eternally dry. By comparison, the wave-spattered hulls of the other yachts at the docks looked crude and stained.

"To be so unblemished!" said Simone softly, feeling afraid that he might accidentally mar the yacht's hull with spittle were he to exclaim too sharply; and Darlington, too, offered up a quiet set of compliments as they mounted the long gangplank leading onto its deck.

Simone experienced a moment of vertigo halfway up the gangplank, and gripped hold of the golden velvet rope to keep himself steady. To either side of him the sea sloshed, making him feel dizzy, and for a brief, terrible second, he was back in the ice-cream parlour watching the new fashion – which he had invented, and which had been stolen from him by Justine – as it spread through the room. Then, the moment passed, and Simone was on board the yacht.

The party certainly seemed exclusive. There were all kinds

of remarkable people gathered at the bow, competing (without looking as if they were competing) for the best of the sunshine, and Simone admired them, feeling the deck gently shifting with the motion of the waves beneath him. There was Gabriel, dressed in a shimmering golden sarong, and he and Darlington shared an air-kiss, Gabriel taking the time to compliment the butterscotch stains currently drenching Darlington's chin and bathing suit. Simone decided that he was not in the mood to exchange pleasantries with Gabriel, but that he was in the mood to consume a considerable amount of champagne, and to find a quiet corner of the deck where he could lounge in the sunshine and take the time to recover properly from the magazine stand and the ice-cream parlour.

There was a long table in the middle of the lower deck, shaded from the sky by the balcony overhead, where there were rows of fizzing golden flutes, and Simone took his time selecting one that would not affect the arrangement. At the centre of the table stood an ice sculpture of the yacht, and Simone observed it as he sipped from his glass, enjoying the way the sculpture's base kept it freezing cold and fixed in place, in defiance of the sun's considerable heat. Just like the yacht itself, not a single errant droplet marred the ice, making it look as if it might just be a chunk of glass.

As Simone admired the sculpture, he noticed a man wearing a pair of trunks the colour of a crab's underbelly approach it, brows arched to suggest thoughtfulness. The man's skin was the colour of bronze, which Simone appreciated because it complemented his trunks – though it did occur to him that it might be more to the man's advantage were his skin to instead be the ruddy colour of a crab's shell, to better match his choice of bathing suit. While thinking these thoughts, Simone watched the man pick up the long silver ice pick resting beside the sculpture, twirling it between his bronze fingers dexterously, as one might a fine lip liner.

Too late, Simone realised what was happening.

Carefully, the man inserted the slender ice pick up one of his nostrils. Then, adjusting it for comfort, he gently tapped the end of it. A small stream of red oozed from the corner of his nose. Quickly, and no doubt for the sake of symmetry, the man repeated the action with his other nostril. Then, replacing the pick and taking hold of a champagne glass, the man took two steps up the staircase nearby so that he was standing in a gush of sunlight, and there he raised his chin and puffed out his chest, to draw attention to the blood now streaming from his nose. Red ran freely from both of his nostrils, dripping in heavy droplets across his lips and down his chin, before falling and splattering on his chest. Within moments, the man was drenched in his own blood.

Simone felt his grip on his glass tightening.

The attentions of those aboard the yacht were inexorably drawn to the man with the self-inflicted nosebleed. Then, one enterprising fashionista, realising precisely how the man had achieved his aesthetic, rushed, as elegantly as she was able, to take the ice pick and inflict the same upon herself. Blood ran from her nostrils, and before she could replace the pick upon the table, a queue had formed behind her. One by one, the glitterati awaited their turn, tapping at their inner nostrils with the pick and making their blood flow, their desire to execute the latest fashion quite overwhelming any disgust felt at having to share the bloodied instrument. The once-immaculate deck of the yacht was very quickly turning red with spattered blood, dislodged from jutting chins, and it was small comfort indeed that the yacht's deck was not as hydrophobic as its hull.

There was a cracking, splintering sound, and Simone shifted his gaze to his hand, which, he noticed, was also bleeding. There were shards of glass embedded in his palm, and the broken remains of the champagne flute scattered in a glittering ruin across the deck beside him. Simone clenched his fist and glanced around, but nobody was paying him any attention: everyone was too absorbed in making their noses bleed. Keeping his fist clenched as tightly as possible, to prevent any blood from trickling between his fingers, Simone slipped away from the table.

Back on the gangplank, he found himself stumbling, made light-headed by the feel of the glass embedded in his palm grating against his bones. There, in the distance, sprawled the white pill-like capsules of the vibro-rail, and he steered himself towards them, keeping his bloodied fist clenched against his chest. Thankfully, the oral aerobics necessary to keep up with the fashion for eating ice-cream also resulted in a fashion for highly flexible cosmetics, so it was easy to retain his smile without ruining his makeup, and he worked his painful fist into his stride so it would seem as if nothing was wrong – as if he was simply so touched by the sight of the glittering sea that he must keep his hand clenched against his chest, to feel his heart beating appreciatively at the view. Simone worked fiercely to retain his decorum because it was in his very nature to do so, and to betray that nature, especially at such a terrible time as this, would be to lose himself completely to his horror, and be rendered as hideous as any of the unfashionables that inhabited the wretched, overcrowded beaches further along the coast, splashing and wobbling in the sea, and letting the sand encrust their cracked skins, and laughing ugly, heaving laughs with each other.

There was blood everywhere, now. The fashionistas along the promenade were using toothpicks to prick their inner nostrils, and the fashionistas emerging from the vibro-rail carriages were using the pointed ends of nail files, and Simone's fist oozed a steady stream of red down his ribs, so that it pooled into his belly button. Simone smiled and smiled and smiled, and all those who smiled back at him did so with red teeth, stained bloody by the new fashion.

The fashion for nosebleeds.

The fashion that Simone had invented.

The fashion that nobody was giving him any credit for.

Inside, Simone seethed.

* * *

The problem with going to the hospital was that Simone would have to cross a street frequented by unfashionables. Normally, Simone would have simply taken the limousine to the hospital, and misted the windows so thoroughly that he would not have to lay eyes upon any of them, but the fact of the matter was that Simone's hand was bleeding rather badly, and he was beginning to feel dizzy. There was a red puddle between his feet, which he was proud to see had a mirror shine to it, allowing him to study his reflection in his blood, but his increasing dizziness would soon render him fashion-impaired if the flow from his fist was not stopped. Therefore, Simone would have to exit the pristine vibro-rail carriage at the station opposite the hospital, and brave the street in between, where the uglies were.

All too soon, the vibro-rail carriage whispered to a halt, and the doors swished open.

The station was clean and bright and currently occupied by a pair of fashionables air-kissing each other with enough vigour to suggest that they were a couple about to be parted. Simone quickly slipped past them before he was noticed, and stepped, as daintily as he could, down the alabaster steps towards the exit. There, a pair of large doors were all that separated him from the world of the unfashionables. It would take only a few moments to leave the station, cross the street and enter the hospital, Simone knew, but he was deeply aware of the kinds of catastrophe that might befall him during that short space of time. What if one of the uglies breathed on him, or, worse, *touched* him? Would he be contaminated with ugliness?

Clenching his bloody fist tightly to his chest, Simone sashayed through the doors. And when they slid aside, they revealed a street far worse than Simone had imagined. He was immediately confronted by a set of worn concrete steps, leading down to a cracked concrete pavement littered with cigarette butts and discarded crisp packets. Immediately beyond the pavement were four lanes of traffic, inhabited by all kinds of squat, paint-flecked cars, their exhausts pouring fumes across the oil-slicked road. The streetlamps were bent, and there were gratings leaking subterranean vapours, and everywhere, absolutely everywhere, the unfashionables lumbered, flinging their legs about in a crude and unrhythmic form of locomotion, propelling them along the pavements and among the cars. And the racket! There was so much noise! Engines revved, and horns honked, and birds cackled, and all the ugly people chatted and chewed and laughed, overwhelming Simone as he stood there, feeling dizzy and small.

The hospital was a shining white building, so clean against all the filth, and Simone forced himself to focus on it as he stepped forward, trying to maintain his composure. His sandals almost slipped against the worn concrete, but he remained upright, trying to ignore the little weeds poking up from the cracks in the pavement, and the sun-bleached posters stuck haphazardly to the brick walls, and, worst of all, the beaten metal cans everywhere, overflowing with lumpy black plastic bags that Simone did not understand but felt himself innately hating. Soon, he was down at street level, and that was when the uglies began to notice him.

They stopped in their tracks, eyes widening at the sight of him. A rotund man wearing a brown trench coat with mismatched buttons drew his dog short, mouth opening in an uneven oval of surprise even as the mutt yipped and yapped at his feet; a woman with a threadbare pram, wearing a grey dress that should never have been worn on a Thursday, or indeed any day at all, gasped, holding an unmanicured hand to her chest while a strange sobbing sound emanated from within her pram; and a man in a blue uniform slightly too large for him, a truncheon dangling like a forgotten accessory from his hip, removed his hat and wrung it between his filthy hands. Simone did his best to hold his head high and walk through them, but he could not prevent himself from noticing their stray hairs. The man in uniform had little brown bits of wire poking out of his nostrils, and the man with the dog had grey sprouting from his inner ears, and the lady with the wailing pram had a collection of black hairs emerging from the brown lump on her upper lip, and Simone could feel those little bits of hair tickling and scratching at his thoughts. Much longer here, Simone knew, and unkempt patches of hair would sprout from every bit of him: armpits, and legs, and even the knuckles of his toes.

The uglies parted before him, clearing a path. So too did the cars, positioning themselves to leave Simone an avenue directly across the broken tarmac and to the pavement beyond. Some of the cars were yellow, and some of the cars were silver, and some of the cars were brown, and the drivers and passengers in all of them stared in wonder at the lone glitterati as he strode between them, trying desperately to imagine that the street was a crude runway, pausing to strike little poses as he went. To Simone, the runway stretched on forever, making it feel as if it took years for him to reach the other side. Yet at last he did, mounting the pavement with as much aplomb as he could muster. There was a puddle of something dark and oily awaiting him, but he avoided it, striding the last of the distance to the hospital's side entrance. The white doors slid open, and Simone fought to stop himself from leaping inside.

At last, as the doors gently closed behind him, he was safe.

The hospital's interior was so clean and white and smooth that Simone felt as if he had stepped inside an egg, but not one of the eggs the unfashionables used (which he knew often arrived freckled, or brown, or speckled with bits of detritus left over from the filthy bird that had laid it). No – Simone felt as if he had stepped inside an egg carefully bleached into an unblemished whiteness, and that he was now an unbroken yellow yolk, shielded from the world beyond his pristine shell. There was a counter not too far away which, much like the room he had entered, had no corners at all, and approaching from behind that smooth counter came two nurses, one presenting male and one presenting female, each clad in the same whiteness as the walls, so that it appeared as if they emerged from those walls as manifest avatars of health. The nurses wore little white masks, and little white hats that looked like origami, and crisp white uniform dresses so well fitted it almost made Simone swoon with gratefulness to look upon them.

Gently, they towed Simone deeper into the hospital.

The wonderful thing about the hospital staff was that, while they were not technically fashionable, nor were they unfashionable, leaving them in a strange aesthetic limbo. The way Simone liked to think about it, the hospital was a timeless place beyond the world, where clean whiteness would always be the fashion, pristine and unaffected by the rhythms of fashion undulating endlessly beyond its walls. Therefore, Simone allowed himself to relax as he was led along a tubular corridor, and around a corner that was difficult to call a corner because it had no edges at all – more of a barely discernible curve that made Simone feel as if he were being led through the arteries of an exsanguinated corpse.

He was gently deposited into a large changing room and told that his doctor would see him soon. Then the nurses left, the round door sliding closed behind them and sealing Simone inside. The changing room was large, and spherical, and the walls were covered in racks upon racks of apparently identical gowns for him to select from. Removing his skirt and sandals with his good hand, Simone then ran that hand through the racks, taking his time to select the right kind of hospital gown to wear. Of course, all of them were the same white as the rest of the hospital and its staff, but the cuts were different, and so were some of the materials, so that Simone found himself lost in the art of selection, momentarily forgetting the throb of his wounded hand. Near the end of one rack was a gown made of a particularly soft material Simone did not recognise, and the label told him that it was a design by Messr Messr, and when he pulled it on, it fit so wonderfully around him that he allowed himself a little gasp of pleasure. Thus satisfied, he perched at the edge of a bench and tried to ignore the way the blood running from his hand immediately started seeping into the soft cloth of his chosen garment.

Taking a few deep breaths, Simone began to relax.

Only, as he continued casting his eye over the endless racks of gowns – a soothing display – one in particular caught his attention. It was just the very edge of a sleeve, poking out from between two crisply ironed specimens, but the colour was wrong. Feeling himself frown, Simone stood and approached the sleeve, only to confirm that he was correct; here, among all these bleached eggshell-white gowns, was a mint-green gown.

Simone felt his composure begin to waver. It was like being back outside, among the uglies. Carefully, so as to not touch the garment intruding upon the waiting room, Simone parted the racks and beheld the robe in all its glory. The whole thing was mint green, and even worse, it was baggy, and draped ungainly across its hanger, the single pocket sewn into the breast hanging as loose as if it were a pocket genuinely designed to have things put into it. Simone uttered another gasp, this time involuntarily, and stepped away from the gown. Here, in this place of healing, the dreadful mint green felt like an infection; the potential source of an unaesthetic disease that might reach out and wrack him with ugliness. Simone knew that he must warn someone about the intruding outfit immediately, before any harm could be done.

Luckily, it was then that Simone's doctor arrived.

Dr Cask had an extraordinary gaze. It was as if he were seeing straight through one's outfit, and makeup, and skin, and examining one's very bones and organs for their aesthetic appeal. Dr Cask's eyes seared through Simone's skull, and if he bore any expression, it was hidden by his white mask. Much like the rest of the staff at the hospital, he wore white and white and white. Only, instead of a uniform, he wore an extraordinarily white suit. Better still, unlike the bleached pale flesh of the nurses, his skin was an unblemished caramel brown, and though his hair was a black wave, and his lashes were scalpel-sharp black blades, both his hair and lashes were tipped with the same frost-white as his suit, as if he had just stepped through a snowstorm and emerged with ice clinging to him in the most aesthetically pleasing areas possible.

"Simone," said Dr Cask.

"My very dear doctor," said Simone, feeling his words slur slightly.

"Your hand is injured."

"Yes," said Simone, presenting his bloodied fist. "I feel as if I have lost rather a lot of blood."

"So it seems," said Dr Cask. Then, "I shall repair you."

"That's very gracious of you."

"Follow me, please."

Simone paused at the door. "Doctor?"

"What is it?"

"You should know…" Simone drew closer, to whisper the dreadful secret. "There is a *green* gown in that waiting area. Hidden among the white gowns."

Dr Cask blinked. Then, he said, "That is unacceptable. I will have the article burned."

Feeling such relief that he almost swooned, Simone said, "Thank you, Doctor."

"Yes. Follow me, Simone."

As they walked together down the white tubular corridor, Dr Cask said, "How is your jawline, Simone?"

"My jawline?"

"Yes. Are you satisfied with it?"

Up until now, Simone had been perfectly satisfied with his jawline. It had a nice curve to it, and his chin was dainty, and he always enjoyed running his brushes down it, enhancing its sharpness with powders. Dr Cask's enquiry, however, had suddenly thrown Simone's satisfaction into doubt. Was he really satisfied with his jawline? Perhaps it would look neater with slightly less of a curve, he thought. And there was currently a fashion for chin dimples. "I suppose I hadn't really considered my jawline recently," said Simone.

"So it seems," said Dr Cask. "Here." Through another round white door was another round white room. Only this one had a long, cushioned table at the centre of it, with plush armrests and soft straps hanging free. "Please lay down on the table."

Simone did as he was told, and the table automatically adjusted itself beneath him, until he was so comfortable that he could not feel a single pressure point anywhere on his body. It was like floating on a cloud. Then, Dr Cask gently pulled the straps over him, until he was fully fastened to the table, with his hands outstretched to either side of him. Simone did not understand the need for the straps, but they did make him feel very safe in Dr Cask's care. Come to think of it, Simone could not remember how the hospital worked at all. He could remember, quite clearly, leaving the hospital on multiple occasions, but the reasons for his visits, and the ensuing healing process, were absent from his recollections. Still – the holes in Simone's memory were not worth dwelling upon. It was perfectly routine and acceptable to have unfashionable memories purged from one's mind.

"Try and relax," said Dr Cask.

Simone's hand throbbed. "What must I do?"

"Please understand that the process is quick, and clean, but very painful. Try and contain yourself as best you can. If you struggle too much, it may delay the process."

Simone felt his eyes widen. "I'm sorry. Very painful?"

"Yes, but it's nothing to worry about." Dr Cask made sure the straps were secure. "Your memory of the injury, and of the process of repairing it, will both be erased in short order, after the process is complete. You will leave feeling perfectly clear of mind."

Simone tried to move, but the straps were very tight around him. "Doctor?"

"Yes?"

"May I have some kind of sedative?"

"There's no point," said Dr Cask. "You will remember none of this." Satisfied with the straps, he returned to the wall near the door, where a set of controls were embedded into the white shell of the room. There, he pushed one of the apparently identical white buttons.

Part of the ceiling slid aside, and a bizarre hand emerged. The hand was certainly a hand, but it was made of chrome and had altogether too many fingers. Some of the fingers weren't even fingers; they were scalpels, or tweezers, or other instruments Simone didn't recognise. The hand, which was attached to a chrome limb with too many joints, descended until it hung above him. Then, swivelling on its various wrists and elbows, it manoeuvred itself into position above Simone's ruined hand, where it hovered, as if considering the glass embedded there. There was a gentle whirring noise that Simone found comforting.

Dr Cask placed a pair of white glasses over his eyes.

Before Simone could enquire as to the metal hand's purpose, it reached out and gripped his own. For a brief moment, he and the hospital held hands. Then, with gentle dexterousness, the hand's many fingers curled around his own, splaying them rigid. And without so much as a pause, or warning, it began to cut. The cutting began at the very edge of his palm, with a single slice, all the way from finger to wrist. The pain wasn't so bad; it was very distant. Then, using a whole selection of different fingers, the metal hand began to peel the skin from Simone's palm. There was even a neat little roller for keeping the flesh tidy. As the metal hand peeled his skin back, tiny tweezers zipped back and forth, nipping at the shards of glass embedded in Simone's flesh and placing them, ever so delicately, into a small tray. With the skin of his palm removed, Simone could see the muscles and tendons beneath, and marvelled at their intricacy. He idly wondered if there would ever be a fashion for removing one's skin. Then, the pain hit.

Agony bloomed in his hand.

The metal hand continued its work, degloving each of Simone's fingers one by one, and unpeeling the rest of his hand. Blood had begun to spray from his palm in little bursts, staining the chrome instruments working at it, and splashing both Simone and the table. Before long, Simone's entire hand had been flayed, and it lay there, a glistening collection of muscles and tendons, twitching with each tiny adjustment. The metal hand plucked every last shard of glass, one by one, and Simone realised he was screaming. The pain was worse than any he could ever remember. He could feel the currents of air in the room, blustering over the exposed flesh of his fingers.

The operation continued, unabated.

With every piece of glass removed, the metal hand began fastening up the wounds in his musculature, suturing them with tiny lengths of silver thread. Each push of the needle was another moment of pain, crackling up Simone's spine and into his skull. Then, with all wounds tightly secured, the metal hand began spraying Simone's exposed muscles with a thick white solvent. Every small gush sent yet more agony through him, until he was almost blind with panic, his limbs shuddering horribly. The solvent quickly billowed and took form, unfolding itself across his skinless hand as a new, fresh layer of skin. The metal hand gently massaged it into shape, giving it folds identical to those the previous layer of skin bore. Within moments, Simone's hand was completely wrapped in a layer of soft and unblemished new skin.

Simone gulped for breath like a drowning fish.

Yet, the process was not complete. As the metal hand turned Simone's hand over and worked at the new skin on the back of it, Simone saw that he was missing nails. The very small part of him not completely overcome by the pain of the operation was instead overcome by the dread that he may not be given nails, rendering his fingers fleshy nubs. The metal hand had not forgotten, however. Simone noticed that all the while it had been working, it had also been carefully unravelling the nails from the flesh of his old fingers. Those nails it now began embedding in his new skin, pulling back at the flesh and installing each without the slightest consideration for Simone's continued discomfort. Stars of agony gleamed across Simone's vision, and he did his best to concentrate on the aesthetic brilliance of them.

Nails restored, the metal hand paused once again, whirring.

Apparently satisfied, it withdrew into the ceiling.

Dr Cask was there, beside the table, removing his glasses. “There,” he said, as he examined the repaired hand. “Completely restored.”

Simone felt himself burbling something. His tongue was no longer working.

“Quiet now, Simone. A few moments longer.”

Dr Cask pressed another of the identical white buttons on the panel beside the door, and another slot in the room’s ceiling opened up, revealing a machine that looked like a motorbike helmet, if that helmet were chrome and bristling with all manner of cables and wires and instruments. The helmet, which was attached to the end of another long chrome limb, manoeuvred itself around until it was resting above Simone’s head. Then, it gently descended over his ears, until it contained his head completely. Dr Cask was still talking, telling Simone something else, but his voice was too muffled through the helmet for Simone to make out. There was another sound, like a drum being beaten, and Simone realised it was his own heart thumping in his ears. Then, there was an almost deafening screech, and a bright flash of light, and the overwhelming smell of burning, and everything seemed to

* * *

Simone awoke feeling ravenous.

His arm was dead beneath him on the pink leather chaise-longue, so he unpeeled it slowly, slick skin sticking, and rubbed the life back into it. The poor thing was tingling with pins and needles, and flopped about uselessly on his lap for a few moments until he regained control of it. Before him, his bed bubbled and glowed, and Simone watched the colourful fish flitting back and forth as he regained his bearings. It felt as if he had just woken from a particularly troublesome dream, the contents of which he could not entirely recall. In fact, the last thing he could remember with any clarity was leaving the hospital, which was peculiar because he had no memory whatsoever of entering the hospital. Further, the last thing he could recall before exiting the hospital was eating ice-cream on the promenade with Darlington. Simone's stomach growled at him as he considered the ice-cream, which was embarrassing because bodily noises were quite out of fashion. Thankfully, the bedroom was empty except for Simone and the bed full of fish which, while aesthetic in themselves, lacked the ability to appreciate beauty.

The most likely explanation for Simone's patchy recollection of the previous day's events was that some of his memories had been erased. With this realisation, Simone relaxed. Memory erasure was perfectly normal: it was like a pore-cleanse for the mind. Whatever it was he had forgotten was certainly not worth remembering.

Stomach still growling, Simone decided to go to the kitchen.

He was wearing a set of cream-white pyjamas patterned with strawberries that made him salivate as he beheld them, and upon his feet were a pair of slippers that made him feel as if he were walking along a road paved with marshmallows. A delicious smell wafted through the apartment which, to Simone, recalled succulent meats carefully spiced for the optimum olfactory experience, and indeed, as he drew closer to the kitchen, he could hear the sizzle and pop of meat being cooked in a manner that emphasised the clarity of said sizzle and pop.

Now that Simone was thinking about it, memory removal was the likely culprit for Wednesday's fortuitous mix-up. Both he and Georgie must have had the entirety of Tuesday erased. This was a rare event – usually, either Simone or Georgie was available to gently guide the other through any resulting confusion, but in this instance they had been unable to help each other: both convinced that it was actually Tuesday. Still, it had worked out well in the end. Idly, he wondered what must have happened on Tuesday to make them both want their memories of the day cleansed, but he supposed it didn't really matter. It could be anything: a sub-par choice of outfits for the day; a car-crash resulting in grievous injuries; bad sex. None of it was worth remembering.

Simone paused at a window overlooking the garden, which was ever so slightly ajar. Through it drifted the sound of gentle laughter and the clinking of champagne glasses (the timbre of which suggested the glasses were nearly full). Beyond the glass, the garden blazed in the red sunset; a thousand crimson suns beamed down upon it, reflected, as they were, in the thousand mirrored windows of the skyscrapers that rose to every side of it. There were fires lit all across the garden; torches, and small fireplaces, and even the smouldering frame of a barbecue, and dark figures drifted between them, their outfits giving them sensuous silhouettes. Simone realised, at last, that Georgie must have organised a barbecue. How marvellous! Once he had eaten something, Simone would have to rush to his wardrobes and select something to enhance his own silhouette.

But first, the kitchen.

As Simone wandered through his apartment, he realised that there was a chance someone might see him in his pyjamas before he had a chance to get dressed, and spent the remainder of the journey formulating his excuse. He decided that he would feign embarrassment, and claim to have just awoken after a particularly taxing night shift at work (which was perfectly plausible: Tremptor Tower was known to be open twenty-four hours a day).

Through a clean white door lay a clean white room with veined white counter-tops, and all manner of chrome machines that, while aesthetically very interesting, Simone did not understand the function of. He supposed that some of them were designed to make things hot, and that there were utensils meant for stirring and whisking and such, but the fashion for cookery, which had occurred a few years prior, had not been about the practicality of the thing. Simone had rather enjoyed wearing aprons, and dusting himself with various powders meant to resemble ingredients, and treating his guests to lavish dinners which he pretended, with such graciousness, to cook, but everybody knew that actual cookery, with all its chopping, and sweating, and fats, was for the unfashionables. Indeed, the marvellous smell wafting through the apartment emerged from a shiny chrome vent in the wall, and the popping and sizzling that he could hear was coming out of a set of speakers artfully disguised as what Simone assumed was a sort of oven. Thankfully, at the very heart of the kitchen stood a pyramid of burgers, situated on a tray beneath a bright set of overhead lights. The burgers, no doubt, were meant for the barbecue outside, but Simone was far too hungry to wait for their eventual delivery.

Fetching a pale porcelain plate, he beheld the pyramid.

The selection was difficult, because none of them were quite perfect. While each burger had its round bun, slightly toasted, and each had a square of cheese, with a layer of moist lettuce and precisely two slices of vivid red tomato, all positioned so carefully above a juicy patty glistening with its own sumptuousness, each was also slightly imperfect; the cheese of one had dribbled down too far, mingling with a bun, and the lettuce of another had a tiny tear, and the juice of a third had dripped down on to the top of a fourth, and as Simone hungrily cast his eyes across the pyramid, he could find no single burger aesthetic enough to satiate him. Until, at last, his gaze settled upon the burger at the very apex of the pyramid. Everything about it was splendid; from its smooth, unblemished bun, to the sharp corners of its cheese, to the crisp moistness of its lettuce (encrusted with tiny droplets of water like dew), to the robust yet tasteful thickness of its tomatoes, and, of course, the glistening glory of its exquisitely charred patty, it was truly a wonder to behold. With care, Simone slid it from the top of the pyramid and on to his plate.

Sliding his lips back from his teeth, Simone raised the burger to his mouth and took a bite. When he lowered the burger, he was pleased to see a flawless bite mark, revealing a splendid cross-section. Satisfied, he began to chew; grinding the flavours together in his mouth and feeling the juices roll down his throat. Savouring every crushing movement of his jaw, he allowed the small piece of the burger to become him, so that he might be restored by its aesthetic brilliance. And then, at last, when the bite was sufficiently chewed, he allowed himself to swallow, feeling the food fill him like a glow from within.

Satiated, Simone left the rest of the burger on the countertop, and went to get changed.

The trick with firelight was to work with its effects; its long, moving shadows, and the wavering tremble of the light itself. Simone settled on a tight-fitting black Hesselhorf suit, with a rich, deep red shirt and tie, which would give him a sharp silhouette and complement the colours of the sky and flames both (it still being a Thursday, the day when nature was in fashion). Then, to accent it, he pinned and buttoned his matching Fogel Filligre cufflinks, tie pin and ring, each of which was black and inlaid with a single enormous ruby, so that the flickering of the fire would reflect from their many facets. Outfit chosen, and completed with a dagger-sharp pair of black dress shoes, Simone then went to his dresser and considered his face.

There was no time to waste in completing his look because Simone had no idea how much longer the barbecue would last, but still he paused, momentarily struck by his jawline. His jawline was fine at a glance, but Simone could not help but notice, with further study, that it could be improved upon. Rousing himself from his surprise, he made a mental note to get in touch with Dr Cask, and quickly got back to the task at hand: choosing how to present his face. Time being of the essence, his look would have to be quite simple, so Simone decided to get to work with his foundation and powders while he formulated the nuances. Foundations and powders in place, Simone quickly completed his look with a set of ruby lashes, and ruby glitter, and ruby lipstick, along with a set of actual rubies carefully glued into place along his cheekbones. It was a rudimentary aesthetic in the bright lights of his makeup mirror, but in the firelight outside, it would serve well. Satisfied, he stood, brushed down his suit, and prepared to make his entrance.

Simone knew something was wrong the moment he stepped outside. There were not many options for making an entrance into the garden, so he had settled on the bay doors, with the glow from within the apartment enhancing his carefully selected silhouette. This entrance had the intended effect; those occupying the garden, and within sight of the bay doors, had turned to see him, and he could see his silhouette reflected in all their eyes.

No – the problem was not with Simone's entrance. It was with the sky.

The sun, which had been a deep red when Simone had last looked, had set, leaving the sky black and starry. The stars were wonderful; an endless glittering reflected from the shard-like protrusions of the mirrored tower blocks surrounding the garden. Only, with the stars had come the moon, which was enormous and yellow. It looked, to Simone, even more sickly than usual, its normal tasteful silver replaced with a feverish pale yellow, and it hung low and heavy and marked with craters like pox scars in the sky, at the precise apex between the surrounding skyscrapers. Worst of all, it was reflected in all the windows of all the towers, so that there were thousands of disgusting moons all glowing down at Simone at once.

Simone felt his bite of burger rising in his throat, and swallowed to keep it down.

Striding over to the deepest shadows beneath the trees, he found some relief from the thousand sickly moons, and there posed beside the glowing barbecue, letting those coals glint in his rubies. There were white wisps of smoke rising from the coals, and they swirled around him as he concentrated on keeping his revulsion in check. Focussing on the coals helped a little; Simone had the vague idea that the barbecue was designed to cook food, but the idea was very strange. Better to warm one's hands upon the heat than one's meal.

Fashionable friends and acquaintances moved around the garden, showing off their own silhouettes, and Simone exchanged pleasantries with them from his place of safety. The exchanges were peculiar tonight, however – because everyone was paying compliments to his crimson shirt and tie. The shirt and tie were excellent, he knew, but they were no more than a mere tile in the mosaic of his complete aesthetic. Eventually, it became apparent that everyone speaking to him was also wearing some shade of red upon their breast. There were wonderful shirts and ties and blouses and dresses, and some even more exotic sources of redness, such as elaborate necklaces or swirls of paint. Some of those attending the barbecue even wore red across their chins, and a little beneath their nostrils.

Eventually Georgie arrived, carrying the pyramid of burgers. She set it down beside the barbecue, and when she air-kissed Simone, he noticed that she, too, had a crimson breast; she was wearing an enormous, glittering cascade of rubies that bubbled from her lips and made their way down her chin to cover the exposed skin of her upper chest. She even bore two rubies in pride of place at the centre of her face, one beneath each nostril.

"Darling…" said Simone uncertainly.

"I'm so glad you're awake!" she said. "I thought you might miss the entire barbecue. But you have come through wonderfully, as usual. Your outfit absolutely complements my own, which is ever so marvellous. I do so love you."

"And I love you."

"Won't you come and see everyone?" She looped her arm into his.

"Georgie?"

"Yes, darling?"

"Why does everyone have a beautiful nosebleed?"

Georgie blinked, dusting her cheeks with a little crimson powder from her lashes. "Why, it's the new fashion, darling. Surely you've seen the magazines? Justine invented it this morning."

"Justine?"

"Yes, dearest. Are you quite well?"

Simone wobbled, overcome by the surge of memories rushing into his brain. He remembered the party, the nosebleed, the flash of the camera, his meeting with Justine, and all the magazine covers he had seen down at the beach all at once, so that it felt as if a burst of recollections had blasted through his dam of sleepy forgetfulness. Simone lifted his hand to his face, and was surprised and gladdened to find that none of the memories had come flowing out of his nose with their sudden ferocity. "Yes, darling Georgie. I am well. I simply must… I simply have to… Is Justine here?"

Georgie paused before some firelight. "No, darling. I'm sure she has a great many more important party invites tonight. Why, she is a fashion genius!"

Simone took a deep breath, ready to protest and declare that it was he who had had the nosebleed; that it was he who had invented the new fashion; that it was he who was the true fashion genius. But then, in the darkness of the garden, a faint sound interrupted his thoughts. It was only very subtle – the merest background noise that would, on any other night, have caused him absolutely no alarm – but he could see, in Georgie's eyes, that she, too, had heard it.

It was the faint sound of glass shattering.

"The greenhouse!" cried Georgie, as softly as she was able.

They swiftly meandered, arm in arm, through the barbecue, exchanging as few pleasantries as politely possible. The torches lining the paths guttered, and the noise of them crackling and fizzing mingled with the affected murmurs of the guests to form a warm background noise which seemed to have mostly masked the sound of breaking glass. Thankfully, sobriety was not in fashion, and being so chemically impaired at a party that one might drop one's cocktail was perfectly acceptable, so it would be easy enough to assume, for anyone who was not Simone or Georgie, that someone at the barbecue had simply had one cocktail too many, and that one of their glasses had slipped from their fingers.

There, ahead, stood the greenhouse. It was far enough away from the fires that nobody was nearby, but it still glowed, crystalline in the night, its myriad panes as starry as the sky above.

Only, tonight, there was a different glinting near the rear of the structure, beside a dark square absent of glass. It was the shattered remnants of a pane, and Simone found himself momentarily distracted by the jagged edges of it, sprawled so wickedly across the grasses, breaking apart the horrible yellow moon with its reflective shards. Only after dragging his gaze from the glass did he notice the deeper silhouette in the grass nearby; the silhouette of a small body, covered in a mushy, glistening substance Simone assumed was yet another bodily fluid, of which the child had a surplus. The body lay still in the grass.

"*It's the denim child!*" shrieked Georgie, beneath her breath. "What ever should we do?"

Georgie was right. Something had to be done. At any moment someone might walk along the paths of the garden close enough to see the small body, and it was very unfashionable to leave a corpse lying around at a party (even though it was, currently, fashionable to be dressed as a corpse at a party). Simone's brain, currently unimpaired by cocktails or white powder, and refuelled by his rest and meal, leapt into action. "Darling," he said softly, "you must do your best to distract everyone at the barbecue."

"Of course, dear heart. But what will you do?"

"I," said Simone, heroically, "will dispose of the body."

"You are so brave, Simone! But won't that mean…"

"Yes, darling. I'm afraid… I'm going to have to touch the child."

Georgie's gasp of horror was almost loud enough to be heard over the murmur of the barbecue. "But, darling… what if you catch whatever horrible disease it has that makes it so small and unfashionable?"

The truth was that Simone did not know if childhood was infectious. "If I begin to feel any less fashionable," he said, reasonably, "then I will immediately go to the hospital."

Georgie nodded. "Very wise."

"Wish me luck, dear heart."

Georgie air-kissed Simone, and then rushed back towards the heart of the party. Simone, meanwhile, stared at the horrible little child, and tried his very best to muster up the courage he would need to not only touch it, but pick it up and carry it all the way to the edge of the garden. Once again, he cast his eyes over the pulpy substance that glistened all over its torso, and found himself shuddering at the idea of being in contact with it. He would have to burn his suit afterwards, and have at least two baths, and a very lengthy manicure. Swallowing the bile rising in his throat, Simone advanced across the crisp grasses, feeling the blades crunch uncomfortably beneath his shoes.

There lay the hideous child, glistening wetly in the ugly moonlight.

Leaning over as gracefully as he was able, Simone slid his hands beneath the small body and, wobbling, hoisted it into the air. Simone had not done much lifting in his life because it had never been particularly fashionable to be seen doing labour (which was largely the domain of the unfashionables), so while he had a great deal of experience hauling things like cocktails and morsels of food, he had never before had the opportunity to appreciate just how heavy a human body was. Staggering slightly beneath the unbelievable weight of the child, Simone began making his way through the darker recesses of the garden.

Ahead, between the trees, he could see a railing, which overlooked the steep drop to the realm of the uglies below.

There was the distant sound of a glass being politely clinked for attention, and Simone glimpsed the silhouettes of his fellow barbecue attendees as they meandered towards the summons. By the sounds of it, Georgie was gathering everyone near the barbecue for what would no doubt be a rousing toast. Simone felt a momentary flash of pride; Georgie was wonderful at toasts; she had a way of keeping everyone's attention, and always made certain she included and complimented everyone present without making it obvious she was subtly complimenting herself most of all. Simone wobbled up to the edge of the garden, preparing to roll the body over the railing.

Suddenly, the child made a noise. It was a small, mewling, coughing splutter, like a wet sneeze crossed with a gargle, and Simone almost flung its body over the railing in surprise. The child was still alive! And somehow even more disgusting because of it. Simone felt his arms tremble in panic, and quickly began to rush through the rest of the garden. It would have been fine to throw a corpse over the edge of the garden, but actual murder was both very impolite and highly unfashionable. He would have to hide the child instead.

There was nobody beside the bay doors, and the silhouettes Simone could see were all angled towards the barbecue and Georgie, whose voice rose above the warm crackling of the torches in a steady stream of compliments and accolades. On quivering legs, Simone swiftly crossed the distance between the dark shade of the trees and the bay doors, and stepped into the bright interior of his apartment. Shuffling out of his shoes to avoid staining the carpets with pieces of grass, he rushed along the hallways towards the distant bedroom. The child lolled precariously in his arms, and beneath the bright lamps of the apartment Simone could see that it was not smothered in bodily fluids at all, but a kind of red seeded pulp that was all over its hands, face and shoulders, and smelled strongly of tomatoes. But of course! The greenhouse was filled with tomatoes! The child must have gorged itself on them.

At last, there was the bedroom door, still slightly ajar.

Unable to maintain his composure any longer, Simone elbowed the door the rest of the way open and flung the child on to the bed, where it bounced a couple of times before coming to a rest. It was making a lot more disgusting gurgling noises, and beginning to twitch, as if awakening from its stupor, so Simone quickly slammed the door shut before it could rise and accost him with its miniature brand of ugliness. Still shaking, he dragged a gilded claw-foot chair from the lounge nearby and propped it up against the door as an extra barrier. Then, at last, he allowed himself to regain his composure, and made his way through to the nearest bathroom.

By the time Simone finished cleansing himself (suit burned, multiple baths poured, and an intricate manicure applied to both fingers and toes), the barbecue was over and the apartment was quiet again. Simone, now wrapped in a red dressing gown with matching slippers, both of which were as soft as a lobster's innards, wandered the halls until he found Georgie, who was sat upon the gilded claw-foot chair in front of the bedroom door, her expression glazed.

"Georgie, darling. You did ever such a good job with your toast."

"Yes," she said distantly. "And you did ever such a good job carrying the child to the bedroom before anybody noticed it."

"Is it… still in there?" asked Simone, daring to believe that the denim child might have simply vanished while he was bathing.

"It was making a lot of disgusting noises," said Georgie, "and I wasn't sure what to do. I thought feeding it might settle it, so I left it the pyramid of burgers and a pitcher of that refreshing blue and yellow cocktail that Darlington likes to mix."

Simone knew the very cocktail Georgie was talking about. "Such a wonderful idea, darling."

"Indeed. It seems to have worked."

Simone considered the bedroom door. "We may have to sleep in the guest bedroom tonight."

"Yes," said Georgie. "I dearly hope the horrible child will be gone by morning."

"Darling," said Simone, leaning over and taking her by the arm. "You have had a trying evening. Why not go and soak yourself in a nice warm bath?"

"Yes. I think I will. Will you be joining me?"

"Perhaps, later on. I have something important to do first."

Georgie's eyes focused, searching Simone's. "What do you have to do, my dearest?"

"It's time," said Simone sternly, "that I confront Justine."

* * *

The current fashion for confrontation was knightly, so Simone dressed in the armoury.

There were an awful lot of guns in the armoury, chrome and gleaming and accompanied by all different kinds of bullet belts, and Simone eyed them regretfully. The fashion for bringing guns to confrontations had been loud, and exciting, and Simone had enjoyed the weight of the pistols and rifles in his hands; they lent his outfits a lethality, as if one might drop dead at the mere sight of him. Still, he supposed the fashion for guns might come back at some point, perhaps in a new form. The previous fashion had come as part of an Old West theme, replete with broad-brimmed cowboy hats and sharpened spurs, and while fashion did not like repeating itself (at least, within the lifetimes of the fashionables who adhered to them), there were certain components that did see reuse. Guns were just another type of accessory, after all.

Simone turned instead to the racks of melee weapons. There were all kinds of maces, and hammers, and flails, and pikes, but he settled on the swords, which were arranged in a row at the very centre of the selection. The trick with confrontations was to choose the correct weapon in proportion to one's opponent, to better complement them and thus improve the aesthetic sensibility of the conflict on all sides. Indeed, Simone would expect Justine to tailor her outfit to complement him in turn. The swords were ideal, because Justine was elegant, and sharp, and well balanced; there was no heaviness or bluntness to her. Settling on a mirror-chrome longsword, Simone swung it about a bit. He supposed, in the distant past when knights used swords to physically murder each other, that they must have been quite heavy, but the longsword was lightweight, made from a material that rendered it strong and sharp without encumbering its wielder. Sheathing it in mirror-chrome silver with gilded trimming, he looped the scabbard into a creamy white leather belt, ready for the rest of his outfit.

Next, Simone weaponised his face. For his eyes, he chose a set of false lashes like needles by Raul Rascale, so sharp that he seemed to slice the air every time he blinked. Then, with silver powders (also from the Raul Rascale Honour and Glory collection), he sharpened his cheekbones and jaws into stern, steely lines, and with silver and gold liners and lipsticks brought his brows and lips to deadly points. When Simone pouted in the armoury's dressing-table mirror, he was surprised the glass didn't crack.

There were several sets of armour up on the racks, but the choice today was obvious. The ideal set for a mirror-chrome with gilded edges aesthetic was designed by Kammpa Starr. First, he donned the gentle layers of under-armour, which were downy on the inside and made of a soft creamy leather. Then he fastened the various pieces of armour into place. The plates – greaves, and vambraces, and pauldrons – took a great deal of time to buckle together, all interlinked as if the armour was a beautiful exoskeleton, but Simone's hands worked automatically at the task; his body knew, in the same way it knew how to breathe, how to dress itself. At last, Simone pulled on his gauntlets, and flexed his fingers beneath the lightweight plating, which made a satisfying metallic noise. Strapping his sword belt into place, Simone picked up his helmet and looped it on the other side of his belt from his sword; the helmet was an essential part of the armour, but no fashionista would ever dare to actually wear one, for fear of affecting or, worse, concealing their features.

Satisfied, Simone took the lift down to the lobby.

Between the vast gold and red pillars of the reception was Georgie, dressed in a silken scarlet dressing gown that matched the draperies and carpet. Her hair was a red rush, cascading across her shoulders, and her lashes were the same gold as the light fittings. "Oh, darling!" she exclaimed, at the sight of Simone in his armour, "you do look deadly."

"Do I, dearest heart?"

"I feel as if you might behead me with a glance."

Simone fluttered his knife-lashes. "I do feel quite deadly."

Georgie leant up against one of the golden pillars, hands to her heart. "I took the liberty of anticipating your choice in armour and programmed the car for you. I do hope you're pleased with it." The red drapes hanging from the pillar billowed dramatically around her. "Also, this morning's magazines arrived while you were readying yourself. I've left you a selection, should you feel a desire to peruse while out on your noble journey."

"Oh, darling. You really do think of everything."

Georgie smiled, gorgeously. "Best of luck, my sweet."

Simone air-kissed his wife, then strode proudly through the awaiting doors of the lobby and into the night beyond. There idled the car, every bit as chrome and gilt as Simone's armour. Why, it was perfect! Simone was vaguely aware that knights rode horses, which felt like a peculiar choice; horses were beautiful, certainly, but they were also intimidatingly large, notoriously untrustworthy, and smelled of things like hay and manure. Knights, thought Simone, as he inelegantly manoeuvred himself into the back seat of his limousine, would have been better off with cars, which were far more modest, and reliable, and smelled of pleasant things like petroleum fumes, leather and car freshener.

"Take me to Justine's house," he said, and the limousine began to move.

There was indeed a large stack of magazines beside the fizzy glasses of champagne, and Simone flicked through a selection. Of course, there was plenty about Justine, and reports indicating that designers everywhere were busy producing collections in honour of the new fashion for nosebleeds, composed of clothing and jewellery designed to really set off one's bloodied chin and chest. Simone quickly tired of the selection; he would confront Justine in person very soon, after all. Thankfully, Georgie had also included the latest lingerie catalogue from Sensua, which had absolutely no mention of nosebleeds anywhere in it.

Simone leafed through the lingerie catalogue and was delighted to see that suspenders and stockings were still in style. He rather liked the way his legs looked in stockings, and the new colours and materials were really quite exciting. Simone made a mental note to update his collection before the next orgy, and flicked through to find the corsets. Thankfully, corsets were also still in fashion, and this month the fashion was for basques. Simone was fond of the fashion for corsets, because Georgie had a marvellous bosom, and Simone enjoyed seeing the extraordinary effects that her collection of corsets had on it.

Indeed, Simone so enjoyed Georgie's bosom that he sometimes considered asking Dr Cask for one of his own.

As Simone admired the various corsets in the catalogue, he realised that he had developed an erection. Thankfully, his armour's codpiece was generous enough to accommodate him, so he continued looking through the catalogue, thinking about Georgie in lingerie, and enjoying the hardness of his penis. Perhaps, when he returned from his confrontation with Justine, he would participate in a very different kind of confrontation with his wife.

At last, the limousine pulled up at Justine's driveway.

Simone slid from the car as elegantly as he was able, and stood before the open gates, his armour shining in the light of the headlamps. Dark clouds had gathered overhead, mercifully muffling the disgusting yellow moon, and the way ahead was lit only by the pale lamps lining the ascent. Tonight, a low mist drifted down the driveway, curling around Simone's sabatons, and it felt fitting that he should make his ascent to the house on foot, to maximise the drama of his approach. Making certain his sword belt was well buckled, Simone stood in the car's headlights for a few moments more (in case there was anyone in any of the other houses nearby watching him), then waded into the rolling mist and up the hill. Ahead, where Justine's house should have been visible, there were only dark clouds stifling the stars.

The trees overhanging the driveway were perfectly still, and the clinking of Simone's armour was the only sound. Feeling wary, Simone drew his shining blade and turned it over in his gauntlets so that it caught the light of the lamps. He could see hints of his reflection in its shiny chrome surface, and he drew strength from it.

This time, Justine's house had no windows at all. The balcony was gone. Instead, there was a single set of double doors, open at the apex of a set of stone steps, from within which the drifting mist slowly rolled. The light inside was dim, and there was no movement. As Simone approached, he expected Justine to emerge from the house, making her grand entrance to the confrontation – but while the mist made for strange silhouettes, none coalesced into the shape of a woman armed and armoured to meet him.

At the foot of the steps, Simone paused, blade in hand. The sky boiled black above him. It was plausible, he reasoned, that Justine had failed to anticipate the confrontation about to occur, and was simply disposing of certain vapours that had accumulated inside her house, but it was unlikely. A failure to appropriately anticipate and prepare for a confrontation was an admission of defeat, and Justine was far too clever for that. It was most likely that the open doors were an invitation.

The mist thickened as he climbed the steps, writhing around his greaves as if it meant to tangle and trip him. The doors were thick, and made of a dark wood the same black as the sky, and beyond them waited an unadorned corridor, dim beneath the gloomy white glow of low-lit bulbs. The walls of the corridor were mirrored, just as they were at the party, so that when Simone stepped inside a multitude of Simones stepped with him. At once, he became more than a lone knight; together with all his selves, he was an entire vanguard, assaulting the oppressive house with his mighty beauty.

The corridor was long, and as Simone ventured down it, the lights behind him began to wink out. Eventually, he was alone with his reflections and the few bulbs above him, revealing nothing of the way ahead. Simone remained alert, treading carefully through the mist to avoid any traps of the kind that might rob him of his marvellous knightly glamour, but none presented themselves. He blinked away the gloom with his knife-like lashes.

At last, the corridor opened into an octagonal room, filled with mists that came all the way up to Simone's waist. The lights were low, but Simone could still see himself reflected in the walls, all of which were mirrored. As he turned, blade steady, so too did all the other Simones, so that he felt as if he were defending himself from every angle. There were no doors, and no more corridors from here; this is where the confrontation would occur.

All at once, the lights went out.

Simone gripped his sword with both hands.

The lights returned, so much brighter, and no longer was Simone surrounded by himself. Every mirror reflected Justine instead.

Tonight, she wore ice.

The ice was a dress frosted across her, crystalline and cold. When she moved her limbs, it moved without cracking, and at her shoulders and wrists it fractured into gleaming icicles that seemed so much sharper than Simone's sword. Upon her brow sat a ring of icicles in a jagged array, arranged into a tiara that complemented her icicle eyelashes. The ice was all crystal clear, and revealed her skin in its smooth facets, except for the places where the frozen dress dripped with a slow-moving stream of blood. Justine's nose ran thickly crimson, down her chin and across her chest, flowing along intricate fracture lines.

"Simone," she said, from every angle of the room. "I hoped you would come."

Simone turned on the spot, but Justine was everywhere around him. "Justine," he said, "you stole my look," but the waver in his voice betrayed his uncertainty. Surely – a small voice was saying in the back of his mind – someone as overwhelmingly tasteful as this would not stoop to stealing. Surely she must have come up with the fashion for nosebleeds all by herself. Just look at her! Look at how beautiful she is!

"My fabulous friend," said Justine sensually. "I have an offer to make you."

Simone felt his grip on his sword weaken. The tip dipped into the mist.

"You are brilliant," continued Justine, her pale eyes as agleam as the ice she wore. "But you don't understand your own brilliance. You are the stuff of raw beauty, but you're incapable of realising your own potential. I, however, can help you. I can see what you are, and I can make you what you dream of being. I can make you… a fashion icon."

The sword hung loose at Simone's side.

"Leave your wife," said Justine, with blood in her teeth. "And I will let you marry me."

It seemed so obvious a thing to do. Of course, Justine was right. With Simone's ability to accidentally stumble into aesthetically innovative situations, and her ability to refine them into fashions, they would be an unstoppable couple.

Simone was close to verbalising his acceptance – so absorbed in Justine's icy gaze that he felt frozen by her – when he remembered Georgie. Georgie, who had stood by him, all through his unfashionable fumbles. Georgie, who was the most beautiful aesthetic weeper he knew. Georgie, who had helped him hide the horrible denim child. Simone dropped his gaze into the mists, ashamed.

The mists temporarily parted, and there was the sword. In its mirrored blade, Simone caught sight of himself, and suddenly he was free of Justine's icy visage. Why, Simone was no fumbling fashion fool, stumbling from glamour to glamour; he was a glorious, stunning fashionista, armoured in his own deliberate beauty!

Gripping his sword tightly again, Simone raised it to his face, so he could admire himself properly. There were his cheekbones, so deadly, and there were his silver knife-lashes, so cutting, and there were his lips, sharpening as he arranged them into a pointed smile.

"No," said Simone, and his voice did not waver. "I will not marry you."

There was a gasp of frustration from the reflected Justines, followed immediately by a sharp cracking noise. Simone glanced across just in time to see the fissure forming across the left arm of Justine's frozen dress, formed by the sudden movement of her tightening her fist. The entire sleeve began to disintegrate, cracking into shards, and the last thing Simone saw before the lights went out was Justine's face, curled into an inelegant expression of humiliation.

When the lights came back on, she was gone, and Simone was once again alone with his many reflected selves. Victorious, he sheathed his sword and retraced his steps along the reflective corridor, pausing every now and then to admire himself. Back out into the night he went, and when he reached the bottom of the steps, he heard the doors leading into Justine's house close behind him with a sigh. With his head high, Simone descended, and by the time he reached his waiting limousine, the mists had completely faded away.

* * *

Feeling fresh, Simone stepped out of the vibro-rail carriage.

Today was Friday, which meant neon. Thankfully, the fashion did not favour any particular shade of neon, which made for quite a nice variety of colours. As such, the mall would be vibrant with garishly dressed fashionistas in every shade of bright. The mall was a wonderful place to visit on Fridays, because a lot of the stores had neon signs and neon decorations, making it very easy to find good places to strike a pose. Simone sashayed through the sliding entrance doors and into the cavernous interior, which bustled with so many brilliantly dressed glitterati across its many tiered floors that the mall felt like a colosseum for fashion.

Simone had opted for a fruity look. He was wearing a pair of cute lemon-yellow shorts with a tiny lemon slice embroidered into the pocket, along with a matching pair of lemon earrings, to complement his neon orange slinky vest and neon orange cheekbones and mascara. Best of all were his neon orange sneakers, which were segmented in a way that made it look as if his feet were wrapped in slices of orange. Ahead, at the top of the escalator, waited the gym – Simone's destination for the morning – and around his wrists were lemon-yellow sweatbands which matched his lemon-yellow nails and shorts. Mounting the escalator, Simone's ascent into the heights of the mall began, and he stretched his arms as he rose, so that everyone below could admire his outfit.

Waking this morning had been wonderful. For the first time in weeks he had slept in a bed, because the guest bedroom, while still nautically themed, had an ordinary emperor-sized mattress instead of a mattress occupied by fish. Better yet, he had awoken to find that Georgie, who must have already left for work, had artfully positioned delicate pieces of clothing everywhere around the room, so as to suggest the sensual undressing and subsequent sexual ravishing that had occurred the night before. There were several bras strategically strewn over lamps and the backs of chairs, and the floor was a veritable field of silken stockings, and each doorhandle had its very own pair of panties, so that Simone could not possibly leave the room without recalling every detail of the many marvellous hours he and Georgie had spent stimulating each other. Indeed, they had shared so many aesthetically pleasing orgasms together that Simone's legs still trembled slightly.

Simone entered the gym, where the glitterati were elegantly arranged over instruments of exercise. Some idly bounced on giant inflatable balls, while others practised their runway walks on the treadmills. A few even posed in some of the more complicated pieces of machinery, which were designed to allow the user to adopt some wonderfully athletic positions. Of course, doing any actual exercise in public was deeply unfashionable, but it was fashionable to be seen appearing to exercise.

Simone spotted Darlington over by the mirrors, and meandered elegantly across.

Darlington's body really was rather marvellous. It bulged in all kinds of interesting places, and the outfits he wore always appeared to be under considerable pressure, as if parts of him might burst through them at any moment. Indeed, Simone had had several fantasies about being held in his enormous arms. Today, Darlington was sat upon a bench and gently pumping a pink dumbbell that matched the rest of his neon pink outfit. He wore a tiny vest top that exposed his rippling musculature, and a tiny pair of shorts that emphasised everything they strained to contain, and his hair was a pink swirl that made it seem as if someone had poured strawberry ice-cream across his scalp.

"Good morning, Darlington," said Simone. "Your hair is wonderful today."

Simone had a sunshine-yellow water bottle, and he sipped from it to give his aesthetic an athletic kinetic element.

"Thank you, Simone," said Darlington. "Your shoes are delicious."

The two men spent a while admiring each other.

"Did you hear about Cynthia?" asked Darlington. "She perished yesterday."

"Oh, how dreadful! She was quite beautiful. Do you know how it happened?"

"From what I hear, she tried to use a six-inch stiletto to give herself a nosebleed and accidentally lobotomised herself." Darlington's expression was wistful. "Apparently, it was quite the sight to behold. She was drenched in blood down to her toes, and her stiletto was embedded so deeply up her nostril that nobody could get it out. All the way to the hilt."

"Gorgeous way to go."

Darlington pumped his dumbbell, and Simone sipped at his water bottle, remembering the fashion for deadly clothes a few years ago. A few of his friends had perished while wearing dresses made of knives, and lipsticks made of arsenic, and other such dangerous pieces of clothing, and their corpses had made it onto the covers of various magazines.

"Ah," said Darlington. "I almost forgot. Justine was looking for you."

"Justine?"

"She's in the dance studio."

"Did she say what she wanted?"

"If she did, it's quite gone from my mind."

"Thank you for letting me know."

Curious but cautious, Simone wandered across to the doors that would take him through to the dance studio. Certainly, he had been victorious against Justine last night – reassuring him that he was the true fashion genius, and that she was no more than fashion carrion, circling him in search of beautiful morsels – but he was still wary. The doors to the studio swished open and Simone paused there, one arm across his forehead, as if he was wearied by all the exercise he had been doing in the gym.

The dance studio was loud with thumping music, and filled with shifting fashionistas. Some flowed like ballerinas, slow and graceful, while others strutted to and fro, striking shapes, and Simone moved elegantly among them, feeling his heart synchronise to the beat. At the far side was a long wooden bar set against a row of mirrors where a group of glitterati stretched themselves into warm-up positions, and there was Justine, resplendent among them. While everyone in the studio was dressed in neon, Justine's neon was an especially neon neon. She wore a lime-green leotard as the centrepiece of her look, and upon her feet were a pair of matching lime-green sneakers, one of which was currently positioned up on the wooden bar. Justine stretched lengthily and luxuriously across her raised leg.

Unable to speak to her over the music, Simone stretched beside her to get her attention, raising his arms over his head as if they were rays of sunshine bursting from his orange and yellow outfit. Justine turned her head to acknowledge him, fluttering her lengthy lime lashes in greeting. Then, lowering her leg and bouncing upon her feet for a moment, she took him by the arm, and together they shifted through the room and back towards the gym.

The doors into the studio swished closed behind them.

"Simone!" exclaimed Justine. "I am so glad to see you!"

"As am I, dear Justine," said Simone cautiously.

"I wanted to apologise for last night," she said, arching her intricately plucked brows to emphasise her regret. "I said ever so many inappropriate things."

"It's quite all right. Already forgotten."

"You're so generous! And your outfit today is simply scrumptious."

"Thank you. As is yours."

She giggled, raising a hand to her face bashfully. "Oh, Simone. You are wonderful, and I am dreadful. To make up for my behaviour, I would like to invite you to a little pool party I'm having this afternoon at my beach house."

Simone felt his heart flutter in his chest. Justine really was very well connected. It would be an opportunity to mingle with some highly influential fashionistas. And besides, it had been ages since he last attended a pool party – especially one beside the sea. He would have to go home immediately and spend the rest of the morning choosing exactly the right outfit to impress everyone with. "Why… of course!" he replied. "I would be delighted to attend."

Justine gave his bicep a little squeeze. "Marvellous," she said. "Simply marvellous."

* * *

Simone hugged his lemon-yellow inflatable water-wings close and shivered. For the pool party, he had opted to wear an eye-catching pair of miniscule neon yellow swimming briefs by Stringham, and little else. Upon his feet were a pair of matching sandals, and upon his forehead was a set of swimming goggles, and, of course, he had his water-wings, but the truth was that he was feeling rather cold in the back of the car. His chilly lemon-slice earrings jostled, and every time one of them swung to touch his jaw, it gave him a little fright. There were a few glasses of bubbling fizz up on the counter, which might have warmed him with their intoxicating golden glow, but Simone was hesitant to touch them for fear the crystal might be as cold as everything else in the limousine. Instead, he huddled up in the leather, which was at least the same temperature as his body, and tried to think warm thoughts.

Beyond the limousine's windows, the highway seethed.

Rust clung to the railings, and grass sprouted from cracks in the paving, and bits of litter fluttered in the wind. There were fields beyond the railings, full of all kinds of untamed growth; the trees were stooped and gnarled, and the crops sprouted like so many dry hairs, and weighty cattle tottered about, their stumpy legs struggling to support their lumpy bodies as they shifted between uneven patches of gnawed grass. Worst of all were the unfashionables, who sweated and laboured in the fields, gnarled limbs struggling, stooped beneath baskets of fruit and working with unmanicured hands at the drooping udders of the cattle, spurting white liquid into beaten metal buckets and all over their worn, dirty clothes. Everyone Simone saw was wearing denim, and every time one of them rose to admire the limousine as it swished past in the sunshine Simone huddled up even tighter in his seat, for fear the very gaze of a farmyard unfashionable might render his skin equally as weather-worn.

Eventually, the fields gave way to uninterrupted citrus orchards, and the view improved considerably. No longer did unfashionables lumber and grope about; instead there were only trees in ordered rows, growing high and bright in the sunlight, their branches bulbous with ripe fruits. There were orange trees, and lime trees, and, finally and most magnificently of all, lemon trees, the fruits of which were so engorged with yellow loveliness that it seemed to Simone as if they were in fact sun trees, with miniature suns growing on their slender branches. Simone drew closer to the window and admired the lemons, but as he did he noticed a terrible detail. The lemons were imperfect! As soon as he focused on a fruit he could see the lumps and dents across its glowing surface, marring its shape. Of course, Simone blamed the unfashionables. Obviously, under their care the fruits were not realising their perfect, unblemished potential.

Suddenly, a singular lemon tree grabbed his attention.

The tree was young. It grew tall, and its leaves were each a crisp greenness. A lone lemon grew from a branch, so heavy and engorged that the whole tree tilted towards it, and not a single errant nodule or scar marred its surface. Better yet, the tree bore no other fruit; it seemed to have devoted its entire purpose to producing a single exquisite specimen.

The lemon swung gently in the breeze.

"Stop!" Simone cried, and the limousine came to a smooth halt.

Emerging from the vehicle, Simone was immediately warmed by the heat of the sun; it was another dazzling day outside. Moving forward, he did his best to ignore the uneven highway. Juddering, coughing cars that resembled piles of scrap bolted carelessly together clattered past, and blackbirds screeched overhead, threatening to spatter Simone with excrement, and the grass and gravel beyond the railing were filthy and no doubt infested with all kinds of maggoty insects, but Simone continued bravely on, stepping over the railing and the low wall beyond, and into the orchard itself, where he was immediately surrounded by the imperfect lemon trees and their single perfect sibling. A few more steps and he was stood before the wonderful tree itself, which seemed to lean down towards him, offering him its bounty.

Simone reached up and carefully cupped the fruit in his hands.

The lemon was warm. It took no more than the gentlest twist of his wrist to pluck it, and then it was free. The tree seemed to sigh, its leaves rustling in delight at having delivered its fruit to such a beautiful recipient, and Simone smiled his thanks in return, fluttering his lashes in deference.

Quickly, he returned to the limousine.

"Carry on," he said, and as the car resumed its journey, he turned the lemon over in his hands. It was the ultimate accessory to his outfit, certainly, but it was also more than that – its warmth seeped into him. No longer did Simone shiver, and no longer was he nervous at the idea of appearing at the pool party; he felt every bit as flawless as the lemon.

It did not take much longer to reach the driveway leading to Justine's beach house. As the car left the highway, the road became smoother and meandered into a rich, well-kept forest, with trees positioned to dapple the forest floor with coins of sunlight, making it appear as if piles of gold had accumulated among the roots. Simone caught glimpses of the sea beyond the trees, and it sparkled as if it were a pot of blue glitter he might use to accentuate his cheekbones. Then, at last, the beach house itself came into view, nestled into a copse close to the seafront.

The house itself was no more than four glass walls with a

flat white roof to protect the white double bed that stood inside. In fact, the house appeared to be no more than an accessory to the pool at its rear, which was quite the event. The pool was a smooth, glassy, unblemished blue, and it was surrounded on all sides by a white stone patio, bedecked with deckchairs. There were flagpoles here and there, upon which guttered and streamed white flags made of such an ethereal material that it was as if someone had captured summer spirits, each desperately trying to escape their confinement. The glitterati surrounded the pool, and Simone felt his heart lift at the sight of them.

Leaving his limousine, which was the same yellow as his swimming briefs, Simone made his way to the pool. A sliver of beach lay beyond, being sucked at by the sea, and Simone found himself momentarily distracted by the lines across the sand; it looked as if someone had raked the beach earlier, but had failed to smooth it over properly. And yet… the longer he spent looking at the lines, the more he grew to appreciate them. They were in neat rows, like bars of sheet music, and the uneven rise and fall of the sea was like a description of sound across them. Simone realised he was listening intently for the song of the sea.

"Simone!" It was Justine, who was waiting beside the gate. "I'm so glad you could make it." She was wearing a one-piece swimsuit that looked as if it was made out of the skin of an enormous lime. At the sight of Simone, she raised her oversized sunglasses to reveal a set of green lashes the same texture and sharpness as the leaves at the head of a pineapple.

"Justine!" said Simone. "I must say, that is a darling swimsuit." She and he air-kissed.

"Why, thank you. It's a new design by Karpa Fishh."

"Do you know what it's made of?"

"Why don't you ask him yourself? He's over by the pool."

Simone felt his heart stop in his chest. "Karpa Fishh? He's here?"

"Of course." Justine bobbed, unable to contain her smile. "I sent him an invite yesterday, and he very graciously accepted. Follow me, and I'll introduce you."

Designers were the saints of fashion, and to have a designer attend one's party was the highest of compliments. Simone had only ever seen two designers before. The first time, he had caught a glimpse of Messr Messr entering a limousine after a fashion show and spent the next two hours pacing the space the designer had temporarily occupied, hoping to catch the faintest whiff of his scent. The second time, he had caught sight of Jill Mill at a gala as she placed her empty cocktail glass down on a table, and, after stealing and subsequently smuggling the used glass home, had spent the next month studying the lipstick stain at the rim. To be introduced to a designer was almost too much for him to handle. Indeed, the very presence of Karpa Fishh at the pool party made everyone else seem hideously unfashionable; Simone was suddenly ashamed of his outfit. Doing his very best to retain his composure, Simone gripped hold of his lemon with both hands, and drew as much strength as he could from its smooth, unblemished surface.

Looking at Karpa Fishh was like trying to stare at the sun. Simone caught glimpses of bejewelled fingers, and the sleeve of a shirt made of neon yellow scales that looked like fingernails, and a jawline so sharp it made every other straight line Simone had ever seen look curved. Justine was saying something to Karpa Fishh, and Karpa Fishh was saying something in return, and then Karpa Fishh's gaze was directed towards Simone, and Simone felt as if his flesh was melting from his bones. Words transcended the gulf between them, and Simone realised he was being spoken to. "That is a wonderful lemon," said Karpa Fishh. Then, suddenly, the encounter was over, and Simone was back on the other side of the pool and recovering, his knees trembling slightly.

The lemon glowed in the sunlight, and Simone admired its loveliness. Karpa Fishh himself had complimented it, so it truly was a blessed object, and Simone's perilous excursion through the field had been worth the risk. Perhaps he truly was a fashion conduit, channelling the raw stuff of beauty. Perhaps Simone was destined for fashion greatness. Perhaps, one day, Simone might even transcend his status as a fashionite and become a designer himself, foregoing his given name for a designer name. Sometimes, late at night, Simone tried to imagine what his designer name would be; maybe Simón Simón, or maybe – now – Simón Lemón.

Simone's dream was disturbed by Justine, who was approaching with a pair of cocktails. The cocktails were made of a yellow liquid and a wispy clear liquid, separated from each other by some trick of chemistry. "Simone, my darling friend. Would you be a dear and take these to Karpa Fishh? I would go myself, but I think they complement your outfit rather more than mine." Pouting, Justine tilted her oversized sunglasses so that twin suns blazed in the lenses.

"Of course!" Simone almost leapt at the opportunity to approach the hallowed designer for a second time. The only issue was that there were two cocktails, and Simone's hands were currently occupied by the lemon. Taking a moment to check his outfit for any pockets he might have missed (of which neither his swimming briefs nor his water-wings had any), Simone reluctantly decided he would have to temporarily leave his lemon somewhere safe. There was an unoccupied deckchair nearby, on which lay a folded fluffy white towel, and when Simone placed the lemon upon it, it felt like the ideal frame to emphasise its yellow opulence. Satisfied, Simone left his lemon bathing in the sunshine, and took the cocktail glasses from Justine.

Orbiting the pool with a casual affectation, as if he were simply taking the cocktails for a stroll, Simone chose a route that would offer Karpa Fishh the best possible view of his approach. Then, suddenly, there was the designer, lounging upon a deckchair between two fabulous fashionites, who were laughing simultaneously at something the designer must have said. Simone synchronised his laughter to theirs, as if he had heard the amusing comment, and gracefully outstretched his arms to offer the cocktails. "These are for you," he said to Karpa Fishh, and what followed was a measure of gratitude so dazzlingly casual that Simone struggled to continue on his way, having delivered his cargo. Why, even the words that left Karpa Fishh's mouth were beautiful! Each syllable a delectable treat for the ears! Simone chose a meandering route back to his lemon, to make certain he would not accidentally swoon into the pool.

There, ahead, stood the deckchair where the lemon lay.

Only… there was no lemon.

Still dizzy from his second encounter with Karpa Fishh, Simone took a moment to collect himself. This was certainly the place he had left the lemon; there was the fluffy white towel which, upon closer inspection, still bore the slight indentation the lemon had left in it. There was a chance a particularly strong gust of wind might have caused it to roll from its resting place, but Simone could see no lemon anywhere nearby – it was neither in the pool, nor on the decking. It was possible that a wretched bird might have snatched the lemon, appreciating it only for its delicious potential, but the sky was empty and so were the trees. The only remaining possibility was that the lemon must have somehow rolled away with enough force to leave the deck and land on the beach below. Reluctantly, Simone went to investigate.

The sand was a gritty expanse at the end of the path. Leaning over, Simone did his best to inspect the beach without getting any grains on him, but he could see no lemon down there. It would surely be a bright yellow beacon, easily visible, but the sand was an unbroken amber.

There was a furore from the party which suggested that something fabulous had occurred, so Simone quickly made his way back to the pool; it simply would not do for him to miss anything important. The scene he met, however, was so overwhelming that Simone quite forgot how to breathe.

Justine had changed her outfit. She now wore a vivid yellow bikini of a design reminiscent of her swimsuit – except, instead of looking as if it were made of the skin of a lime, it looked as if it were made of the skin of a lemon. So, too, had she altered her face, so that her lips were neon yellow, matching the contours emphasising her cheekbones. Yet for all this, it was her jewellery that was the most remarkable part of her outfit. From each ear dangled an exquisite spiral of lemon peel, which bounced with her laughter, and threaded upon a slender golden chain around her neck, and rolling a single, aesthetically pleasing droplet of juice between her breasts, was a slice of lemon.

Of course, Simone recognised the peel. Of course, he recognised the segment.

Everyone was applauding her outfit, and paying her compliments, and Simone almost leapt the distance between them, ready to tear the butchered pieces of his perfect lemon from her. But then there was Karpa Fishh, at the head of the congregation of fashionites surrounding her, offering her compliments of his own. The world whirled around Simone, and he finally remembered to breathe, sucking in air with such an unaesthetic desperation that it was to his advantage that nobody was paying him any attention. Indeed, everyone was fixated on Justine. Simone clenched and unclenched his fists helplessly, listening to the praise that should have been his being lavished upon her. He stood there for as long as he could, but it was finally too much.

Lemonless and seething, he left the party.

* * *

Simone went for a makeover to try and cheer himself up.

At the heart of the silver skyscrapers in the centre of the city was a bright arcade full of salons that felt like something of a sanctuary. Simone began at a hair salon, where a team of hairdressers teased and tousled and trimmed his hair from one shape to another; he had no particular preference for the shape of his hair at that moment, but the act of having it worked upon was usually quite soothing. Unfortunately, today it was having little effect on his mood, and his hands remained clawed on the leather armrests of his chair.

At the next salon, he found himself snapping irritably at the manicurists working at his fingernails. Normally, he preferred to ignore them. The occupants of the salons, who worked at the beautiful bodies of the glitterati, were not really people after all. Each of them was no more than an elaborate, person-shaped tool, honed to do one specialised task exceptionally well. But today they were sloppy, and Simone snatched the file from a particularly clumsy manicurist in order to finish the job himself. Of course, Simone was perfectly capable of administering an excellent manicure, but that wasn't the point in the salons; they were meant to be a pleasant pastime, where one might go and feel like a statue being chipped away at by a team of sculptors.

Finally, Simone went to get a pedicure, and there sat rigidly in his chair, glaring out of the window at the fountain at the centre of the arcade, which ejected water through the sunshine in patterns that made it look as if diamonds were spurting from its various faucets. And, just as he was beginning to get irritated at the various grovelling pedicurists handling his beloved toes so roughly, he spied a group of especially ugly unfashionables intruding upon the pristine district.

They were gangly, and wore ill-fitting garments that appeared to have been designed to offend the eye of a fashionable onlooker. Some wore odd shoes, and others had a surplus of piercings in a variety of improbable places. Their cosmetics looked smeared on, and the gang's apparent ringleader, who strode around on platform boots with the gait of a man with inexplicably heavy pockets, wore his hair in gigantic spikes. They raised their hands in crude gestures, and spat on the clean white concrete, and yelled at the salons: "Fuck you, fashionists!"

Simone gripped hold of his seat harder than ever, almost tearing clean through the leather. Thankfully, it was then that the doors of the salons opened and almost every hairdresser and manicurist and waxer emptied into the arcade, brandishing the implements of their trade. Within moments, the sight of the unfashionable gang had been swept away beneath the rush of beauty specialists. Arms rose and fell, and the shouts of the unfashionables were replaced with screams, and a little blood was visible, spattered across the white concrete.

Normally, Simone would have drawn great satisfaction from seeing unfashionables being treated so rudely, but today he could find no comfort in the sight.

* * *

Simone continued to seethe through dinner.

The restaurant, which was called Banquet Dilué, was

overflowing with flowers. Bunches dripped from the ceiling and chandeliers, arrangements drenched the tables and windowsills, and even Simone's chair crunched as he sat down, crushing brightly coloured specimens. The petals and leaves of the plants were made of a silken meta-material that Simone did not recognise, but did appreciate for its luxuriance and luminosity, the result of which was that the restaurant resembled a super-real, overgrown garden. Yet, for all the wonder of the extremely exclusive restaurant (it had taken Simone weeks to get a reservation), he simply could not enjoy himself. Instead, he swirled his water around in its tumbler and did his very best to refrain from making it shatter against the nearest wall.

"Darling?" Georgie was seated opposite, but the flowers were so thick that they could not see each other. Parting the floral barrier, she emerged, and today her hair was a blue so bright that Simone felt as though he were beholding a summer sky through the foliage. "Are you well?"

"Of course, dearest heart."

"Are you quite certain? You're awfully quiet."

Simone tried to unclench his teeth. "Justine… has gone *too far*," he said.

"What has she done this time?"

"She stole my lemon, and wore it."

Georgie's hand emerged from the flower arrangement, palm upwards. "I'm so sorry, darling. Was it a particularly beautiful lemon?"

"It was the most perfect lemon I have ever seen."

"That dreadful girl!"

At that moment, the chef arrived with their dinner. Chefs of a calibre considered fashionable enough to serve the glitterati were so rare that it was quite extraordinary to see one, and this chef was no exception. His whites were so unblemished that he looked as if he had never so much as thought about the preparation of food in his life, and as he leaned over to place a small crystal phial first before Georgie, and then before Simone, Simone spent a moment appreciating his skeletal bone structure, which suggested his taste in food was so particular that he hardly ever ate anything.

With the chef's departure, Simone ate his meal. Of course, he did not exactly *eat* his meal because it was homeopathic. Right now, it was fashionable to have the contents of an entire banquet liquidised and diluted down to the point where it was basically water, and then carefully dropped on to one's eye. And indeed, as Simone raised his dropper on high, pulled his lower eyelid down and allowed a single, glinting droplet of food to splash on to his eye, he made several appreciative noises, as if the droplet were delicious. Then, because he was feeling especially famished, Simone even went so far as to drop a second drop on to his other eye. For a few moments, Simone's vision was blurry, and he very carefully blinked until the food was fully absorbed into his eyeballs.

Afterwards, Simone parted the flowers on the table just in time to see Georgie delicately dabbing at her lower eyelid to clear it of any stray dinner. "Darling," he said decisively. "I have decided I must take action."

"That's wonderful, dear heart." Georgie's eyes gleamed, either with the remains of her dinner or delight.

It was at that moment that dessert arrived, which was very convenient because while Simone had absolutely decided to take action, he was not yet certain what form of action he would take. The chef placed a large white plate before Simone, which was empty but for a tiny crystal. Simone gently pressed his finger to it, so that it stuck. Raising it to his face, he admired the delicious-looking morsel, which was an entire wedding cake crushed down to the size of a diamond. Placing it on his tongue, he felt the crumb melt and fill his mouth with its pungent sweetness. The chef returned and cleared the table, leaving Simone and Georgie with a saucer each, upon which was a spherical white breath-mint of ordinary size. Rolling his mint around in his hand, Simone decided he would wait for inspiration to strike.

Inspiration did not strike in the limousine on the way home. The low evening sun glowed through the windows, warming Simone's lap and illuminating the bubbles rising in the champagne flutes on the counter, and he felt nothing but a sharp pang of grief for his lost lemon.

Inspiration did not strike in the elevator up to the apartment, either. The problem was the lighting, which was far too harsh. Hot white bulbs beamed down upon the lift's occupants, revealing every tiny flaw, and there was no escaping one's ill-lit reflection in the multitude of mirrors, forcing one to confront one's every microscopic imperfection. Simone could not remember ever having taken an elevator with good lighting (even the elevator in Tremptor Tower gave him trouble), and after an incident involving no less than eight return trips to the apartment to fix a particularly troublesome set of lashes, Simone had decided to simply stare at the carpet whenever he was in one. Today, in a bid to open himself up to inspiring thoughts, he dared to peek, and saw the Simone in the mirror peeking back. The eyes, he had to admit, were very fetching, even in the harsh lighting, but he found no inspiration in them. Beautiful and empty.

Despite Simone's desire to fling himself into a soothing bubbly bath and wash the day away, he paused in the apartment's entrance hall. Georgie bustled about, and the soft lights were a soothing balm compared to the horrible glaring bulbs of the elevator, but something felt ever so slightly off about the apartment that he could not place. "Georgie?"

"Yes, darling?"

"Have you been doing some decorating?"

"No, darling." Georgie avoided Simone's gaze.

The fixtures and fittings all appeared to be in order. The carpets were still a lush expanse. Simone removed his hat and cast his eyes across the furniture, searching for the flaw as readily as he regularly searched for flaws in his own features.

There. On the leg of a cabinet. A smudge.

Simone leaned over and examined the smudge. It was very small, and composed of a black powdery substance. "Georgie?"

"Simone… I…"

There was a handprint on the wall, beside the cabinet. Simone gasped, stumbling backwards. The handprint was black, and slightly smeared, and very small. "Georgie!"

"I can explain!"

A sound interrupted Georgie's explanation, emanating from an open door a little further down the hall. It sounded like the sickly burbling of a polluted stream. Gripping hold of the rim of his hat as if he might use it as a shield, Simone hesitantly ventured to the doorway.

Decorating one's living room to a safari theme had been in fashion for a while now, and the living room was composed of zebra-skin carpets and lion-skin sofas, and arranged around the wood-panelled walls was a selection of taxidermy heads, belonging to all kinds of exotic and endangered species. Indeed, it was a fashion Simone was quite fond of; he rather enjoyed sashaying up and down the length of the living room, testing his outfits out on the glass eyes of the dead animals on the walls to see how it felt.

The living room was in ruins.

There were stains on the rugs, and handprints all over the sofas, and somebody had made a poor attempt at applying cosmetics to the taxidermy heads; an elephant wore lipstick on its trunk, and a crocodile wore drooping eyelashes, and there was an uneven pair of brows drawn on to a tiger, giving it an alarmed expression.

The culprit, and source of the horrible burbling, lounged in the corner.

It was the child.

Making all manner of wet noises to itself, the child continued to apply black smudges to its surroundings using the powdery remains of a jar of coal-black eyeshadow. Some of the eyeshadow was smudged into its own face, giving it a deathly look.

"Georgie!" Simone could barely breathe.

"It's all right, darling," said Georgie. "It's perfectly harmless. I promise."

"But it's ruining everything!"

"That's what I thought at first, too." Georgie went into the room, and approached the child, making small cooing noises. "After you left for your party, I decided to see if it was still in the bedroom. And what I found quite astonished me. Not only was the child still there, but it had managed to get into one of your wardrobes, and was trying things on."

"It touched my clothes?" Simone's legs felt weak.

"Yes, darling! At first, I was horrified. But then, I started to watch what it was doing. And…" She paused, dramatically. "It was matching colours together."

"It… was?" This was a peculiar development. Certainly, colour matching was a very rudimentary element of fashion, but it was something most unfashionables displayed no understanding of whatsoever. Indeed, the child was no longer wearing its grotesque denim ensemble, and was instead clothed in a crude toga made of white scarves.

"It was fascinating to watch," said Georgie. "Eventually, I offered it some of my cosmetics, just to see what it would do."

"What did it do?"

"Watch this." Retrieving a silver tube from the selection of cosmetic items strewn across the room, Georgie crouched in front of the burbling child, and held it out like an offering. "What's this?" she asked, gently. "Can you tell me what this is?"

The child ceased burbling, its watery eyes fixed upon the chrome tube. Then, it reached out with its grubby hands, grasping the tube and marring its silvery brilliance. "Lipdick!" it exclaimed. "Lipdick! Lipdick!"

"Do you see?" said Georgie.

"It can speak!"

"It only seems to know a few words. But it knows what lipstick is, and eyeshadow, and eyelashes." As if to demonstrate this, the child had managed to remove the top of the lipstick, which was a fetching shade of sunset purple, and was busy smearing it in the general region of its own mouth. "It took me a while," continued Georgie, "but I began to realise that a child is just a very small drunk person."

The slurred words. The strange noises. The crude understanding of fashion. "Of course!" Suddenly, the child made so much more sense to Simone. While he had no experience with children, he did have extensive experience with drunk adults. "Have you had to…?"

"Yes. It needs help going to the bathroom, and cleaning itself, and feeding itself," explained Georgie, and Simone could remember a great many occasions when he had drunk too many cocktails, and was in need of help with those things himself.

The child righted itself, and clumsily wobbled over to a wall, where it began to paint the lips of a leopard. It even walked like a drunk person! "How long do you think it will take to sober up?"

"I'm not sure. Years, perhaps."

"Well, then." Now that Simone knew childhood was just a prolonged period of drunkenness, his horror was fading. "Perhaps we should go and sit in the garden? I always enjoy fresh air when I've had a few too many cocktails."

This time, instead of shooing the child with his slippers, Simone simply ushered it along as he might a drunk person, with endless patience for its slovenly meandering. The child continued to play with its lipstick as it went, getting purple all over its fingers, and by the time they reached the garden it had painted most of its lower jaw. They would need to bathe the child shortly, but that was fine; Simone had helped to bathe Georgie many a time after she had arrived home too drunk to bathe herself, just as she had bathed him in similar situations.

As soon as Simone slid the glass doors aside, the child rushed out onto the lawn and immediately began to roll around in the grasses, staining its white toga green. The mirrored windows of the skyscrapers each reflected a different part of the great blue sky, so that it appeared as if a thousand skies surrounded the garden, and those thousand skies, and the sight of the child among the grasses, provoked a memory in Simone. It was one of his very first memories, from when he first arrived at his father's magnificent house. His father had thrown a garden party to celebrate Simone's emergence into fashionable society, and the fashion had been for sequins. Simone had spent almost the entire day finding the right outfit, before settling on a matching jacket and skirt, each made with so many silver sequins he felt like a mirrorball come to life. He had even spent a few hours meticulously securing silver sequins to his cheeks, and lashes, and eyelids, and lips, and fingernails, so that his every movement twinkled. When the time came for Simone to make his entrance, he had emerged triumphantly along the veranda in his father's garden, and blown little glittery kisses at his father's fashionable friends. There had been such applause. Applause for the brilliant new fashionite. Simone had felt transcendent, as if he were the most beautiful creature in the world.

At last, inspiration!

"Darling," said Simone, as Georgie joined him on the patio.

"Yes, dear heart?"

"I think I'm going to throw a garden party. And at that party… I'm going to upstage Justine."

* * *

Simone peered at the cathedral from the window of the limousine. It was a collection of fine white windowless cylinders that looked like the contents of a well-stocked cabinet of moisturisers, and for a few moments he found himself absorbed in the way that the clouds above it looked like squirts of cream. At its base, a seething throng of demi-fashionables heaved against the velvet ropes keeping them from the red carpet. Every Sunday, demi-fashionables congregated here to watch the beautiful glitterati attend church, and Simone had to admit he had something of a soft spot for them. They wore a jarring mixture of past-season fashions, and they painted their faces with crude cosmetics, and they all desperately wanted to cross the velvet rope and enter the cathedral with their aesthetic superiors. They were still unfashionables at heart, which was all too evident in their imperfect features and crude approximations of current fashions, but Simone admired their aspirations. At least they were aware of their own hideousness, and were trying to transcend it, unlike the rest of the unfashionable population, which was entirely too unaware of its aesthetic inferiority. It was not unknown for a demi-fashionable to be welcomed into fashionable society, either – it was a rare event, certainly, but Simone had a deep respect for anyone who managed to develop the same instincts that came so naturally to those born fashionable.

There was a queue of limousines waiting to arrive at the red carpet.

Today, there were several photographers in among the demi-fashionables, and their cameras captured the arrivals. It being a Sunday, everyone wore feathers. From the limousine's window, Simone caught sight of Darlington, who sauntered down the red carpet in a corset made of gloriously pink flamingo feathers. He wore matching gloves, each finger delicately wrapped in flamingo down, and there were even more feathers worked into his moustache and brows. There was something marvellous about the way he had worked his hair today, brushing it and moulding it and teasing it into a flowing pink swirl which complemented his look so well – and the demi-fashionables roared their delight, and cameras flashed again and again, immortalising his wonderful look.

The limousine lurched forward one last time, and slid to a halt at the foot of the red carpet. Simone emerged, shaking his shoulders to make his own set of feathers shimmer. Today, he had decided on a peacock-feather dress designed by Dramaskil. He turned on the spot, so that the hem, which was lined with the eyes at the heart of each peacock feather, floated across the red carpet – an action which he hurried through as quickly yet graciously as he was able, in his eagerness to head inside and execute the first part of his plan to upstage Justine. Georgie was wearing a three-piece suit made of corvid feathers by Nanci Drake, and she was swift to join him, clearly sensing his impatience.

Arm in arm, they sauntered down the red carpet together.

At the steps of the cathedral, each fashionable paused, posing before the doors, and Simone was no exception, placing his hands on his hips and peering over his shoulder with a pout, as if to regard the throng of demi-fashionables one last time. The heaving crowd roared its appreciation, and so many cameras flashed that Simone's vision was overwhelmed with bright orbs, and he found himself delicately blinking as he entered the cool interior of the cathedral's vestibule. Georgie, beside him, dabbed delicately at the undersides of her eyes with a jay-feather handkerchief, despite her eyes being unable to produce enough moisture to damage her cosmetics. "I do so admire the plight of the demi-fashionables," she said charitably.

"As do I, darling. We simply must clear out our wardrobes and find them a few morsels to wear." Of course, Simone had no intention of donating any of his past-season looks (in case they somehow ended up in the hands of the dreaded unfashionables), but it was Sunday, and it was fashionable to appear charitable on Sundays.

Entering the cathedral proper, Simone took a breath of fresh air.

Cutting-edge fashion technology had granted the cathedral's interior more spaciousness than its exterior. Its every wall and archway had been fitted with chameleonic screens, and today they depicted the city and sky beyond the cathedral, so that it appeared as if the cathedral had no walls at all. The sky was a vivid blue, and the sun was a hot white, and the city was exactly the same as it was outside except for one very important detail: all of the unfashionables were gone. There were the silver towers of the glitterati in the distance, and the soft curl of the beach beside the bright blue sea, and the jagged spine of the mountains to the north, and the silver threads of the vibro-rail lines arcing through the sky from fabulous destination to fabulous destination, but instead of the ugly architecture of the unfashionables, there was a simple, lovely carpark. There was an awful lot of carpark; indeed, almost the entire city was an expanse of smooth black tarmac divided into endless rows of parking bays, but it was a significant improvement over the boxes the uglies lived in. The sight of all those empty, uniform bays was a delight to behold. There was even the slightest scent of freshly laid tarmac in the air, as if the ugly parts of the city had been paved over very recently, and Simone took several deep breaths of it, indulging in the fantasy that the city really had been cleansed.

Simone was not entirely aware of the theological minutiae behind any of the rituals he took part in on Sundays, but they were all quaint enough. It was currently the fashion to practice a sort of symbolic cannibalism by drinking wine in place of blood and a wafer in place of flesh. Of course, the wine was white (nobody would dream of staining their teeth by drinking red), and the wafer was a chocolate mint (bread was far too prone to producing crumbs), and Simone would have much preferred a simple glass of champagne, but he had to admit that these rituals were far more bearable than last year's, which had involved a lot of kneeling and had blemished his delicate knees with bruises that looked like bunches of grapes. Taking a wine glass and wafer from a table, he placed the minty morsel on his tongue and washed it down with a sip of white, idly wondering who it was he was symbolically cannibalising.

Swirling the remainder of his wine around in its glass, Simone peered around the spacious cathedral at the gathered glitterati, in search of Justine. She proved very easy to spot, wearing a tremendous downy yellow dress that looked as if thousands of ducklings had been plucked bald to make it so soft. She was sipping at a glass of her own, and posing beside an altar, where the sun was casting a particularly complementary ray of light down upon her. Simone sashayed across.

"Justine!" he cried. "I do so adore your dress."

"Oh, Simone! How delightful to see you! Is that a Dramaskil? Very fetching."

They air-kissed.

"The city looks so much better from in here," Simone mused.

Justine glanced out over the carpark. The limousines the glitterati had used to arrive at the cathedral were visible nearby, idling in what looked to be a much older carpark. "It fills me with hope," declared Justine. "For a better future."

"I had hoped to run into you," said Simone.

"Oh?" Justine sipped at her wine.

"I have decided to throw a little garden party on Thursday, at my father's old place, and I thought I would invite you along as thanks for so kindly introducing me to Karpa Fishh."

Justine's eyes seemed to gleam, no doubt at the opportunity to once again take advantage of Simone's fashion instincts. "Why, I would be delighted to attend, Simone. How very thoughtful of you." She ran the tip of one finger around the rim of her glass. "Would you mind awfully if I invited Karpa along? I'm sure he would love to see you again."

This was more than Simone had hoped for. "Of course!" he cried, doing his best to retain his composure. "Nothing in the world would make me happier than to see you and he at my party."

"Wonderful." Justine smiled an immaculately composed smile. "I look forward to it."

"As do I." Simone sauntered away with his heart beating hard against his ribs.

Wine in hand, Simone calmed himself by beholding the clean version of the city inhabiting the walls of the cathedral. If he were, one day, to be a designer himself, he would oversee this particular transformation personally, driving all the uglies out of the city and over the mountains, where they could live beyond the sight of the fashionables. He would take great pleasure in demolishing their homes and paving them over. Perhaps he would even paint the parking bays himself, each white line a meditation on beauty's triumph.

* * *

Simone spent the next three days at work strategically spreading the word about his garden party. There was an art to disseminating gossip in the office, and it revolved around the water-coolers, each of which served as a node in Tremptor Tower's complex rumour network. The water-coolers were lumps of frosted crystal containing icy seas, positioned in well-lit thoroughfares throughout the tower, so that any fashionista seeking a public place to be seen could do so with the excuse of seeking refreshment. Simone systematically struck wearied poses beside each water-cooler he had access to, and artfully exclaimed to any and all who approached how difficult it was to organise such a lavish and well-attended garden party, and how much of a burden it was to have to cater for the likes of Karpa Fishh, who had promised he would attend. By Tuesday afternoon, the rumour that Simone was hosting an essential event appeared to have reached every water-cooler in the building. A steady supply of fashionites dropped by his office with work-related excuses (Do you have any spare staples? Have you seen this month's productivity reports? My printer has run out of ink – can I use yours?), and Simone assured each and every one that of course they were invited to his little soiree. Eventually, word reached Simone that Trevor Tremptor himself was professing to being torn between attending Simone's garden party and a mountain retreat being organised by legendary designer Messr Messr.

* * *

Simone's father's house squatted monstrously against the high hills, the product of a time when architectural fashions subscribed to labyrinthine excess. It had far too much of everything: too many windows; too many turrets; too many gargoyles; more wings than there were points on the compass. Simone's first few years as a fashionite were spent trying to navigate its endless corridors and failing, ending up lost in this wardrobe or that wardrobe because his father had lived through a time when it was fashionable to keep past-season looks instead of throwing them away, hoarding them like a fabulous dragon. Entire wings of the house were devoted to storing the gorgeous excess of the glitterati, and it had grown fat on fashion. It was a wonder Simone had ever managed to find his way out of the house to attend parties.

At its perimeter were endless gardens; entire forests with fairytale towers rising from their hearts; hedge mazes so grotesquely complex as to be unsolvable; a statuary corpus large enough to populate a small city. So, too, were there no end of chapels, and wells, and pool houses, and stables, and garages, and so many tennis courts that one might never have to play on the same court twice. Not that Simone had ever played tennis, of course; the courts were for the implication that the owners partook in sport, and were, perhaps, sporty, thus enhancing any sport-based aesthetics that might come along. The limousine rolled smoothly down the opulent driveway, between trees and bushes sculpted to look like beautiful people, and Simone felt dwarfed by it all. It had been a great many seasons since he had last ventured back to his father's house, and he had forgotten just how much of it there was. He was tempted to reverse the limousine and leave immediately, out of fear he might become permanently lost in the place.

Of course, it was the perfect place to host a garden party.

Tasteful bunting was already hanging around the patios, and an assembled assortment of tables and chairs were draped in white cloth, suggesting that the house had anticipated the party. But that had always been the way with the place: one had only ever to voice a fabulous thought aloud for it to manifest itself. Soon, Simone knew, those tables would fill with tall glasses of bubbly drinks, and trays laden with finger-foods that no fingers would dare touch, and tiers of tiny cakes and sandwiches no teeth would ever blemish, and pleasant music composed of stringed instruments would waft warmly over it all. There were still a few hours left until the first attendees would begin to arrive, however; Simone had come early to plan precisely how to make his entrance.

Leaving the limousine parked on the driveway, Simone sauntered along a winding path between immaculately kept trees to the most decorated part of the garden, where the focus of the party would be. He emerged onto a large lawn of fashion-friendly hypergrass, which was not only springy and soft, but extremely tough and stain-proof (from what Simone knew, each blade, while still the proportion of an ordinary blade of grass, possessed the strength of a small tree). There were more tables laid out across the lawn, and an entire pavilion, upon which stood an array of stringed instruments. Simone so loved stringed instruments that once, in the wild fashion passion of his early years at the house, he had deigned to try and learn how to play the cello – a notion swiftly quashed by his horror at the way callouses began to form on the tips of his fingers. Still, his brief time attempting to learn the instrument had left him with a wealth of knowledge about how to pose with it. Perhaps he would pose with a cello today, should it complement his outfit.

Inspecting the lawn, Simone could see three good options for making his entrance. First of all, arcing gracefully across the pond at the far end of the lawn was a bridge made of a rich varnished wood with an underside polished so well that it reflected the gentle movements of the pond's waters. Second, there was the grand arched stone entrance to a nearby hedge maze, which was covered with carvings of naughty nymphs and backed by the leafy richness of the maze itself. And thirdly, there was the crystal shape of one of the house's conservatories, which backed out onto the lawn, resulting in a set of thick glass doors that pleasingly distorted the conservatory's contents, making them a colourful blur, as if the conservatory's interior was an impressionist painting. Each of these options had a downside, however. The bridge led to a croquet lawn, offering Simone no place to lie in wait for the opportune moment to make his entrance, and while waiting in the maze was certainly an option, Simone knew he would not be able to see the party from within it, and thus accurately judge the right moment to arrive. The problem with the conservatory was that it meant he would have to enter the labyrinthine house, which Simone was reluctant to do. But if he did enter the house, he knew he would be able to watch the party's progress from a window, and thus time his entrance for the most opportune moment.

Simone made his way hesitantly inside.

The conservatory was pleasantly warm, and neatly decorated. Simone knew that when he sashayed through he would become an impressionist blur, aided by the colour of his outfit. It being a Thursday, the fashion was now for nosebleeds, but Simone was still uneasy about following a trend he had invented and received no credit for. As such, the nosebleed aspect of his outfit was rather subtle. He wore a simple crimson dress, and hanging from his neck was a ruby necklace so opulent that it still sparkled brightly on moonless nights. He also wore matching ruby earrings, and an enormous septum piercing with a single ruby, to suggest the idea of a nosebleed. The dress, which was from a recent Nanci Drake collection, was so understated that all attention would be drawn to Simone's jewels. When he made his entrance, he knew that all eyes would be drawn to him.

Through the conservatory was the house's interior proper, and Simone sauntered through, to a dizzying muddle of corridors and staircases and elevators.

Part of the problem with the house was that parts of it tended to shift around. Simone was aware that quite a few wings featured walls and staircases that would routinely change positions, giving the house a new layout every few hours or so. Worse, those walls and staircases only shifted when nobody was paying them attention, and were so cunningly disguised it made the shifting nearly impossible to anticipate. There were entire wings of the house Simone had avoided during his years here, having become seriously lost on more than one occasion, and to this day the vast majority of the house was unfamiliar to him. This wing, for instance, which was filled with statues of discus throwers and hung with desert landscapes, was a part of the house he did not recognise. Regarding the staircases and corridors and elevators with suspicion, Simone was glad he would not have to delve too deeply. All he needed to do was go up one floor and find a window that faced the lawn.

It took Simone less than ten minutes to become lost.

Opening doors on endless bedrooms, drawing rooms and ballrooms, every single window he beheld showed a different exterior, or overlooked one of the house's countless courtyards. Nowhere could he find a view of anything he recognised, and worse, when he decided to backtrack the corridors appeared to have changed, leading him to ever more libraries and game rooms, none of which had the view he was seeking. Eventually, after much frustrating trial and error, he stumbled across some of the house's overstuffed wardrobes, and only there did he slow, momentarily enchanted by the railings. Walking through wardrobe after wardrobe, he had to admit that some of the neatly preserved past-season fashions were still beautiful. There were so many gorgeous pieces of clothing that Simone felt tempted to forego the party altogether, and spend his time secretly trying on outdated fashions. At last, he stumbled through a door and into a large dressing room, where some of the most choice specimens of the huge collection were draped across mannequins, and there Simone gaped, amazed at the ancient beauty. There was a dress that looked as if it was made of spider silk, and a suit composed of thorns, and a gown made of cracked pieces of glass, and each was so utterly, overwhelmingly beautiful that Simone mourned the passing of their fashions. Of course, it would be a faux pas to be seen in any of them, but Simone tried to make a note of the dressing room's position, so that he might return and just try them on, to see what they felt like.

Even as he moved on, the dressing room lingered in his mind.

At last, he came to a turret that overlooked the garden party, and was astonished to see he had spent so much time wandering the halls of the house that the party had begun. It was still fairly early – a queue of limousines wound down the driveway, depositing fashionistas – but there was a decent selection of beautiful people gathered on the central lawn, posing among the tables, and up on the veranda. Glasses of champagne glinted in their fingers, and even from here Simone could hear the gentle stringed music intermingling with gentle compliments. Searching the crowd, Simone saw Georgie, who had arrived with several of her friends, and Darlington, who was making the rounds with his husband. And there… there was Justine. And with Justine was Karpa Fishh.

Simone knew instantly that his plan to upstage her had failed.

Today, Justine wore a white ballgown that swished along the hypergrass, beaded with pearls and fitted with frills which complemented her tall white hair. And the entire dress was running with blood. It fell from her nostrils, and down her chin, and splashed onto her chest, and it dripped from her pearls, and soaked her frills, and there seemed to be more blood covering her dress than there was available in any human body. Of course, there was no way it would all be her own blood, but the effect was still magnificent; it was a nosebleed so outrageous that she embodied the very fashion she had supposedly started. Even Karpa Fishh, who was wearing a stunning pale suit that appeared to have veins, looked like a mere accessory next to her. There was no way Simone would be able to compete.

From up high, Simone could see the perfect place to make his entrance. There was a small copse of trees glowing green in the sunshine, surrounded by a gush of wildflowers, and emerging from their shade would make him an avatar of summer; the ideal way to enter a sunshine-soaked garden party. It would mean sneaking across to the copse without being seen, but there was a golf course to the rear that appeared navigable. Simone was crushed, of course – no matter how elegant his entrance, Justine's outfit was just too gorgeous to compete with – but he still had to arrive at some point. It was his duty, as the party's host. Thus resigned and defeated, Simone dragged himself back into the house, in search of a route that would lead him down to the golf course.

On his return through the house, Simone paused in the dressing room he had passed through before. The spider-silk dress, and thorny suit, and glass gown were each brilliant, and admiring them uplifted him. In fact, it felt so good to be in their presence that he continued to linger, their beauty calling to him in a way he had not felt since he possessed his lemon.

With a gasp, Simone realised he could try wearing one of the outdated pieces. In the same way his instincts had led him to find a beautiful lemon, they were now telling him to see what the spider-silk dress felt like against his skin. Quickly slipping off his inferior crimson clothes, Simone carefully removed it from its mannequin, expecting it to crumble into dust with age. Yet it held together, the softness of it so pleasurable against his hands. Hardly daring to breathe, Simone shuffled into the spider silk, feeling it whisper against his skin, and like a fantasy, like a dream, it settled onto his shoulders and fit him perfectly. Simone felt it swish against him luxuriously, the fabric unused for decades now. Of course, it was out of date, but there was something about the way it was so completely past season that gave it a peculiar charm. Simone felt nervous – appearing at the party in a past-season dress would ordinarily invite humiliation

– but his instincts were insisting he was beautiful. The only thing left to do was accessorise.

The gush of sparkling rubies would no longer do; they would overwhelm the delicate dress. Simone settled instead on wearing only the septum piercing – the small red jewel just beneath his nose paying tribute to the fashion for nosebleeds in such an understated way that it allowed the beauty of the dress to take centre-stage. There was a mirror positioned before a wide set of windows, and Simone turned to and fro in it, admiring the way the spider silk moved across him, silvery and delicate. The dress looked as if it should fall apart at the slightest agitation, but it held together strongly, and Simone wondered how many thousands of spiders must have been farmed for their silk to make this one piece. Satisfied and giddy, Simone quickly made his way through the house, in search of a way out. He was ready to make his entrance.

It took Simone far longer to leave the house than he would have liked. Stumbling through several galleries, parlours, drawing rooms and no less than three ballrooms, he at last emerged from a wine cellar, having somehow accidentally descended into a basement. In the distance he could hear the party, and he knew he was running out of time. If he took much longer, he would be considered embarrassingly late instead of fashionably late. He swiftly navigated a handful of rose gardens, greenhouses and water features to the edge of the golf course, and there he paused, his foot hovering above the grass.

The golf course was a magnificent green sea, rippling gently in the breeze. So, too, shifted the trees at the edges of the course, casting their intricate shadows over the golden curls of the sandbanks. To Simone, the golf course was always a wonderful landscape to admire, and from a distance he had always assumed its immaculately kept lawns were composed of astroturf, or hypergrass. But Simone was wrong. The golf course was composed of *regular grass*.

Clouds passed overhead, and Simone did not move. He knew the moment he so much as touched the golf course, loose blades of grass would fly across and ruin his outfit. Gently, he lowered his outstretched foot back on to the concrete patio.

Desperately, he searched for a path across. He was running out of time.

There! An answer.

At the far edge of the patio was a row of small, clean white vehicles with chrome wheels, white canvas roofs and plush leather seats. Selecting the outermost golf cart, Simone slipped in behind the wheel. Of course, he had no idea how to drive a golf cart – it was not fashionable to drive, after all – but if ugly people could do it, how difficult could it be?

There were only two pedals at his feet, and Simone carefully pressed the first with the very tip of his toe, as an experiment. The cart sighed beneath him, and he felt a slight tingle of delight up his spine; it was responding to his touch! He gently toed the second pedal, and the cart swayed slightly and made a sound like a low purr, sending another tingle up his spine. Slowly, and with gradually more pressure, Simone worked the two pedals, resulting in ever more sensual noises and movements from the vehicle beneath him; one pedal made it thrust gently forward,

and the other brought it to a smooth res
confident enough to apply his entire foot
the silky, springy slide of the accelerator
surged forwards, making Simone gasp wi
Feeling quite breathless, Simone glance
rear-view mirror, and saw he was a littl
to drive the golf cart was far more thrilli

The cart hummed beneath him.
the grassy expanse. The slope was g
meandering set of hills, but to Simo
more perilous than it had before. One
would be spoiled; all it would take w
or grain of sand.

Simone pressed the accelerator
patio behind.

The sea of grass swished arou
against the canvas roof, making i
sail. Simone rode the gentle rise a
his route so that it carefully mea
and at the top of a slope he glim
of trees at the edge of the party.
flag protruding from a hole in t
it, appreciating its sharp colo
everywhere, before continuing

Over the next slope was a
with white balls. Only, as Si
realised with horror that they
breathing rabbits, nibbling at

lip like a jewel upon a pillow would glint in the sunlight. The enchantment Simone had felt in the copse swept across the lawn, and where it went the glitterati were enraptured. They paused, drinks in hand, to regard Simone, and the music rose and fell, rose and fell across them, and Simone's sweeping hands came to a rest beneath his chin, and he turned his eyes to the sun so that they, too, would glint.

The music faded to silence. The enchantment held.

There was a soft tinkling sound, and Simone turned to see, through the yellow sunspots burned into his eyes, Karpa Fishh tapping his claw-length nails against his glass of champagne. The sound echoed as other fashionistas made their own complimentary noises: nails against glass, and fingers against palms, and appreciative throat sounds. Then, new suns bloomed in Simone's vision as the party's photographers snapped pictures, lenses sliding into place and immortalising his entrance. Simone went out into the party affecting a casual air, because it was fashionable to be humble about one's beauty.

"Simone, darling, you look beautiful!" It was Georgie, and she and her friends circled Simone, admiring his dress from every angle. Darlington arrived, and he and his husband each gushed over Simone's outfit, offering him glasses of champagne, and tiny cucumber sandwiches, and thumbfuls of white powder, all of which he graciously turned down. Fashionites approached alone and in groups to pay him endless compliments over his party and his aesthetic, and Simone swept from table to table, swishing the hem of his dress to make the spider silk shimmer.

At last, he came to Justine. Blood continued to pool from her nose, staining her teeth red. "Such a marvellous outfit," she said graciously, and Simone noticed she was clutching her glass with such ferocity that tiny cracks had formed in the stem. "You simply must tell me who designed your dress," she continued, and too late, Simone saw the trap she was luring him into. "It would take a brave designer indeed to work with such an outdated material."

"It's vintage," said a voice, and Simone turned to see Karpa Fishh, smiling brilliantly.

"Vintage?" Justine sounded as if she disliked the flavour of the word on her tongue.

"Yes," continued Karpa. "Like wine. Sometimes, an outfit needs time to mature."

The word was cast like a spell across the party. Nearby photographers scratched it into notepads, and fashionites muttered it to each other, and even the very breeze seemed to say it, swishing through the trees. *Vintage.* The dress was vintage. What a novel and innovate concept. Karpa Fishh drew closer, and the rest of the party faded away, until Simone's whole world was the small patch of hypergrass he and the designer occupied together.

"It's good to see you again, Simone," said Karpa Fishh. "First, you show me a beautiful lemon. Then, you wear a vintage dress. I'm looking forward to seeing what you do next."

Simone had never felt more beautiful in his life.

* * *

Simone fortified his father's house.

The garden party had come to its natural end a few hours ago. When the wind picked up enough to begin threatening hairstyles, everyone had made their polite excuses and quickly retreated to their vehicles – except for Simone and Georgie, who had decided to spend the night in the enormous house instead. The wind whirled across the gardens, swaying the trees and sending leftover sandwiches tumbling, and Simone went from window to window, drawing the curtains and shutters closed. The party had been a tremendous success, and now came the consequences. Simone had upstaged Justine so thoroughly that there was no doubt she would confront him tonight. So, he drew up the drawbridges (of which the house had three), lowered the portcullises (of which the house had five), and admired the emerald crocodiles patrolling the moats (of which the house had a multitude). Peering from the windows of one of the bedrooms overlooking the central driveway, Simone expected to see chariots thundering towards the house at any moment, but there was only the rustling of the bushes, and the stillness of the dark beneath the trees.

The house had several armouries, and Simone armed himself. This time, he dressed for a siege. Instead of plate armour, he clothed himself first in an underlayer of slick dark leathers, and then an outer layer of delicate silver chainmail, which made Simone feel as if he was wearing jewellery like a dress. He chose a silver lipstick to match, and a set of curled silver lashes the same thickness as the chainmail's rings, which enmeshed every time he closed his eyes. Back when he had confronted Justine, his reflective sword had been the perfect offensive weapon, giving him the strength to resist her icy charm, and now he needed a defensive tool of similar power. A shield would be ideal, but none of the shields in the house's armouries quite satisfied Simone's aesthetic instincts. It was only when he entered the en-suite bathroom of the final armoury that he found a worthy aegis, hanging above the sink. The mirror was a large silver oval, framed with matching floral silverwork, and when Simone took it down from the wall, the wire strung up across the back was thick enough that he could comfortably use it as a shield, gripped tightly in his leather-bound fingers. Locating a second mirror in one of the hallways nearby, Simone admired his outfit – he was ready to defend himself.

The interior of the house was aglow with fireplaces, chandeliers, lamps and lanterns, and Simone found Georgie settled into a parlour positively dripping with candles. Unfortunately, there was also a second, much smaller figure in the room, dipping its fingers into the wax and smearing it across the delicate woodwork of the fixtures. "Darling?" said Simone.

Georgie looked up from her book. In all likelihood, she was not actually reading the book – indeed, she and Simone had each secretly confided in the other that the idea of a magazine with no pictures and altogether too many words was ghastly – but Georgie was renowned for being an especially aesthetic reader, and could make her apparent absorption in a book something quite splendid to behold. "Oh, Simone. You look wonderful! I like your shield."

"Thank you, dearest heart. But why is the child here?"

"I thought it might like to see your father's house, so I brought it along."

"Isn't that… risky?"

"Nonsense. Nobody's seen it, and there's plenty for it to play with."

As if to demonstrate this, the child took a globule of warm red wax in its pudgy fingers and proceeded to smoosh it across a landscape of a moor. In fairness to Georgie, Simone did much prefer knowing where the child was – there was no telling what kind of damage it could do unsupervised. "Will you be all right looking after it while I deal with Justine?"

"Of course, darling. I was just about to show it today's magazines."

"A splendid idea. I do like to look at magazines when I'm drunk."

"Precisely my thought."

"Marvellous. I love you, Georgie."

"And I love you, Simone. You did such a splendid job today. I'm very proud of you." Returning to her book, Georgie pressed two fingers against her temple and adapted an expression of absorption, as if she were wholly transported into the narrative. The child, meanwhile, had begun to peel the wax from the portrait, and was giggling maniacally. The moor disintegrated at the child's waxy touch.

Simone returned to the bedroom overlooking the driveway, and there stood before the last remaining set of unshuttered windows, peering into the darkness in search of the sparks or headlights heralding Justine's inevitable attack. Yet, no attack came. The wind whooshed through the dark trees, and pieces of the party tumbled over the driveway, and Simone began to wonder what was taking her so long. It was considered terribly impolite to confront one's enemy any later than supper.

At last, a figure emerged from the dark beneath the trees, but when she stepped into the light, Justine was nothing like Simone had expected. Instead of armour, she wore a simple polka-dot dress with a matching polka-dot hood, and instead of weapons, she carried what looked like a pie. The lipstick she wore was the same red as her dress, but the shade was too bright to be considered bloody, and the polka-dots suggested that she had dressed not for confrontation, but in a manner considered appropriate for a greeting. In fact, now that Simone thought about it, the fashion for the cordial welcome of one's new next-door neighbour was for polka-dots, because they seemed to say that the wearer was fun and possibly a little quirky (but not in a bothersome way).

There was the abrupt clamour of bells, gongs and various other alarms throughout the building as Justine pressed the doorbell, and Simone allowed himself a moment before shuttering the last window and making his way downstairs. The act of shuttering the window was useless, of course – by wearing polka-dots instead of armour, Justine had successfully circumvented all of Simone's fortifications – but it comforted Simone to know that the window in question matched all the other windows belonging to the same bedroom.

Simone opened the front door. "Justine! This is a surprise."

She stood on the doorstep, smiling so warmly that it was impossible not to return it. "Good evening, Simone. I wanted to stop by with a peace offering."

"How thoughtful of you. Won't you come inside?"

Justine's heels clacked on the marble of the central hallway, and her red smile glowed in the light of the chandeliers. "I like your chainmail," she said.

"Thank you. Your dress is darling."

"Isn't it just?" She give a little twirl, and then offered up the pie she was carrying. Hot cherries gleamed and steamed inside a crispy, flaky crust, and a measure of steam rose from it, as if to suggest it was fresh out of the oven. "I made this for you," she said. Of course, she had not made the pie.

"What a lovely pie," said Simone cautiously. "Thank you."

She perched it neatly upon an empty plinth, of which the hallway had a multitude. Then, bustling past him, she stood in the pool of light at the base of the grand staircase and surveyed the enormous hall. "I did so admire your father," she said. "He was fabulous."

Still unsure of Justine's intentions, Simone kept his mirror shield raised. It was true that Simone's father had been fabulous. "A splendid man," he said carefully.

"Anyway," said Justine.

Simone braced himself. "Yes?"

"I think…" Justine turned to face him. "We should be friends."

"Friends?"

"Yes. I have been ever so monstrous to you, and that changes now. Do you think we could be friends, Simone?"

Simone relaxed his grip on his shield. "I suppose…"

"Splendid!" Justine cried. "I'm sure you will warm to me in time. Now, then. I must depart. You must have much celebrating to do after your big success today." Heels clacking, she strode across and subjected Simone to a prolonged series of air-kisses. Then, she said, "Take care now!" and vanished back into the night, leaving Simone alone at the empty doorway.

Pieces of bunting shifted across the dark driveway.

Shutting (and bolting) the door, Simone leaned against it and regained his composure. The confrontation, as peculiar as it had been, was done. Resting his shield against a sculpture of a man throwing a discus, he retrieved the pie and went in search of Georgie.

"That was quick, darling," said Georgie, peering at him from over her book.

Placing the pie on the coffee table, Simone sank into the leather sofa beside her. The pastry still steamed, and Simone peered at the glistening fruits visible beneath the crust.

"She gave me a pie," he said.

Georgie turned a page. "Poisoned, do you think?"

"Most likely." Removing his coif, Simone allowed himself to relax, at last. It had been a successful day, and he was looking forward to seeing tomorrow's magazines. A warm quiet fell over the room, punctuated by the crackling of the fireplace.

There was a clatter, waking Simone from his snooze. At first glance, the pie appeared to have fallen on the floor. Given a moment to awaken fully, however, revealed that the pie was on the floor, the table, the sofa, and both inside and outside the child. It sat at the apex of the delicious explosion, attempting to fling handfuls into its mouth with varied results, and within moments the entire pastry had vanished, leaving only a mess of crumbs and jam.

Then, with a hiccup, it fell asleep.

"Simone?" said Georgie.

"Yes, darling?" he replied, softly, so as not to disturb the child. So far, it was still alive.

"I could have sworn I just saw a face at the window."

Simone leapt from his seat, and dashed across to the bay window. Beyond the pane, there was darkness. Loose leaves tumbled across the driveway, and hedgerows swayed, but there was nobody outside. "Could you have been mistaken, darling?"

Georgie shrugged, and turned the page of her book. "Perhaps it was a ghost."

This was a satisfactory explanation. Simone had never seen a ghost before, but there had been a fashion for spiritualism a few years ago, and he was aware that the spirits of ugly people sometimes lingered in the world after death, restlessly wandering the houses of fashionable people in search of something nice to wear. "How ghastly," he said, and went to bed.

* * *

Sunlight streamed through the high windows of the divan room, and Simone felt every bit as glorious as those heavenly rays. Throwing off the pillows he was partially buried in, he stood, stretched and attempted to spot Georgie. No pillows stirred, and there was no obvious sign of anyone sleeping among them, so Simone very carefully navigated his way to the door, testing every step in case a scrap of silk turned out to be Georgie's pyjamas.

Daylight poured into the house through skylights, drenching

it in a warm glow, and for a few moments Simone allowed himself to enjoy stepping on light feet through it, luxuriating in the brightness filling his father's house. Then, he went in search of the mail room. There were no end of libraries and studies and other paper-based rooms in the house, and by the time he stumbled across the mail room, the excitement he had felt upon awakening had built up to a crescendo. Stacked up in neat piles all across the tables and desks of the enormous mail room were today's magazines, still so fresh that they smelled of newly dried ink, and Simone almost screamed at the sight of them.

SIMONE: FASHION GENIUS, read one.

OLD IS THE NEW NEW, read another.

VINTAGE IN VOGUE, read a third.

Simone was on the cover of almost every issue, pictured in his spider-silk dress. Behind him, the copse was a verdant green against the vivid blue sky, and at his feet crowded wildflowers. The red jewel resting on his top lip gleamed, a star of white light at the centre of each image. Grabbing armfuls of magazines, Simone dashed through the house in search of Georgie, rushing from dining room, to tea room, to kitchenette until he found her in a banquet hall.

"Georgie, look!" The breakfast buffet filled the banquet hall from wall to distant wall, a sea of food. There were lakes of baked beans and yoghurt and orange juice, and basins of bacon and muesli and pancakes, and Simone came to a halt beside the egg selection (scrambled and fried and poached), offering his armfuls of magazines.

At a dining table, they sat together and pored through the articles.

"Oh, darling. This one says you're at the frontier of fashion!"

"This one says I may have started a fashion revolution!"

There was a clattering from the cereals section, and Simone looked up from his magazine to see the child stuffing handfuls of something marshmallowy into its mouth. It appeared to be content, so he went and made some breakfast for himself. Pouring a very small glass of orange juice, and searching through a dish of waffles for a symmetrical specimen, he drizzled a suggestion of syrup on top and returned to the table, nibbling at the morsel (carefully, to prevent crumbs) as he turned over the front page of another magazine. The articles all praised his fashion daring, and Simone felt effervescent. "Darling," he said decisively. "We simply must do something to celebrate."

"I agree," said Georgie, who was watching a blob of butter melt on her toast.

"What do you suggest?"

"How about you and I do some shopping?"

"Oh, that's a marvellous idea!"

There was another crash as the child spilled a tray of sausages over the carpet.

"What do you think we should do with the child?" asked Simone.

"I'm sure it can entertain itself," said Georgie. "It looks perfectly happy."

Indeed, the child was throwing sausages at the silverware with such enthusiasm that it seemed rather a shame to spoil its fun. Sausages successfully chucked, it turned its destructive joy on the pastries, sometimes cramming morsels into its mouth, but mostly placing them in the juice jugs, where they slowly sank.

Simone sympathised; food became considerably more fun when he was drunk.

"I'll throw on something to wear," said Simone.

"And I'll have the limousine brought around," said Georgie.

* * *

The Boulevard, which was a long stretch of road occupied almost exclusively by fashion boutiques and their clients, bustled in the hot sun, busy with fashionistas. Simone admired them from the rear of the limousine; the way their armfuls of bags resembled wings, and the way the palm trees cast pleasing shadows over them as they passed to and fro along the sidewalks. Their vibrant neons – yellows and oranges and greens – glowed in the sunshine, and they lounged on the intricate white trellised chairs outside cafés, casting appraising eyes over one another's treasures. Most prominent of all were their handbags, of course – because nobody would dare to go shopping without one – and Simone spotted no end of extraordinary specimens. There was a handbag which looked as if it was made of the feathers of a particularly downy cardinal, and there was a handbag that looked as if the strap was made of a human spine, and on Simone's lap was his own handbag, which was a yellow Messr Messr that looked as if it were composed of diamonds but moved like leather.

The limousine slid to a halt at a crossroads, where the Boulevard split into four, and it was there that he and Georgie slipped out onto the sidewalk.

"Where to first, darling Georgie?"

The Boulevard's boutiques changed hands so frequently that it could be difficult to keep track. Sometimes a designer would occupy a boutique for years, but that was rare; normally, designers tended to occupy a boutique for no longer than a week at a time to retain the exclusivity of their brand (Grantis Granto had once famously occupied a boutique for less than twenty minutes). As such, the four branches of the Boulevard were currently unfamiliar to Simone, who had been rather busy over the past few days and was thus woefully behind on the latest layout. Thankfully, Georgie seemed to know where she was going. Today, she wore a neon blue three-piece suit with a pair of oversized white sunglasses, and her hair was a white swirl that looked like a cloud.

"This way, dearest heart."

Georgie led Simone through a series of new boutiques hosted by severe ladies and gentlemen wearing samples of the fashions on display, and Simone was dazzled by the selection, just as he always was. Of course, he already had an enormous selection of clothes back at the apartment, but fashions were fleeting enough that there were already so many new styles to choose from. Today, there were a few new boutiques devoted exclusively to vintage fashions, and Simone was welcomed into each like a hero.

Something felt strange about Simone's tour of the Boulevard today, however. As he shopped, he began to notice that he was far more discerning than usual. Normally, Simone left each boutique with armfuls of new clothes (most items of which he would wear only once, or not at all), but he found himself dithering among the racks, sliding items aside and dismissing them one by one.

There were still a few items that caught his eye, but they were unusual pieces, hidden away and overlooked by the rest of the fashionable population.

Finding new clothes felt like finding rare treasures today, and Simone decided to enjoy the sensation, picking oddities up wherever he went: a necklace made of teeth; a dress made of popcorn; stockings that made his legs look as if they were made of wood.

While most designers did not constrain themselves to designing a single item, most did specialise, and there was a district of the Boulevard where the boutiques belonging to designers famed for their shoes tended to congregate. Pumps and sneakers and slippers gleamed temptingly in the windows, and Simone passed them by, dissatisfied by the selection on display. He watched Georgie slide into brand-new sandals and stilettos as he surveyed the shelves, searching among the boots and brogues for inspiration.

There was a gasp from Georgie. "Simone!"

Simone paused, midway through lacing up a pair of knee-length boots that had caught his eye (they looked as if they were made of glass). "Darling?"

"A new boutique is about to open across the street!"

Simone drew himself to his feet, balancing precariously upon the glass heels he was half strapped into. "Can you see who it is?"

"It looks like…" Georgie's eyes widened. "Dramaskil!"

"Quickly, Georgie! There's no time to waste!"

Indeed, the need to cross the street was so urgent that there was no time for Simone to remove the boots, which were almost certainly a size too small. Hobbling as quickly as he could, he dashed across the baking pavement and into the road, following the hurrying Georgie, whose hair wisped around like a cloud caught in a breeze. Already, other fashionites were spilling out of boutiques up and down the Boulevard and rushing as graciously as they were able to towards the brand-new boutique. Its every brick had been painted sky blue, and the letters DRAMASKIL had been stencilled across the window in powder blue, and everything beyond the window was also blue, so that it looked as if a fabric sea were swishing around inside. A stern-looking woman wearing a blue suit stood astride the door with an enormous pair of scissors, about to cut the royal-blue ribbon hung up across it, and as Simone reached the pavement, the flashing blades of the scissors sliced and the ribbon fell away.

Georgie was the first inside.

Two other fashionistas managed to make it through the door before Simone could reach it, handbags swinging wildly as they momentarily fought each other for space, and then Simone was in and confronted by the boutique's blue interior. The words DRAMASKIL: THE BLUE COLLECTION were picked out in neon above a mirror painted with swirls like waves, and beneath the mirror were racks and racks of blue clothes. Simone caught sight of Georgie, whose hands were a blur as she pulled garments aside, searching for the exclusives. More fashionites barrelled inside, almost sending Simone sprawling with the force of their entry, hands outstretched and grabbing. There was a clattering of coat-hangers as they slid across railings, but Simone found himself momentarily paralysed by indecision. Normally he would have swept through, hoarding armfuls of clothes and snatching at anything that might be remotely exclusive, but today he realised that he was scouting the selection, searching for anything worthwhile.

Fashionites continued to pour into the store around him.

There! Nearby was the aquatic glimmer of a sequinned jacket with potential. He leapt into action, sending a mannequin tumbling with his handbag as he went. The mannequin was immediately trampled as two other fashionites attempted to grab the jacket at the same time, but Simone was there first, and shielded the jacket with his body, almost tearing it from its hanger.

With the jacket over his arm, he noticed a shoe rack nearby, heavy with tiered aquamarine heels that seemed as if they might complement the jacket. There was a scrum of fashionistas to either side, blocking him in, so he dived through a long rack of silken shirts, and when he emerged he saw he had accidentally gathered a few on his way (which was not a terrible thing – they seemed promising). The rack of shoes was before him, and while he was not certain which would fit, he had little time to decide. Grabbing a few specimens, he turned and saw a section devoted to suits made of materials that moved like seawater, almost hidden behind a display. Dashing across a floor alive with fallen fashions and unbalanced fashionites, he narrowly avoided tripping over the dislocated arm of a mannequin.

Like bowling skittles, the mannequins beside the suits burst apart as a fashionite smashed through, snatching with manicured hands for the only one that looked as if it was in Simone's size. Simone lashed out with his heel and managed to trip the fashionite, sending him sprawling among the scattered limbs. Stepping over the fallen body, he quickly grabbed the suit from its display and added it to the stack of clothing he was accumulating. Then, after tumbling through a collection of hats, he danced precariously through a set of blue curtains and into the cool safety of the changing rooms. There, ahead, was a single unoccupied booth, and he rushed into it before anybody could take it, closing the door behind himself.

Catching his breath, Simone tried on his treasures.

It was so pleasant, pulling the garments on. Some did not fit – like the shirts, and most of the shoes – but the suit was close enough that it would be perfect with a few small adjustments (which seemed to happen magically whenever he put an ill-fitting garment in his wardrobe), and the sequinned jacket was so snug it was as if it had been made for him. By the time Simone had made his selections and hung up the clothes he did not want, the noise outside was beginning to die down. There would be no exclusives left unclaimed in the building, but Simone was pleased with his findings. The jacket, at the very least, had to be unique; every sequin looked individually placed.

His treasures across his arm, Simone re-entered the boutique.

There were bits of mannequin and clothes strewn everywhere. A few fashionistas still searched the racks, diving deep among the remnants of the opening. The stern woman who had opened the store was behind the counter, looking dazed, and as Simone approached, she awoke from her stupor. Wordlessly, she folded up Simone's selections, wrapped each in tissue paper, and placed them in a blue paper bag.

Georgie was outside, with several blue paper bags hanging from her elbows.

"Did you find anything, darling?" she asked.

"A few things," said Simone.

"Wonderful." She air-kissed the tips of her fingers and blew the kiss across. "I do love Dramaskil. I was disappointed to have missed the opening of the Yellow Collection last month. I'm so glad we managed to catch the Blue Collection."

Simone and Georgie continued to shop long into the afternoon, and as their expedition continued, Simone noticed that he was accumulating significantly fewer new clothes than his wife. Trousers of every cut, and shirts and blouses of every style, and dresses inspired by every era were whisked from shelves into bags at Georgie's behest, along with everything from swimwear to ski-wear, while he continued to pick up only the occasional, inspiring piece. Still, he was pleased with his selection, and relished returning home and trying on all of his new treasures again (normally, he preferred to throw all his new clothes into his wardrobe and simply get on with his day). Shopping with a discerning eye felt good. And by the time Simone and Georgie had finished, the rear of the limousine was so full of shopping bags anyway that there would have been no room at all had he been less discerning. Driving home would be a squeeze, nestled in among all their new outfits.

Exhausted by their long day of shopping, Simone and Georgie settled at a table outside a nearby café. Simone placed his handbag on the table, so that passers-by would be able to admire it, and affected a casual pose, reclining in his chair as if he were glamorous but entirely unaware of his own glamour. Small cups of coffee arrived on the arm of a gaunt waiter, who placed them on the table with such an air of indifference that it felt as if he were dismissing the coffee from his presence. So, too, did he place a tiny tray of pastries, each of which was so intricately crafted that they looked like edible pieces of jewellery. Of course, Simone would not dream of tasting any of the pastries, some of which had components capable of leaving disastrous stains and crumbs upon outfits, but they were so fiercely gorgeous that he was of the belief he could taste them simply by admiring them.

As Simone and Georgie lounged, a peculiar sound became audible, gradually rising in volume as it progressed. Simone was well acquainted with the various gentle sounds of the city – the humming of traffic, and pitter-patter of feet and the soft murmur of polite conversation, accented by the distant calling of birds and rumbling of passing planes – but this noise was unfamiliar to him. It sounded like the wailing of a distressed machine, and as it drew closer, it was accompanied by a metallic grinding and groaning. The fashionites occupying the café all paused between sips of coffee, exchanging puzzled glances, and those glitterati on the sidewalks nearby had also stopped, and were glancing to and fro across the Boulevard in search of the source of the noise disturbing their shopping.

Suddenly, three cars came into view, roaring down the Boulevard.

They were angular, beaten-looking things, painted black and white, and the guttural spluttering of their engines rattled the tables of the café as they approached. Upon the roof of each flashed a set of blue and red lights, spinning with wild abandon, and from each emanated a piercing wail that echoed from all the boutiques. Fashionistas clutched their ears against the shrieking of the cars, throwing themselves against the walls to escape the noise of their passing, and Simone found himself gripping hold of his handbag with both hands, as if he might use it as a shield against the approaching vehicles. The gratings in the front of each looked like silver grimaces.

Just when it felt as if the cars would deafen Simone, they came to a screeching halt outside the café, leaving long black skid-marks down the previously immaculate street. The coughing of their obviously diseased engines continued, as did the wild flashing of their rooftop lights, but the shrieking suddenly ceased, and from each emerged an ensemble of uniformed unfashionables, waving dull black guns and unpolished badges at everyone in sight. Simone was too horrified to move, hands frozen around his handbag as he cast his appraising eyes over the uniforms of the uglies. Not a single piece of clothing fit properly; shirts were too loose or too tight, and trousers dragged or revealed too much ankle, and they wore belts fitted with a selection of grim-looking tools: dented batons and tarnished bracelets.

From the third car emerged an unfashionable not in uniform. This man wore a drooping brown hat, an enormous trench-coat several decades out of fashion, and an ill-fitting grey suit that looked as if it had been worn several times without being cleaned. His moustache was a tangled brown mess infesting his upper lip, and his unshaven jowls quivered as he grimaced. Thankfully, the man's eyes were hidden behind a large set of mirrored aviators, which reflected the Boulevard back at itself in their shining lenses. This man swept the street with his gaze, before settling on the café, and then, finally, Simone's table.

"Simone and Georgina St Claire?"

Simone shrunk back in his seat. Somehow, the unfashionable knew his name.

The man in the trench-coat approached, flanked by uniformed uglies. "Simone St Claire," he said, his voice so hoarse and guttural that it sounded as if he had never once thought to clear his throat in his life, resulting in decades of accumulated phlegm. "I'm placing you under arrest for the kidnapping of Louise Gram." Reaching beneath his coat, he withdrew his own set of dented metal bracelets. "You have the right to remain silent. Anything you do say may be used against you in a court of law." A pair of uglies grabbed at Simone arms, their calloused, unmanicured fingers rasping at his soft skin, and hauled him upright. "You have the right to a lawyer," continued the man in the trench-coat, as the uniformed uglies twisted Simone's arms behind his back, "and if you can't afford one, one will be appointed to you." There was a horrible, metallic scraping, followed by the ungainly weight of the bracelets as they were snapped around Simone's wrists. Wriggling slightly revealed that the bracelets were joined together, leaving Simone utterly at the mercy of the gang of uglies. "If you decide to answer questions without a lawyer, you have the right to stop answering at any time." The man in the trench-coat brought his face down, so that it was level with Simone's, and though his breath stank, Simone was grateful for the opportunity to see his own reflection, which was beautiful. "Do you understand?"

When Simone opened his mouth, only a low wail emerged.

"That'll do. Take him away, boys."

Simone's legs were refusing to work properly, so the uniformed uglies had to carry him to their rearmost vehicle, the lights of which were leaving blue and red streaks in his vision. Shoving one of the back doors open, which creaked with rust, Simone was bundled inside. The door slammed shut behind him, leaving him trapped in a prison of stinking, worn leather, scuffed plastic and sticky armrests. Even the window was cracked and scratched, and as Simone stared out of it, he saw Georgie being loaded into another one of the cars.

The last thing he saw before the car began to move was his own handbag, fallen to the ground beside his seat in the café. It gleamed luxuriously in the sunshine, and as the Boulevard slowly rolled away, he tried to keep it in his vision for as long as possible, feeling as if it might be the last beautiful thing he would ever see.

* * *

Of course, Simone was aware of the police. There had been a fashion for law-enforcement uniforms a few seasons back, and he had worn an outfit featuring gleaming silver adjoined bracelets and a polished black truncheon, and several other tools he had assumed were sexual in nature (indeed, he and Georgie had explored the carnal possibilities of the handcuffs and truncheon with much abandon), but so far as he knew, the police themselves were no more than a type of ugly person appointed by other ugly people to keep the filthy mess that was unfashionable society functioning. This made sense, of course: the unfashionables had to have laws preventing them from murdering each other, and stealing from each other, and who better to enforce those laws than the unfashionables themselves – their betters, the glitterati, were far too busy getting on with the important job of being beautiful. It had never once occurred to Simone that the police might dare to try and enforce their laws against him. Let alone for something like kidnapping. So far as Simone was aware, he had never kidnapped anyone.

The deeper the car travelled into the city, the uglier the city became.

Rain crawled down the windows, blurring the sight of the buildings that squatted like uneven rows of teeth to either side of the road, and Simone was overwhelmed by the notion that they might snap shut at any moment, the city swallowing him down like a delicious, beautiful morsel. No matter how still Simone tried to sit, the car jostled and jarred him, leaving new stains across his once-vivid canary-yellow suit; much longer, and he would look like a polluted sunset. Worst of all was the ache in his shoulders, caused by the way his arms were twisted behind his back, fastened together by the rusted cuffs that rasped at his soft skin. Each bounce of the car crushed his fingers against the cracked, worn leather, and Simone desperately tried to keep his fists clenched to preserve his manicure.

Eventually, the car came to a halt. The drumming of the rain grew louder, and a mob of unfashionables flung themselves at the car, their faces distorted by the water down the windows. Some held crude approximations of cameras, which flashed relentlessly, and there was even more yelling as Simone's door was yanked open, letting in a spray of intermingled rainwater and spittle. Two more uniformed uglies – police officers – yanked Simone from the car and into the crowd, which was composed of the tatty, lesser cousins of the fashion photographers he was so familiar with. The press of reporters barked incomprehensible questions, and took even more pictures, and the rain slapped across his skin, making his cosmetics run. With each arm in the grip of an unfashionable police person, Simone was dragged towards a tall building so blocky and unremarkable that it could only be their destination.

The interior swarmed with police, and Simone was led, dripping, past desks overloaded with chipped ceramic ornaments and scribbled-on bits of paper, down a corridor that stank of smoke and sweat and stale coffee, into a room where he was uncuffed and forced to press each of his fingers into a squashy pad of ink, and then roll them across a piece of paper. Given no time to rub away the black mess clinging to the tips of his fingers, he was then hauled over to a white wall with unflattering horizontal lines, handed a piece of slate with some numbers chalked across the front, and positioned before yet another camera. Of course, Simone did his best to strike a pose, but there was very little he could do with the backdrop and slate, and with his fingers and face and suit so marred by his journey, the best he could hope for was that his natural beauty might shine through. Simone pouted, and turned his face to the light, and tried to affect an air of having accidentally stumbled into the shot. The officer behind the camera was silent, giving him no encouragement or compliments.

Once again Simone was cuffed, this time with his hands in front of him, and escorted bodily along a corridor and into the heart of ugliness at the centre of the building. This room was no more than a set of cages made of coarse metal, and trapped in each were some of the most repugnant unfashionables Simone had ever seen. They leered, and keened, and slobbered, their eyes following the fashionite as he was hauled past them, numb to their catcalls. An officer waited at the end of the corridor, holding open the door to a cage, and Simone was deposited inside, shaking fiercely. The cage door shrieked shut, clattering with a finality that filled him with the certainty that it would never open again, and hands reached through to uncuff him. Then the officers left, chuckling with each other as they went, and Simone was alone with all the other uglies that inhabited his cage. They sprawled and squatted across the concrete and splintering benches, and Simone backed away as far as he could, into the rearmost corner of the cell. There, he hunched down, wrapped his arms around his legs, and gulped heaving sobs into his knees. The fabric of his trousers was soft, and still smelled like home – a beautiful home that Simone feared he would never see again.

* * *

Time passed, and Simone felt filthy.

The walls of the cell were dank with mire, and the unfashionables inhabiting it seemed to seep ugliness from their grotty pores. The bars of the cell at Simone's back grated against his suit, trapping him in place. Every now and then an unfashionable would gibber something incomprehensible across at him, spraying him with a fine layer of spittle, and Simone wondered how long it would be before he began to transform into one of them. Perhaps it would be pleasant being unfashionable – blissfully ignorant of his own ugliness – but he knew that even a glimpse of the glitterati would be like torture: beholding beauty he would never again attain. Every now and then, a police officer entered the long chamber and dragged an unfashionable from its depths, which suggested to Simone that he would not be condemned to live in his cage forever. The thought did not give him much hope, however; it felt inevitable that whatever came next would be worse still.

Eventually, he heard a faint rumbling.

The rumbling was subtle enough that the cells' occupants ceased their slobbering conversations one by one to hear it better. Soon, all the cages were quiet and listening to the rumbling, which was gradually becoming more intense as time passed. Listening intently, Simone thought he could discern an intermingled cacophony of footfalls, papers being rustled, doors being slammed, and voices being raised.

All at once, the doors at the far end of the cells slammed back and a flood of men and women wearing sharp suits poured into the room. They were all yelling at once – at the officers guarding the cells, at the occupants of the cells, at each other – and they brandished briefcases and wads of official-looking paper at every set of eyes turned their way. Simone's breath caught in his throat as he watched them advance down the corridor. They were clearly not fabulous – but nor were they unfashionable. Their suits were impeccable, and clean, and so were their hairstyles and shoes, and even their voices seemed harmonious as they argued their collective way into the room. And while the tide of semi-fashionables were mostly interchangeable, each wore a unique tie, by which Simone was able to tell them apart. A gentleman in a maroon suit with a red satin tie was shouting at a pair of police officers with such ferocity that they cringed back against the wall, and a woman in a grey suit with a peacock-feather tie was thrusting a set of papers at one of the caged unfashionables, and a blonde fellow in a coal suit with a gold-leaf tie was the first to sweep into Simone's cell after it was unlocked.

"Simone, yes?" the gold-leaf tie man reached out a hand.

Still shaking, Simone allowed himself to be drawn to his feet. "Who… Who are you?"

"We," said the man, as more semi-fashionables poured into the cell, "are your lawyers."

There was further yelling from elsewhere in the station.

"What's happening?" asked Simone.

"We are having you moved to a more appropriate cell."

There was a shift in the collective shouting of the lawyers, and Simone was swept along among them, out of his cage and back into the station. The lawyers surrounded him like a shield against the ugliness of the place. Everywhere he was taken, he saw police being accosted by lawyers; they shrunk back at their desks, and hid behind their hats, and shivered together in the corners of their grotty offices, as reams of official papers and streams of verbose proclamations pinned them in place. Simone was led up several flights of stairs and into an enormous office with a large wooden desk and wood-panelled walls. It was still a far cry from the impeccable architectural fashions of the glitterati, but everything was clean, and Simone was afforded a comfortable-looking green leather chair.

"This was the chief's office," said the lawyer with the gold-leaf tie.

"It's very..." Simone sought the right word. "Quaint."

"Quite. Does anything displease you about it?"

Simone cast his eye around the place. "That statue is quite ugly."

Two lawyers grabbed the heavy-looking bust of a frumpy man, while a third opened the room's window. The statue was immediately flung out into the rain, and Simone was satisfied by the noise of it shattering on the wet concrete below.

"Anything else?" asked the lawyer.

"The wallpaper is a little drab."

A team of lawyers immediately began tearing the wallpaper from those parts of the walls that were not wood-panelled, using the edges of their clipboards and tie-pins to get purchase. Within moments, another mass of lawyers arrived bearing rolls of a yellow wallpaper designed by Manchodroi, and were swiftly pasting it over the bare patches.

"Much better," said Simone, finding comfort in the wallpaper's patterns.

"Very good," said the lawyer with the gold-leaf tie.

Another team of lawyers then poured into the room, with Georgie in their midst. She looked every bit as filthy as Simone felt; her outfit was stained, and her makeup was smeared, and her hair, which had so resembled a fluffy white cloud, now looked more like a storm cloud. At the sight of Simone, she sobbed and flung herself across him. Usually, he would have appreciated a little more decorum, especially in the presence of so many semi-fashionables, but he was grateful for her touch.

"Oh, Simone, it was dreadful!" she declared.

"I know, darling. I know. They kept me in a cage."

"What horrible, ugly people."

"I am so glad to see you, Georgie! I feared I might never set eyes on you again."

They clung to each other for a few moments longer.

"Wonderful wallpaper," mumbled Georgie, into his lapel.

The lawyer with the gold-leaf tie cleared his throat. "Good afternoon to you both," he said. "My name is Mr Vivian, of Vivian and Associates."

("Marvellous name," remarked Simone.)

"You have my sincerest apologies for everything that has occurred, and my reassurance that your doctor is on standby to erase your memories of it as soon as this is all over."

"Thank you, Mr Vivian," said Simone, who wanted nothing more than to forget the police station forever. "But why have these horrible people arrested us? They mentioned kidnapping?"

"You are indeed being charged with the kidnapping of Louise Gram."

Simone gasped dramatically, because it seemed appropriate.

"Of course," continued Mr Vivian, "this is nothing to worry about. We will prove your innocence and have you returned home as soon as possible." Another bustling mass of lawyers somehow squeezed into the office, and Mr Vivian turned to consult with them.

"Georgie, darling," said Simone. "He must mean the denim child!"

"It has a name?" asked Georgie, baffled.

Mr Vivian turned back. "Now, then. Let me explain what's going to happen. We are, of course, going to trial. We should be able to set a court date no more than three months from now, and the nature of the charge against you means that it will be a jury trial. I have full and complete confidence that we will be able to convince a jury of your innocence."

"What evidence do they have?" asked Simone.

"From what I've seen, they have videos, photos, and extensive eyewitness accounts. But trust me when I tell you that these things don't count for much against persons of your calibre."

"That's very reassuring," said Simone, who was more reassured by the quality of the man's tie than the quality of his words. "Thank you, Mr Vivian."

"Don't thank me yet, Simone. The prosecutor who took your case managed to get a warrant signed by one of the most notorious justices in the city, and that judge is going to be overseeing your bail hearing."

"Is he handsome?" asked Simone.

"The prosecutor, or the judge?"

"Either. I do love a handsome villain."

Georgie nodded sagely. "It's true. He does."

Mr Vivian blinked rapidly. "I'm afraid not."

"Such a pity."

"Yes." Clearing his throat, Mr Vivian continued. "The issue we have is that Judge Grout is an outspoken anti-fashionist, and will be biased against you."

Simone frowned. "An *anti*-fashionist?"

"I'm afraid so. It's a growing political movement in the city. I believe that she was persuaded to sign a warrant for your arrest on the grounds that she might be able to make an example of you."

"How dreadful!"

"Quite. Therefore, we must do our best to make you seem sympathetic."

"How might we do that?"

"I'm going to need you to appear unfashionable."

Simone and Georgie gasped simultaneously. "But… Mr Vivian!"

"I know, I know." Mr Vivian raised his hands defensively. "But trust me. If you can act unfashionable for just twenty minutes, then I can have you home this evening."

Simone exchanged a glance with Georgie. Of course, it would be horrible pretending to be unfashionable, but it was certainly preferable to returning to his cell. There was nothing Simone wanted more in the world than to return his apartment, run a bath and soak in it for several weeks.

"Very well," said Simone begrudgingly.

"Fantastic." Mr Vivian clapped his hands and even more lawyers squeezed into the room, bearing some heavy-looking briefcases. "I have had several outfits prepared. Please choose the clothes you find the least aesthetically appealing."

* * *

Thankfully, there was a small courthouse attached to the police station, which meant that they would not be seen in public. The lights in the courthouse were a glaring white, banishing every shadow as Simone limped into the room, Georgie in tow.

Being unfashionable was far more than simply wearing ugly clothes. Being unfashionable was a state of mind, and it was one Simone took to reluctantly – one thread of clothing at a time.

First, there had been the underwear. There had been no underwear on offer, but Simone had insisted on some being provided because underwear was foundational to an outfit – it dictated the shape of one's body beneath one's clothes, and subtly informed one's attitude (when Simone wore lingerie, for instance, it made him strut). After much deliberation, he chose a pair of Y-fronts two sizes too large, which rode all the way up to his waist, and were giving him something of a limp. Then he chose socks from two different sets and slipped them on, wriggling his well-manicured toes into the mismatched fabrics. The suit was a double-breasted lavender affair that fit relatively well everywhere but the sleeves, which were far too long and kept slipping over his hands. If there had ever been a label, it was long gone, and the whole thing smelled faintly of sour milk. There was a pair of brogues so well-worn that the soles had absolutely no grip, turning his limp into something of a shuffle, and Simone had chosen a sad grey tie to finish it all off, which hung like a dead fish from his throat. The outfit rasped against his skin, and as he entered the courthouse he slouched as deeply he could, relaxing every muscle in his arms and legs and face in an effort to make it appear as if an aesthetic thought had never entered his head.

Georgie's own outfit had a lot of ruffles in unexpected places. There were ruffles protruding from her jacket and sleeves, and there were ruffles cascading down her lapel, and even her shoes were ruffled, as if the offending shirt went all the way down to her feet. Simone had to admit that she looked very convincing as an unfashionable person. She was currently excavating a nostril with abandon, and her expression was one of such vacancy that he felt compelled to lead her along, lest she somehow lose her way through the benches.

Those benches were empty, as was the rest of the courtroom but for a handful of figures near the front. Mr Vivian was waiting, gold-leaf tie agleam like a beacon of beauty in an ocean of ugliness, and beside him was a man with altogether too many veins in a drab brown suit. The veins were red and blue, and they pulsed beneath every inch of his transparent skin, making him look like a map of the vibro-rail. Both Mr Vivian and the man with too many veins stood before the high bench where the judge sat, and the judge was far worse than anything Simone had imagined of an anti-fashionist.

The problem, so far as he could see, was the lighting. Judge Grout sat at a confluence of several hot spotlights, and their collective radiance had made her moist. Perspiration glistened on her forehead, and beaded her top lip, and pooled on her chin. There was a ragged grey wig perched upon her head, and what few strands of grey hair emerged beneath it were plastered to her skull. Huge wet stains were visible at her underarms, and when she raised her gavel, held lightly between her fingers, it was a wonder it didn't slip from her lubricated grip and fly across the room.

"Follow me," said Mr Vivian, leading Simone and Georgie to a table nearby, which was so stained with coffee rings that it might have been a map of the solar system. Then, whispering beneath his hand, "Just let me do all the talking, okay?"

"Of course," said Simone, who wanted nothing less than to converse with either the judge or the man with too many veins. He stood behind the table and preoccupied himself by pretending to be unfashionable, scratching liberally at his chin, as if his stubble were irritating him.

There was the clatter of the gavel, and the bail hearing began.

"I decided to close the court because I was informed that your clients were glitterati," said Judge Grout. "But now I see that I was ill-informed."

"My clients are far from fashionable, your honour," said Mr Vivian.

"So I see." Clearing her throat, she turned to the man with too many veins. "Do you have anything to add, Mr Farmer, or should we begin?"

Mr Farmer's face reddened as more blood poured into it. "Nothing from me, your honour."

"Good." Judge Grout flicked through several sheets of paper. "Your clients are being charged with kidnapping, Mr Vivian. How do they plead?"

"Not guilty, your honour."

"Very well. They will be tried by jury three months from now. I set bail at—"

"Your honour!"

"What is it, Mr Farmer?"

"I believe the St Claires to be a flight risk."

Judge Grout's brows oozed together. "How so?"

"If your honour would be so kind." Advancing, Mr Farmer slipped a sheet of paper across the high bench, which Judge Grout examined. "The St Claires own four jets, three helicopters, two zeppelins and have their own airfield."

Simone wistfully remembered the fashion for zeppelins. He had so enjoyed floating over the city, so far above the ugliness below. Emerging from the memory, Simone noticed that everyone was staring at him, and immediately realised his mistake. He had inadvertently adopted an aesthetically pleasing expression of wistfulness to match his remembrance!

Judge Grout's eyes narrowed. "What say you, Mr Vivian?"

"My clients have no interest whatsoever in fleeing!" cried Mr Vivian. "They are innocent, and wish to prove themselves innocent."

But it was too late. Judge Grout was examining every inch of Simone's face, and Georgie's face. "If I didn't know any better," she said, "I would say that your clients were indeed glitterati, and that you have taken pains to de-glamourise them."

"Of course not, your honour!"

The gavel rose, and the gavel fell. "Bail is denied."

Everyone reacted simultaneously. Mr Vivian's eyes widened, all the blood rushed from Mr Farmer's face into his fists, Georgie's finger froze (buried knuckle-deep in her nostril), and all the air left Simone's lungs with such finality that he felt as if he might never take another breath again.

"Mr Vivian?" said Georgie.

"I'm sorry," he said, shaking his head. "I'm so sorry. But it's only three months, and once it's over, and we've proven your innocence at trial, all your memories will be erased."

"Memories of what, Mr Vivian?" Simone still didn't understand.

Taking Simone's hand in both of his, Mr Vivian looked him in the eye. "Prison, Simone. You're going to prison."

* * *

Prison was full of ugly people. The guards were ugly, and the prisoners were ugly, and even the visiting families and lawyers that Simone occasionally glimpsed through several layers of reinforced glass were ugly. He quickly grew to rely on Mr Vivian's daily briefing as a relief from the relentless ugliness, focusing on the lawyer's golden tie in an effort to maintain his appreciation for beauty.

While Simone had at first felt relief at shedding his unfashionable court outfit, he had instead been given an orange jumpsuit, which did absolutely nothing for his complexion. Worse, he had been equipped with several pairs of identical socks and sandals.

Time moved strangely in Simone's cell. The walls were concrete, and his bed was made of unadorned iron, and the sheets were threadbare cotton, and while there was a clock visible beyond the bars of the door, all three of its arms were hanging limp at six, as if it had given up all hope of telling the time. Without glossy magazines or snatches of gossip to keep his mind moving, Simone was beyond time, stuck in a place where the outfits were always the same, and the faces were always the same, and the slow crawl of the sun across the concrete was the only way to mark the passing of days.

Some of Simone's fellow prisoners were clearly of the same anti-fashion opinion as the dreadfully sweaty Judge Grout, patrolling the dining hall in search of anything pretty to demean, and he spent much of his time alone practising his ugliest expressions to blend in. After a few days, it became apparent that several particularly hideous prisoners were beginning to suspect him of being beautiful, so Simone polished a patch of his cell's toilet bowl to a mirror shine and spent an entire night learning to relax his face to the point of complete expressionlessness. The suspicious anti-fashion prisoners promptly ceased their inquisitive glares, but Simone had never felt so wretched and unappreciated in all his life.

Then, Simone began to notice the fashions.

There were fashions among the prisoners, and they were most prominent during the recreation hour and mealtimes, which were the prison equivalent of social gatherings. The fashions were subtle – limited by the identical orange jumpsuits and lack of cosmetics – and Simone spent his hours carefully cataloguing them. First, there was the way people wore their jumpsuits; some prisoners wore their sleeves rolled up to their elbows, and others worse them rolled up to their shoulders, depending, it seemed, on the relative musculature of the inmate. Secondly, there was the way people wore their hair. The larger gentlemen tended to shave it all off completely, and the smaller gentlemen tended to slick it back across their heads, using such generous amounts of gel that their heads glistened. And lastly, there were the tattoos.

There had not yet been a fashion for tattoos among fashionable people, mostly due to their permanence. Tattoos were essentially just another type of scar – a needling violence administered by one ugly person to another in a feeble attempt to liven the latter's skin. Yet, in prison, tattoos were everywhere. They were largely crude and colourless, but there were discernible trends: poorly rendered animals on biceps, crosses and teardrops on faces, and tally marks on wrists. And there were a great many symbols Simone did not recognise, the discussion of which occupied a large part of the prison population.

After five days, Simone plucked up his courage and approached a man with a prominent tattoo of an eagle across his forehead, who was tattooing the base of another man's neck with a tattoo gun that looked as if it was made out of several toothbrushes.

"Excuse me," said Simone.

The man with the eagle tattoo ceased his work and glanced up. "Yeah?"

"I just wanted to say – your eagle is very fetching."

There was a pause. The man with the eagle tattoo was wiry, and there was very little hair to be slicked back across his scalp, and one of his eyes twitched slightly, as if to emphasise the intensity of his gaze. He appeared to be searching Simone's face for any sign of beauty, but Simone had come prepared, and was wearing an expression of such slackness that he felt as if he were wearing a pair of ill-fitting trousers for his face. "Thanks," said the prisoner, at last. Then, gesturing at his toothbrush tattoo gun, "Want one?"

"That would be very kind of you."

"Watcha want?"

Simone had spent all morning, and most of the previous day, considering what his first prison tattoo would be. In the end, he had settled on something symbolic of his love for Georgie. She was in a different prison right now, perhaps even getting her own prison tattoos, and Simone wanted to remember her at her best. He recalled the last night he had seen her before the child had arrived in their lives, back when his biggest worry had been the fish mattress. He remembered the way she had been curled up on that mattress wearing a thematically relevant silken pyjama set, which made her look like a beautiful prawn. "I would like a prawn," he said.

The eagle man's eye continued twitching. "Sure. Where?"

"On my right foot, please."

"Right." The tattooist turned back to his current client and made a few last jabs at his neck before sending him on his way. Then, he invited Simone to sit.

So far, Simone had not worn his socks and sandals together because it would have been an affront to beauty. As such, Simone did not have to remove his sock, and he simply placed his foot into the lap of his artist. Without any warning, the eagle man began to stab Simone's foot with the needle end of the toothbrush tattoo gun. The sensation was rather like being stung by a wasp repeatedly, but it was far from unpleasant, and within minutes the shape of a prawn began to form. By the time the buzzer sounded to mark the end of recreation, the prawn was complete.

"Thank you ever so much!" gushed Simone. "Wonderful work."

The man with the eagle tattoo grinned.

The prawn was crude, and a little blood seeped from it, but that night, as he lay on his bunk, Simone let the moonlight from his cell window illuminate it and thought of Georgie. And for the first time since he arrived, he drifted away to a peaceful sleep.

* * *

Just as Simone was beginning to get comfortable with prison, something extraordinary happened.

He had just awoken, and was trying to determine precisely how far up his arms he should roll his sleeves for the day, when a buzzer sounded and the door to his cell swung wide. Simone was well acquainted with the buzzer for food and the buzzer for recreation, but this particular buzzer had a timbre he had not heard before. There was murmuring as the prisoners gathered in the hall, and Simone joined them, trying to gauge how he should feel by the expressions on their faces (Simone was getting steadily more confident when it came to reading the emotions of ugly people). Most of the prisoners appeared unperturbed, and were exchanging their usual pleasantries, but a few appeared to be quite excited, and were in the process of licking their lips and rubbing their hands together as if they were anticipating a banquet. So far, prison food had proven to be mostly indigestible, and a banquet would be nice, Simone had to admit.

The prisoners were arranged into rows by bored-looking guards, then shuffled through the corridors of the prison, and for the first time, Simone saw just how enormous an institution it was. There were cells upon cells, arranged in endless rows and columns, and there were countless guards up on the walkways brandishing shotguns. Simone wondered if there was enough room in the prison for all the unfashionable people in the world. It would certainly be a neat solution to the problem of public ugliness.

At last, the queue of prisoners arrived in a particularly large chamber, which echoed like a warehouse. Long cables dangled from the distant ceiling, bearing bright bulbs which illuminated hundreds of square tables, and upon each table was a machine Simone did not understand, along with a pile of vividly green fabric. The fabric looked so luxurious that Simone longed to rush across and fling some of it across himself like a makeshift cloak, but he remained in line, and awaited his turn as the prisoners were distributed among the tables. One by one, each prisoner sat down at his appointed desk and began to shuffle through the papers beside their machines, and within moments Simone had been directed to a table of his own. There was a metal chair, and as he settled into it, he ran his hands over his pile of green fabric.

It was every bit as soft as he had imagined. Like the outside of a tennis ball.

There were some scissors, and spools of thread on the table, along with a few sheets of paper, which depicted some kind of blueprint. One of Simone's neighbours was cutting at his green fabric, and the other was drawing some thread through his machine, and as Simone peered closer at his blueprints, he realised he could see some familiar shapes.

These were instructions for making a pair of trousers.

There was a clattering as the first machines started, and Simone spent a while simply observing what everyone else was doing. Most were still cutting, but a few had begun to feed lengths of material into their machines, which knitted the fabric. But of course! These were sewing machines! Simone turned back to his own and felt a great warmth filling his mind. These were sewing machines, and this was fashion, and fashion was something he understood. Taking a spool of thread, he spent a while examining his machine, and studying the movements of his fellow prisoners for clues as to its operation. After he had managed to successfully thread it, he glanced over the instructional blueprints he had been given and began to cut his green fabric into appropriate lengths.

The sensation of his scissors gliding through the soft green material was so luxurious that the rest of the room faded away, leaving Simone alone with his table. Then, slowly – so slowly – he constructed his first pair of trousers. Every now and then, he accidentally pricked the tip of a finger with a needle, and dabbed at it with a cloth until the bleeding stopped, but the sight of his own blood did nothing to disturb him. Discovering he could make clothes made him feel as if he had snorted an entire mountain of white powder.

Then, at last, Simone had a finished pair of trousers. They were a little uneven – the product of an unpractised hand – but pride bloomed in Simone's mind like a flower.

Beneath the pile of fabric was the final element of the trousers: the label. They were pre-fabricated, and came in a little envelope, which Simone gingerly opened. The design of the trousers was gorgeous, yes, and they were made of a luxurious material, but they subscribed to no current trend, and he had assumed they were meant for the demi-fashionables. But when he saw what was inscribed into each label, Simone felt his eyes grow wide.

DRAMASKIL, read the labels. THE GREEN COLLECTION.

* * *

In the days that followed, Simone continued his prison routine in a daze. There were mealtimes, and there was recreation time, and he spent countless hours alone in his cell. But every now and then – every few days or so – the buzzer would sound, and the prisoners would queue up, and they would all go to the workshop and make designer clothes together.

Simone spent his next two trips to the workshop simply absorbed in the sight of his fellow prisoners at work, and there was no doubt about it – they were ugly. They worked with unmanicured hands, and subscribed to coarse prison fashions, and every now and then one of them would cough or sneeze into the clothes they were working on. But as the hours progressed – each prisoner wearing an expression of intensely ugly concentration – beautiful clothes emerged, improbably constructed by those same unmanicured hands. The pre-fabricated labels changed each time (Simone recognised the name of each designer), and each fashion was new – intended for weeks and months ahead (he could picture the completed designs on the racks of the shops lining the Boulevard), and the fabrics… If Simone had any doubts whatsoever about the authenticity of the clothes, they were satisfied by the fabrics, which were always of such luxuriousness that there was no questioning their quality. These were indisputably designer clothes.

It was true, then. Designer clothes were made by ugly people.

Eventually, Simone's horror began to subside. The clothes were always beautiful, no matter how calloused and hairy the hands making them – and he had to admit he had thoroughly enjoyed making that first pair of trousers. So, he tried making another piece of clothing. This one was a shirt, and the fabric was a flowy, silky expanse; his scissors whispered through it, making him gasp at the sensation.

As he made the shirt – carefully following the blueprints – Simone thought back on his wardrobes. He now knew that they were full of clothes made by ugly people. His father's house: a thousand rooms, filled with beautiful clothes made by generations of unfashionables. Mere weeks ago, he would have fled to the hospital and begged them to have his memory erased, but here he was, in a hall full of unfashionables, rather enjoying the rhythm of his sewing machine as he drew his silky shirt through it. It did make sense, he supposed – he knew that ugly people built the houses the glitterati occupied, so why not the clothes they wore?

Simone considered Karpa Fishh's hands, which had made quite the impression on him at the garden party. Those hands had been encrusted with rings and lengthy false nails, and his skin was soft and clearly well moisturised. Simone's hands, meanwhile, were being pricked and scratched by the tools he used to make his shirt, and he had no doubt that, as the weeks progressed, they would become calloused and worn. Of course Karpa Fishh did not make the clothes he designed himself. It would have compromised his own beauty.

Satisfied with this line of reasoning, Simone allowed himself to become absorbed in his work. No longer did he watch his fellow prisoners making designer clothes, preoccupied with the implications; he was too busy enjoying the process of making them himself.

* * *

Gradually, Simone felt something shift inside himself.

The communal showers started to become something of a guilty pleasure. At first, Simone had found a corner and stayed there, staring at the tiles. Yet as the weeks progressed, he began to notice that some of his fellow prisoners were actually quite attractive. There was a fashion for weightlifting in the prison, which meant there was quite a lot of musculature on display. Nobody had a body quite like Darlington's, but there were, perhaps, enough well-toned limbs to add up to one entire Darlington's worth of attractiveness among them. Soon, Simone found himself admiring a few choice specimens from the corner of his eye, enjoying the steam rising from their bodies, and tracing the soap as it slipped and slid across their abs and biceps and thighs. It felt strange to take so much pleasure in seeing naked ugly people, but Simone supposed not all unfashionable people were quite as ugly as he had imagined them to be.

Even mealtimes began to be something of a treat. Each meal was composed of cubes, and each meal's cubes were different. Sometimes the cubes were crunchy, and sometimes the cubes were slippery, and sometimes the cubes were spicy, and they came in a whole variety of different colours. Simone began to look forward to certain combinations (the red crunchy cubes were his favourite), and as the days continued he found his appetite growing. There was a trade among the prisoners for the most sought-after cubes (green spicy and blue sugary were in high demand), and Simone even found himself saving some of his cubes to exchange with his fellow inmates for favours. On days when his legs and face were itchy with stubble, he would trade some food cubes for the use of a shiv and shave in the showers, enjoying the smoothness of his skin afterwards.

If showers were a guilty pleasure, and mealtimes were a treat, then the hours Simone spent in the workshop were a splendid dream. Simone had never done any actual work before, and he was surprised by how satisfying it was to labour at manifesting gorgeous pieces of clothing. As soon as he sat down, he immediately became immersed in his work. And as the weeks progressed, Simone's skill improved. His scissors slipped through the fabric confidently, and his sewing became neat, and the skin of his fingers toughened until he no longer bled when he pricked them.

As his life beyond the prison slowly became distant, Simone realised he was happy.

* * *

The door opened, and there was Georgie at last.

The first time Simone had set eyes on Georgie, it was at the launch of Crostay's Sensuous Silks collection. The launch was so sensational that it was practically a riot, and several items of delicate clothing had been spattered with blood. Simone had been sifting gingerly through the remains of a shattered glass display cabinet, and when he looked up, there she was. At first, he had mistaken her for a mannequin. There was something about the way she was posed, her hands so delicate, her eyes so vacant, and she was stood between two disembowelled mannequins as if she were the only survivor of a mannequin massacre. To Simone, she looked like the most beautiful mannequin he had ever seen. And then, she moved! Her skin, which had at first appeared to be plastic, was in fact well-moisturised flesh, and though her eyes remained vacant, there was a sparkle to them when she met his gaze. They stood there for what felt like an eternity, admiring each other while the chaos of the launch continued around them.

Three months in prison had done nothing to diminish her loveliness. At a moment's glance, Simone saw it all – her chipped nails, her grown-out roots, her unplucked brows. She wore the same orange jumpsuit he did, and the same sandals (without socks, of course), and it was then, admiring her, that Simone realised that Georgie's loveliness was not due to any cosmetic features at all. Georgie's loveliness was in the way she stepped up on her toes to receive him, and the way her eyes softened at the sight of him, and the way she set aside all decorum when she embraced him, clinging to him as tightly as he clung to her.

"Oh, Georgie," he said. "Life without you is like a shoe without shine."

"Simone," she said gently. "Life without you is like a shirt without cufflinks."

Mr Vivian cleared his throat. "I'm sorry to interrupt, but we don't have much time, and I need you both to be as fabulous as possible for your trial."

The rest of the room – one of the prison's largest meeting chambers – was alive with lawyers arranging racks upon racks of designer clothes. Already, Simone could see several enticing outfits.

"But I thought Judge Grout was an anti-fashionist?"

"Judge Grout is no longer overseeing your trial," Mr Vivian preened. "You will be glad to know that I managed to get her recused on the grounds of bias."

"Oh, that's wonderful."

"Yes. Her replacement should be far more amenable. But please – I have a plan, and my plan requires you to look your very best. If you can do that for me, then I can have you back home by this evening, I promise. We even have your doctor on standby, ready to erase your memories of this whole ordeal the moment it's over."

Several lawyers wheeled in a bathtub. It was only a small bathtub – just about big enough for two people – and after it was filled with steaming water, and surrounded by curtains, Simone stripped down to his skin and sank in. Georgie shuffled out of her jumpsuit and joined him, sinking into the water with a sigh and nestling up against him. Together, they gently scrubbed the prison from themselves. "Look, darling," said Simone. "I got a tattoo."

Georgie peered at his foot. "Is it a croissant?"

"It's a prawn. I got it to remember you by."

Georgie turned, and kissed him on each of his cheeks. "You darling man. I love you."

"And I love you, Georgie." Simone kissed her back. "Let's go home."

* * *

One simply had to wear a fabulous wig to court. It was the done thing.

Simone's wig was an enormous set of white rolls and curls tied together with lengths of yellow ribbon, which brushed the roof of the car. Georgie's was equally as large, but arranged to resemble a two-storey house, with hair windows and hair archways and hair chandeliers. Warm lights glowed within Georgie's house-wig, which suggested life inside, and Simone was reminded of the many doll's houses he had enjoyed playing with at his father's house after he had first arrived, a fresh eighteen-year-old fashionite; dressing the tiny, fabulous people, and having them attend parties; practising polite conversations between them to keep his social skills honed. Of course, both he and Georgie wore sharp suits as well. Simone's suit was canary yellow and criss-crossed with the same kind of ribbon as his hair, and Georgie's suit was a sky blue that made her wig look like a cloud house. The colours had been deliberate choice (suggested by Mr Vivian) because they were the same colours that Simone and Georgie had been wearing the day of their arrest, which had the effect of making them look like mighty, renewed versions of themselves before the city.

Yet, as fabulous as he knew he was, Simone felt strangely uncomfortable in his regalia. His suit was tight around his joints (where his prison jumpsuit had been baggy), and his false lashes felt heavy on his eyelids, and his feet felt confined, as if each of his shoes was a foot-sized prison, keeping his toes in cells. Worst of all, his wig was fiercely itchy, and he longed to scratch at his poor scalp. Simone pressed his hands together, in an effort to retain his decorum.

Beside him, Georgie was looking equally as uncomfortable.

The steps leading up to the courthouse were crammed with reporters, tripping over each other to get pictures of their arrival. Mr Vivian was the first to emerge from the vehicle, holding the door ajar for its fashionable cargo, and Simone felt shy as he stepped into the drizzling rain beneath a canopy of umbrellas. Cameras flashed again and again, and a scrum of lawyers appeared, forming a protective circle around him and Georgie as she joined him on the steps.

Simone was no stranger to court. Indeed, the glitterati had their very own system of courts for disputes between fashionites (which were mostly resolved by who wore the most fabulous outfit). This courthouse, however, was somehow even more unfabulous than the one attached to the police station, where Simone and Georgie had had their bail hearing. Its rain-stained pillars were worn, and looked barely capable of holding its dull stone roof overhead. Instead of chandeliers, there were strip-lights illuminating the interior, visible through the blocky building's grimy windows. Only the silver threads of the vibro-rail overhead served as a reminder of their pre-prison life. A carriage swished silently through the rain, showering the gathered reporters, and he glimpsed the beautiful people in their glowing white transport pill.

Simone and Georgie were swept along by their lawyers.

Inside, officers and clerks hid behind desks and water-coolers as Simone's team filled the lobby, and then flowed, like a legal liquid, through a tall set of doors into a courtroom proper. This courtroom was significantly grander than the court attached to the police station, but still barely resembled the courts Simone was used to: here, everything was stained and dull; the pews baked under unflattering fluorescent lights, and the windows showed nothing but streaks of rain and the grey sky, and even the grand justice's desk was made of worn wood, splintering at its corners. Simone and Georgie were led along a red carpet so trodden down that any trace of fluffiness was long gone, through a small wooden gate and up to an equally dull desk with a set of angular wooden chairs behind it.

"No," said Mr Vivian. "This simply will not do."

He nodded at the mass of lawyers waiting in the pew, and a handful leapt from their seats and rushed from the room. Simone took the time to survey the rest of the space, and noticed that the entire left side of the chamber was filled with his legal team: his lawyers squeezed together, binders and briefcases at hand. Meanwhile, the right side of the room was occupied largely by reporters, all of whom were scribbling fiercely in notebooks. At the prosecution's desk were a woman whose face was mostly frown lines, and the familiar, intricately veined face of the prosecutor, Mr Farmer. And beyond them, in two rows, fidgeted the jury – the twelve people chosen to pass judgement on Simone and Georgie.

"Mr Vivian?"

"Yes, Simone?"

"The jury…"

"Yes, I know. Not to worry."

The lawyers returned, carrying a freshly carved oak desk, while a second team leapt over the pews and demolished the current table with tiny silver hammers, pocketing the splinters. The new desk was put in place, swiftly followed by a set of matching chairs, each featuring a brand-new, unblemished red leather pillow. Yet, as Simone sank into his seat, he was surprised by how uncomfortable he was in it. He had grown too used to the hard metal chairs of the prison cafeteria.

Georgie sat, squirming, and placed her fingers on Simone's palm.

The door beyond the justice's desk swung back, and a man wearing a wig and robe emerged. "All rise for Justice Slouch!" cried a clerk, and everybody in the room rose to their feet except for Simone and Georgie.

In the courts of the glitterati, fashionites took turns at being the judge, a role so fabulous that it was only fair that everybody got to have a go (it was a marvellous excuse to be the centre of attention, and wear one's most outrageous wig), but this judge looked as if he had spent his entire life sitting behind his desk. His skin hung loose from his flesh, which made him look as if he were slowly melting into his chair, and his wig was small, and dusty, and perched at angle that made it seem as if it might slip off into his lap at any moment.

The judge slapped his gavel against his desk. "You may be seated."

Everyone sat, except for Simone and Georgie, who were already seated.

The judge sorted through his papers. "Today's case is *The People vs. St Claire*. The charge is kidnapping, and the plea is not guilty. Mr Farmer, your opening statement?"

Mr Farmer stood and cleared his throat.

"Your honour?" interrupted Mr Vivian, before Mr Farmer could utter a word.

"Yes, what is it, Mr Vivian?"

"Side-bar, if I may?"

The judge raised his brows. "Already?"

"Yes, your honour."

"Very well. Come forward."

Both lawyers approached the judge's desk, and everybody else in the room leaned forward, straining to listen.

"What is it, Mr Vivian?" asked the judge.

"It's the jury, your honour."

"What about them?"

"They are plainly unfashionable."

All eyes in the room turned to the twelve sitting in the jury's stands. There was certainly no disputing that they were unfashionable; they slouched, and gawked, and wore all manner of crudely knitted and poorly sewn garments, thrown together without any aesthetic regard.

"What of it, Mr Vivian?"

"The law clearly states that the accused is entitled to be tried by a jury of their peers."

Mr Farmer frowned. "I fail to see the problem."

"The accused are fashionable, your honour. They are entitled to a jury of fashionites."

"This is absurd," said Mr Farmer, his face reddening.

The judge was quiet for a few moments. Then, he said, "No, Mr Farmer. Mr Vivian is quite right. The accused are indeed entitled to be tried by their peers, and this jury is clearly not suitable. Mr Vivian – how long do you imagine it would take to arrange for a fashionable jury?"

Mr Vivian nodded, humbly. "I have a selection of alternative jurors waiting outside."

"You can't be serious?" said Mr Farmer. "Your honour? Surely the defence can't be allowed to select its own jury?"

"On the contrary," said Mr Vivian, producing a piece of paper and sliding it across the desk, "I ran the selection process through with the district attorney this morning." Judge Slouch examined the paper. "This is indeed his signature."

"But… how?" Mr Farmer was aghast.

"We play golf on Fridays."

"Very good." Leaning back, the judge called across to the current jury. "Thank you all for your time. You are dismissed." Then, to the bailiff, "Please call the new jurors in."

The chamber brightened as the glitterati entered. There were perhaps twelve of them, but Simone did not count; he was too busy considering their wigs, each of which was towering. This was the first time he had set eyes on a fashionite in months, and the view was almost overwhelming. They sauntered along in gleaming shoes, their cosmetics so vividly rendered that Simone could not keep his eyes from them, and they each treated the courtroom like a runway, finding the optimal patches of light in which to pause. Lawyers bustled around them, laying lengths of soft carpet for them to tread on, and leaving drapes and pillows across the juror stands to disguise the worst of the worn wood. Eventually, the lawyers managed to herd all of them into the stands, where they sat and posed and paid each other's wigs little compliments.

"Mr Vivian?" said Simone to his lawyer, who had returned to his seat.

"Yes?" whispered Mr Vivian.

"How did you persuade them to come?"

"I have a cache of Karrat cosmetics to give them in return for their cooperation."

"Karrat? Which collection?"

"The Scuba Selection."

Both Simone and Georgie gasped. Karrat's Scuba Selection was legendary, and so exclusive that several fashionites had been gravely injured at the launch.

The judge slapped his gavel against his desk again. "Mr Farmer – do you have any objections with this selection of jurors?"

"No," said Mr Farmer, through his teeth.

"Marvellous. Then you may begin your opening statement."

Mr Farmer took a deep breath, and stood. "Ladies and gentlemen of the jury," he said. "The prosecution intends to prove to you all that the accused, Mr and Mrs St Claire, did kidnap and confine two-year-old Louise Gram for seven days, during which time they kept her locked in various rooms, and fed her alcohol." There were gasps, but specifically from the side of the court where the reporters sat. The glitterati were not paying attention. "Ladies and gentlemen of the jury," he repeated, "if you will give me a moment of your time, then I will take you through the events that took place three months ago, when Mr and Mrs St Claire kidnapped the unwitting child."

The jury gave no indication that they were inclined to give Mr Farmer a moment of their time, but this did nothing to prevent him from attempting to take it anyway. "On the sixteenth of June," he continued, "a gardener by the name of Frederick Gram, in the employ of Mr and Mrs St Claire, arrived to work at their property with his two-year-old child, Louise Gram. Normally, Mr Gram would drop Louise off with a babysitter or Louise's mother while he worked, but that day both the babysitter and Louise's mother were unavailable. It was perfectly reasonable, however, for Mr Gram to assume that Louise would be happy enough playing in the sunshine in Mr and Mrs St Claire's garden while he got on with his work, which was a solitary enough pursuit. Unfortunately, while engaged in his work, Mr Gram suffered a massive heart attack. This went unnoticed for some hours, until Mr Gram's relief arrived and called for help. Mr Gram was immediately transferred to an ambulance, where he sadly passed away. It was of no fault on the part of Mr Gram that his fellow gardeners were not aware that Louise was still in the garden, playing by herself on a different lawn."

"We have gardeners?" whispered Georgie, beneath her breath.

Simone had always been uncomfortable with the idea of unfashionable people tending to his garden – so much so that he had preferred to imagine that the garden manifested its own beauty due to its proximity to its fabulous owners. Yet having seen what unfashionable people could do with a pile of fabric, a sewing machine and some instructions, he knew that they were, in fact, perfectly capable of making a garden gorgeous. It seemed so elementary now.

"Indeed," continued Mr Farmer, "the first people to find Louise were Mr and Mrs St Claire themselves, who, instead of notifying the authorities that there was an unattended child in their garden, chose to confine her." Mr Farmer turned and pointed an accusatory finger at Simone and Georgie. "Members of Mr and Mrs St Claire's own household, including maids, cooks and security guards, were surprised by the sudden appearance of Louise in the house, but chose not to intervene, assuming that the child belonged to Mr and Mrs St Claire. Since learning that Louise was the child of Mr Gram, they have provided the prosecution with overwhelming witness and video testimony of Mr and Mrs St Claire's crimes. These testimonies provide comprehensive evidence of abuse, showing Mr and Mrs St Claire luring and locking Louise into their baking-hot greenhouse, locking Louise in their bedroom, and feeding her alcohol. At no point during that time did Mr and Mrs St Claire tell anyone about Louise, leaving her mother frantic about her whereabouts and well-being. In the end, it was one of Mr St Claire's close personal friends who informed the authorities about poor Louise."

"Who do you think he means?" whispered Georgie.

"I'm not sure," whispered Simone, who was still coming to terms with the idea that there were not only gardeners maintaining his property, but maids and security guards. Just how many unfashionable people did it take to maintain his fabulous lifestyle? The more Simone thought about it, the itchier his wig became.

"Ladies and gentlemen of the jury," said Mr Farmer, for the third time. "If you have any sympathy at all for poor Louise Gram, then you will, on the basis of the overwhelming evidence I am about to show you, find Mr and Mrs St Claire guilty of kidnapping." Clearing his throat, and adjusting his drab tie, he returned to his dull table. "Thank you, your honour."

"Very good, Mr Farmer. Mr Vivian – your opening statement?"

"Thank you, your honour." Mr Vivian stood with much aplomb, and sauntered over to the jury. For the first time, the glitterati up on the stands started paying attention to anything but themselves; their eyes were collectively drawn to Mr Vivian's golden tie. "My wonderful, gorgeous, marvellous jury," he said, and they preened at the trio of compliments. "My argument is simple. My clients, Mr and Mrs St Claire, are innocent. They could not have possibly kidnapped a child, because they do not know what a child is."

"Objection!" cried Mr Farmer.

"What is it, Mr Farmer?" asked the judge.

Mr Farmer rose from his chair. "Mr Vivian is lying to the jury. How is it possible that Mr and Mrs St Claire do not know what a child is? They were once children themselves!"

"A fair point," said the judge. "Mr Vivian – please explain yourself."

"Of course," said Mr Vivian, graciously. "It is quite elementary. Among the glitterati, trauma is considered unaesthetic. Therefore, fashionable people routinely have traumatic memories erased." Placing his hands behind his back, he paced. "Not so long ago, it was agreed that childhood is traumatic. As such, fashionable people, including my clients, have all memories of childhood erased. They are introduced into fashionable society as fully realised adults."

Mr Farmer laughed. "You can't be serious?"

"I am perfectly serious, Mr Farmer. My clients, and every member of this jury, do not remember being children."

"Are you really suggesting that your clients are so wealthy that—"

"My clients are also unaware of their own wealth."

Mr Farmer's face was extremely red. "How?"

"Knowledge of economic systems is also considered traumatic," Mr Vivian explained, patiently. "My clients have had all memories of capitalism erased."

"Are you…" Mr Farmer took a moment to gather his thoughts. "Are you saying that your clients, and the jury, *don't know what money is*?"

"Correct," said Mr Vivian. "Their wealth is so profound that not only does it perpetuate itself, but it allows them the luxury of employing people, such as myself, to run their estates on their behalf, so that they may live their lives without knowledge of it. In fact, once this trial is over, both my clients and every member of this jury will have their memories of taking part in it erased."

Mr Farmer's mouth remained open, but no more sounds emerged from it.

Simone squeezed his hands tightly between his knees to prevent himself from scratching at his scalp. This further revelation – that not only was he unaware of just how many unfashionables were maintaining his life, but that he was equally unaware of such concepts as childhood and (what was the word that Mr Vivian used?) capitalism – made him feel as if the wardrobe of his mind was missing more than a few items of clothing. Items of clothing he was only now returning to their rightful places on the racks.

"Therefore," continued Mr Vivian, addressing the jury once again, "Mr and Mrs St Claire could not have possibly kidnapped a child, because they do not know what a child is. And as such, I recommend that you beautiful people of the jury find Mr and Mrs St Claire not guilty of kidnapping." Returning to the freshly varnished desk of the defence, he sat down beside Simone and Georgie. "Thank you, your honour."

Justice Slouch squinted down at the court. "Thank you, Mr Vivian. Most enlightening. Mr Farmer – you have witnesses to call and evidence to present on behalf of the prosecution, yes?"

There was no reply from the prosecution. Mr Farmer was busy sorting through the stacks of paper on his desk, his expression one of furious concentration.

"What is he doing?" whispered Georgie.

"I believe that Mr Farmer is re-evaluating his evidence," whispered Mr Vivian.

"Mr Farmer?" prompted the judge.

"Yes, your honour," said Mr Farmer at last, pushing all of his papers aside. "The prosecution would like to present a witness."

"Go ahead, Mr Farmer."

"The prosecution calls Ms Justine Featherstone to the stand."

The doors at the far end of the court swung back, and there was Justine in the bright lights of the hallway. Her wig was cathedralesque, composed of white hair teased into spires and turrets and laced with purple threads that matched her purple suit. Her lips were a luscious, gleaming purple, and she wore oversized purple sunglasses, and as she sashayed down the carpet, all eyes turned to follow her. At the gate she stopped and struck a little pose (affecting impatience) until a bailiff rushed across and opened it for her, and she paused on every step leading up to the witness stand, taking the time to make certain that everybody could see every angle of her outfit. Purple jewels sparkled on her fingers, and when she removed her sunglasses, she revealed more purple jewels dripping down her cheeks, as if she were weeping gemstones.

"Ms Featherstone?" said the judge.

"That is I," said Justine.

"Do you swear to tell the truth, the whole truth, and nothing but the truth?"

"Of course, darling."

"You may proceed, Mr Farmer."

Mr Farmer rose from his desk and approached the witness stand. "Ms Featherstone. It was you who reported Louise's kidnapping to the authorities. Would you like to take the court through the events of that evening?"

It was Justine who had called the police about the child? The itching of Simone's wig suddenly subsided, as a heat rose from his feet all the way up to his ears.

"Yes, yes." Justine dabbed at her gemstone tears. "It was all so dreadfully upsetting."

"What time did you arrive at Simone St Claire's mansion?"

"Oh, it must have been nearly seven o'clock. I was wearing one of my favourite polka-dot dresses, and was visiting in the spirit of kindness, to congratulate Simone on throwing a wonderful garden party. I even baked him a pie."

The jury nodded and muttered appreciatively among themselves. Word of Simone's garden party must have reached all corners of fashionable society.

"When I arrived, there was nobody there to greet me, and the door was ajar," she continued. "So, I entered the house, and called aloud."

"What happened next?"

"I set the pie down upon a table and checked my lipstick in a mirror. It was flawless, of course. I was flawless. But it was then that I saw it."

"What did you see?"

"I saw… the child."

There were gasps from the jury.

"What did the child look like, Ms Featherstone?"

"It was hideous," said Justine, lip curling in distaste. "It was very small, and very ugly. And it was wearing denim."

More gasps from the jury.

"What did the child do, Ms Featherstone?"

"It rushed across the room and threw itself upon my pie. It grabbed handfuls, and stuffed them into its mouth, and sprayed crumbs all over the room."

The jury's expressions were all of horror.

"What did you do, Ms Featherstone?"

"I fled, as quickly as I could!"

"And did you see Mr or Mrs St Claire anywhere?"

"Yes, I did, as I was running from the house."

"What did you see?"

Justine heaved a sob, and moved her face so that her gemstone tears would glitter in the light. "I saw them rush down the stairs and fall upon the pie themselves. It was all three of them – the child, and Simone, and Georgie, gulping down mouthfuls of pie, and spilling bits of it everywhere. *And they were all wearing denim*."

Several members of the jury pretended to faint.

Simone's fists were clenched tight and trembling beneath his table.

"What did you do next?" asked Mr Farmer.

"I went straight home, and spent the night tossing and turning in my bed, terrified of what I had seen. Then, first thing in the morning, I called the police."

"Very good, Ms Featherstone. Thank you for sharing your story with us."

"Quite," said Justine, still sobbing.

"No more questions, your honour," said Mr Farmer.

"She's lying," hissed Simone to Mr Vivian. "None of that is true."

"I would *never* wear denim," whispered Georgie, emphatically.

"Not to worry," whispered Mr Vivian. "I have it in hand."

"Mr Vivian," said the judge. "Do you have any questions?"

"Only one, your honour."

"Go ahead."

Mr Vivian stood with such aplomb that the jury's attentions were immediately drawn from Justine. Their expressions softened at the sight of his golden tie. "Ms Featherstone," said Mr Vivian. "Please, for the court, tell us the flavour of the pie."

Justine seemed startled by the question. "Pardon?"

"The pie. What flavour was it?"

There was a lengthy pause. "I believe…" she said carefully, "that it was… apple?"

"Are you sure?"

"It may have been rhubarb."

"You are unsure?"

"I was quite overwhelmed by the horror of it all," she said tartly, but it was too late. Her uncertainty was not playing well with the jury. They muttered to one another, and even indulged in small frowns. After all, if Justine could not remember the flavour of the pie, then what else was she misremembering? Justine let out a few more sobs, but it was clear she had lost them. Simone relaxed his fists and exhaled.

"Thank you, your honour," said Mr Vivian. "No more questions."

"You are dismissed, Ms Featherstone," said the judge.

Replacing her oversized sunglasses, Justine sauntered back the way she came.

"You may call your next witness, Mr Farmer," said the judge, but Mr Farmer was once again leafing through his piles of paperwork with an expression of defeat.

"Mr Farmer?" insisted the judge.

"I have no more witnesses," the prosecutor said quietly, "and no more evidence to present."

The judge gave him a withering look. "Very well. Mr Vivian, would you like to call your first witness?"

"I would like to present a character witness, if I may."

"Go ahead."

"The defence calls Mr Harry Darlington to the stand."

The doors swung back, and there was Darlington, oiled muscles shining in the light.

Simone's breath caught in his throat. Darlington's wig was an understated set of white waves that matched his frosted moustache, and he wore a tight white tuxedo cut short at the arms and legs to show off his biceps and thighs, which he flexed as he walked into the court. There was a small round of applause from the jury as he made his way up to the stand, and he winked at them, so that the white powder dusting his lashes fell like snowflakes across his cheek. Simone felt Georgie squeeze his wrist, and they exchanged a hopeful glance.

"Mr Darlington?" said the judge.

"Absolutely," he said, twirling the end of his moustache.

"Do you swear to tell the truth, the whole truth, and nothing but the truth?"

A pause. "All of it?"

"Only the parts relevant to the case at hand."

Darlington looked relieved. “Oh, yes. Of course.”

“You may proceed, Mr Vivian.”

“Mr Darlington,” said Mr Vivian. “Thank you so much for agreeing to come and testify on behalf of Mr and Mrs St Claire. The court sincerely appreciates your time.”

“It’s a delight to be here,” said Darlington graciously. “They are very dear friends of mine.”

“What is it,” continued Mr Vivian, “that you would like the court to know about them?”

Darlington splayed his fingers beneath his chin, turned his eyes to the ceiling as if enraptured by remembrance, and said, “Simone and Georgie are two of the most fabulous people I know. Both are aesthetically impeccable, and I am glad to count them as close friends. On more than one occasion, Georgie has loaned me some of her false eyelashes and helped to oil some of the more hard-to-reach muscles on my back.” The jury murmured appreciatively. “Simone regularly joins me at the gym, and gives me plenty of encouragement. And at work, he often takes the time to recommend me his favourite magazine articles.” There was yet more appreciative murmuring – this was impeccable etiquette.

“Your honour,” said Mr Farmer wearily. “I have to object. What does this have to do with the charge of kidnapping?”

“Sustained. Mr Vivian, please direct your witness with a little more focus.”

“Of course, your honour. Mr Darlington – do you believe Mr and Mrs St Claire capable of kidnapping and abusing someone?”

Darlington took the time to consider Mr Vivian’s question

seriously. Simone held his breath. Then, he said, "Not without consent."

Simone exhaled.

"Wonderful. Thank you, Mr Darlington. I have no more questions, your honour."

"Thank you, Mr Vivian. Mr Farmer, do you have any questions for Mr Darlington?"

"No, your honour," said Mr Farmer, the network of veins beneath his skin visibly pulsing.

"Then you may go, Mr Darlington."

Darlington paused at the table for the defence on the way out, to exchange some air-kisses with Simone and Georgie. Simone returned each one in kind, with unabashed enthusiasm, and Georgie blew a few kisses across. Then, in a haze of white powder, he sashayed away.

The heat that had risen through Simone was almost all gone now – soothed by Darlington – and his wig began to itch again.

"Mr Vivian," said the judge. "You may call your next witness."

"I have no more witnesses, your honour," said Mr Vivian.

Simone tugged gently at Mr Vivian's sleeve. "Do you not want our testimony?" he whispered.

Leaning over, Mr Vivian smiled. "There's no need. You've been giving your testimony the whole trial. The way you look says more than words ever could."

Judge Slouch peered first at Mr Vivian and then at Mr Farmer. "Neither of you have any more witnesses or evidence to present? Are you certain?"

"Yes, your honour."

"Yes, your honour."

"Very well. I may be home in time for dinner. Closing statements. Mr Farmer?"

Mr Farmer rose from his desk, and stood before the jury, looking thoughtful. The jury continued to pay him no attention whatsoever, which was fine because he wasn't saying anything anyway. Eventually, he said, "Beautiful ladies and gentlemen of the jury," and a few impeccably decorated eyes turned his way, drawn by the compliment. "According to the… fabulous testimony of Ms Featherstone, Mr and Mrs St Claire have been seen wearing denim." Yet more eyes began focusing on Mr Farmer. The jury were listening to him at last. "As you well know," he continued, carefully, "it is… outrageous to be seen wearing denim." The jury nodded. It *was* outrageous to be seen wearing denim. "Therefore, if Mr and Mrs St Claire are capable of wearing denim, imagine what else they must be capable of. Such as kidnapping." Jurors murmured their agreement with each other. This was flawless logic. Who knew what depraved acts denim-wearers might commit? "As such, if you believe the testimony of Ms Featherstone, then you must find Mr and Mrs St Claire guilty – of wearing denim, and kidnapping Louise Gram. Thank you. The prosecution rests."

Mr Farmer returned to his seat with an air of triumph.

Judge Slouch turned to the defence. "Mr Vivian?"

Mr Vivian rose from his chair once more, and the jury ceased their muttering so as to best hear his rebuttal. "My darling members of the jury," he said. "According to the sworn statement of Mr Darlington, Mr and Mrs St Claire are fabulous. Do you really believe that any self-respecting fabulous person would be seen wearing denim?" The jury shook their collective heads. Of course not. "In which case, I would invite you to reconsider the testimony of Ms Featherstone, who must have been mistaken about what she saw. Remember that she was unable to recall the flavour of the pie in her story." The jury were taking Mr Vivian's argument very seriously, but there were a few doubtful expressions among them. "While deliberating, I ask you to consider the question of the misremembered pie, and what it means for Ms Featherstone's testimony. I say: 'If she can't remember the pie, then the denim must be a lie.' Again: 'If she can't remember the pie, then the denim must be a lie.'" Several members of the jury mouthed the couplet along with Mr Vivian, and even the most sceptical among them appeared to be convinced by it. After all – things that rhymed sounded pretty, which made them more likely to be true.

"Thank you all for your kind consideration," said Mr Vivian. "The defence rests."

"Very good," said the judge. "Thank you, both." He turned to the jury. "Ladies and gentlemen of the jury, you are now invited to consider all of the evidence put before you, and come to a verdict as to the charges laid against Mr and Mrs St Claire. Bailiff – you may lead the jury to their chambers, for the duration of their deliberations."

The jury slowly began filtering out of the room, which took a while because each insisted on making a fabulous exit, turning to and fro to show off their outfits.

"This court is now in recess," said the judge when they were gone, and he slapped his gavel against his desk with finality, as if he were adding a particularly emphatic full stop to a sentence. The judge rose, as did the rest of the court (except for Simone and Georgie), and disappeared through the same doors he had entered by. And, with his departure, the court erupted into chatter. Lawyers chattered with other lawyers, and reporters chattered with other reporters, and lawyers and reporters attempted to rush from the room at all once, forming a queue at the exit.

"What now?" asked Simone of Mr Vivian. Pushing his fingers beneath his wig, he scratched his poor sore scalp. Surely it wouldn't be much longer until he could take it off.

Mr Vivian was looking quite pleased with himself. "We wait for the jury to come back with a verdict. I don't imagine it taking very long."

Georgie was settled back in her seat, arranged in a way that made it look as if she were in repose and accidentally beautiful, and Simone did likewise, determined to remain composed until the very end of the trial. Mr Vivian wandered over to the prosecution's shabby desk.

"Mr Farmer," said Mr Vivian.

The prosecutor glanced up from his papers, looking flustered. "Yes?"

"Andrew Vivian. It's a pleasure." Mr Vivian advanced his hand.

Mr Farmer took it, with a puzzled expression. "Ralph. Ralph Farmer."

"You did a sterling job today, Ralph."

"Do you think?" Mr Farmer did not look very convinced.

"You did extraordinary work adapting your case as you went along. Indeed, agreeing to prosecute this case was very brave.

Were you to have succeeded, it would have made your career. I admire that kind of bold ambition."

"I might still win."

"You and I both know you lost this case the moment you agreed to it."

Mr Farmer's face was reddening again. "If you hadn't—"

Mr Vivian raised his hands defensively. "I'm not here to argue with you, Ralph. I'm here because my compliments are genuine. You did some really wonderful work today, and I see a lot of potential in you. I'd like to offer you a job at my firm."

"You can't be serious. Why would I ever agree to that?"

Mr Vivian smiled. "Consider your current salary."

Mr Farmer didn't reply, but his expression dimmed.

"Now," said Mr Vivian, "add a zero to the end of it."

Mr Farmer's eyes widened.

"There's no need for an immediate response," continued Mr Vivian. "Representing the glitterati is not something to be taken lightly, but believe me when I tell you that the benefits are quite excellent. Here's my card." Mr Vivian's card was black with gilded lettering, and it matched his suit. "Call my secretary when you've made up your mind, and we can set up a meeting."

Mr Farmer did not respond. His eyes simply rested upon the card, the redness draining from his face as he considered the golden curls upon it.

The court gradually quietened to a low murmur, and Simone realised that he was hungry. He had missed the regular prison lunch time. There was no food in immediate sight, and he had no desire to disturb Mr Vivian, who was busy consorting with some of his fellow lawyers, so he decided to imagine the first meal he would have once he was back at home, in an effort to satiate himself. First, he imagined a lovely crispbread starter, with fresh butter and duck pâté. Closing his eyes, he imagined the various ingredients, manifesting their flavours on his tongue. It was a delicious starter, but Simone did not dwell on it for very long, because he did not want to fill up before his main course. Thankfully, the first part of the main course was quick to arrive, because it was imaginary, and it was a rich, creamy carrot soup, sprinkled with croutons, and as Simone imagined spooning it into his mouth, he could almost feel the warmth of it sliding down his throat and filling his belly – satisfying in a way the prison cubes never were. Accompanying the imaginary soup was an imaginary beef steak, glazed with honey so thickly that it crackled when he attacked it with his imaginary knife and fork. The steak was so tender it melted on his tongue, and went down as easily as the soup did. At last, Simone came to his imaginary dessert, which was an enormous creamy trifle, each layer of which—

"All rise for Justice Slouch!" cried a clerk, interrupting Simone's dessert. He opened his eyes just in time to see everyone else in the room, except for Georgie, stand up, as a mass of lawyers and reporters fought to return through the far doors. The judge with his shabby wig once more emerged, looking more melted than before, and as he settled behind his desk the rest of the room returned to their seats.

"I have been informed," said the judge, "that the jury has reached a verdict."

Georgie placed a hand upon Simone's knee, and he realised he was nervous. Not about returning to prison – which had, in the end, been a surprisingly pleasant experience – but about being separated from Georgie again.

"Bailiff," continued the judge. "Please invite the jury to return."

And return they did, every bit as fabulous as before. They took their time, making their entrances one by one, until, eventually, the jury stands were once again filled. They preened, and admired one another, and appeared entirely unaware of the court beyond their benches.

The judge tapped his desk with his gavel, which was enough to draw their attention. "I have been told," he said, "that you have come to a verdict?"

"We have, your honour," said a member of the jury languidly.

"Is your verdict unanimous?"

"It is."

"Then, if you would, please present your verdict to the court."

There was a tense silence as the member of the jury speaking on their behalf stood, and pouted in the bright lights. Simone placed his own hand atop Georgie's, afraid it might be the last time he would ever do so.

The fashionite who stood cleared his throat. "The jury finds the defendants…"

A pause, for dramatic effect.

"Fabulous."

* * *

The interior of Mr Vivian's car felt too bright. Glasses of champagne bubbled on the counter-tops, warm music floated in the air, and the miniature chandelier swung perilously about. Georgie and Mr Vivian shared empty small talk, and sipped at champagne, and snorted little bumps of white powder together, but Simone found he could not altogether relax, despite having removed his wig. Rain rolled down the windows, distorting the city streets that loomed darkly to either side of the car, and ahead lay the hospital, where Simone and Georgie's memories of everything since the arrest would be erased. Yet, instead of comforted, Simone felt uneasy. Tomorrow, his most pressing worry would be his outfit; a thought that made him frown. Unfashionables lumbered about in the rain, hunched against the heavy sky as if they were carrying the weight of it on their backs, and Simone watched them, sipping half-heartedly at a glass of champagne and listening to the chiming of the chandelier.

Two shapes emerged from the gloom: an adult pulling a child along by the hand. The adult was a woman, and between the raindrops rolling down the window Simone could see that her umbrella was broken and useless, so that neither she nor the child had any shelter from the relentless sky. The woman's unkempt hair was plastered across her shoulders, and the child trudged through the puddles in her wake, its head lolling with every step. There was something gripped in the child's free hand, and it was this object that caught Simone's attention, because it was wholly unlike everything else on the street. All was rain-slick, and dull, and rusted, and beaten, except for that slim silver tube, which gleamed chromatically between the child's pudgy fingers. The car splashed through a puddle, spraying the woman and child, and it was then that Simone realised who they were. The woman was the same woman who had been sat beside Mr Farmer during the trial with a frown, and the child was the denim child, snot oozing down its upper lip, tube of lipstick clutched tight.

"Stop the car!" cried Simone.

The car swooshed to a halt.

"Georgie – look! It's the child!"

Georgie shuffled across, and peered through the raindrops. The woman had stopped her advance, and was squinting at the car, the last scraps of her useless umbrella flapping in the wind. "Why – I think you might be right, Simone. But who is that woman?"

Mr Vivian sipped at his champagne. "I believe that to be the child's mother."

"Poor little creature," said Georgie sympathetically.

"It is a shame," said Simone. The child was staring balefully at the vehicle, tube of lipstick held close to its chest. "The child has so much potential."

Georgie nodded. "A pity it has such an unfashionable mother."

"Perhaps…"

"Yes, darling?"

"Perhaps we could look after it? Teach it how to be beautiful?"

Georgie swirled her champagne around thoughtfully. "I suppose I did rather enjoy its company. I would not be opposed to the idea. But what of its mother?"

Simone pressed the button to wind down the window, and there was an electronic whine as it slowly descended. A little rain pattered across the leather interior, and Simone leaned out. "You there!" he called. "Unfashionable woman with the child!"

The mother's frown somehow deepened.

"My wife and I believe that your child has aesthetic potential," said Simone, speaking slowly to compensate for the woman's aesthetic impairments. "We would like to look after it, and teach it how to be beautiful. We can save it from a lifetime of ugliness."

The woman drew closer to the car. "You want Louise?"

This close, Simone could see the woman's uneven teeth, and crow's feet, and grey strands of hair. "Yes," said Simone. "We can show her how to be fabulous."

"Perhaps," said Mr Vivian, from behind Simone, "we could trade?"

"A trade?" said the woman.

"Yes. What would you like, in exchange for your child?"

This was very enterprising of Mr Vivian, and Simone was glad to have his lawyer present.

The woman's entire face shrunk into a frown, as if she were a grape shrivelling into a raisin. Her eyes turned first to the child, and then to Simone. "Your shoes," she said.

"My shoes?"

"Give me your shoes."

Simone studied his shoes. They were a brand-new pair of bright yellow Scalia loafers, and they were deeply uncomfortable compared to his prison sandals. "Would they even fit you?"

"She doesn't want to wear them," explained Mr Vivian, patiently. "Your shoes are worth a great deal of money. She can sell them, and live very comfortably off the proceeds."

Simone still wasn't entirely certain what money was, but he did appreciate the value of living comfortably. "I see," he said. Then, slipping his shoes from his feet (sweet relief), he presented them through the window of the car. "They are wonderful shoes. I hope you enjoy them."

Letting go of the child, the woman snatched the shoes from Simone's outstretched arm and hugged them close. The child peered blearily up at its mother, and then up at the limousine.

"Would you like to get in?" Georgie asked the child.

The child nodded, once. Then, it presented its silver prize to her. "Lipdick," it said.

"Yes, very good. Lipstick." Swinging the door open, Georgie reached out and helped the child clamber on to a soft leather chair. "Mr Vivian, darling, could you pass me some napkins? The child is absolutely filthy."

Swinging the door shut against the rain-slick street, Simone wound the window back up. Safe against the city, he watched as Georgie and Mr Vivian attempted to wipe the worst of it from the child, who gurgled and burbled happily at the attention being lavished upon it. As the car swept from the pavement, Simone caught sight of the child's mother one last time, standing at the edge of the road with Simone's shoes clutched tightly against her chest. Her frown looked as though it had spread from her forehead to her entire figure, and Simone was glad to have rescued the child from her. Taking a glass of champagne, he relaxed into his seat, laughing as the child waved its lipstick triumphantly around in the air like a crude baton.

* * *

It felt good to peel off his clothes.

The hospital changing room was large and round, and once again Simone felt as if he were undressing inside the shell of a bleached egg. He felt reassured by the sight of all the gowns, which were the same crisp white as the walls. One by one, he neatly folded his canary-yellow clothes into a pile. Then, with various creams and wipes, he began to remove his cosmetics. Soon, he was every bit as immaculate as the rest of the room. There was a clean set of white leather chairs in the centre, and he sat back in one, thinking about the blessed cleanliness he would know when his memories were erased.

Only… since leaving court, Simone had been troubled by his empty wardrobe of memories. The wardrobe itself was huge – a multi-tier expanse representing all the years of his life. Yet his memories only occupied the very lowest rungs, hanging beside the door. The rest had been removed – as one does with unfashionable items of clothing. The last few months had begun to fill some more of the racks.

At last, a set of nurses arrived, faces hidden behind white masks, and Simone was led through the white tubular corridors of the hospital, feeling like a chewed-up piece of food being transported through an immaculate set of bowels. He was deposited into another large egg of a room, along with Georgie and the child, both of whom were wearing their own crisp hospital gowns. This room had a set of three large white leather chairs, above which dangled three enormous chrome helmets, bursting with all manner of silver wires and cables.

Dr Cask entered the room, flicking through the contents of a clipboard. Today, he was wearing a well-fitted white suit beneath his white lab coat, and his mask was of a slightly higher quality than those worn by the nurses and orderlies of the hospital. Simone had never seen beneath Dr Cask's mask, but the way it lay across his face suggested an extraordinarily sharp bone structure. His eyes, like scalpels, dissected the pages he read, and Simone was delighted to see that Dr Cask's hair and lashes were frosted white at the tips, which complemented the rest of his outfit. "Good evening to you all," he said.

"Dr Cask," said Georgie. "It's so good to see you."

"You are looking glamorous today, Doctor," said Simone.

"Quite," said the doctor. "I have been informed that your memories of the past three months are to be erased. Do you have a specific time or moment you wish me to proceed from?"

"Before we begin," said Simone, "I have a question."

"Of course." Dr Cask's eyes did not leave his notes.

"How many of my memories have you removed?"

The full force of the doctor's gaze made Simone feel as if the skin were being peeled from his bones. There was a long pause, and then he said, "Most of them." There was another pause. "Now, then. Do you have a specific moment you would like me to proceed from?"

"How about the morning of the arrest?" said Georgie. "At the café? We were enjoying ourselves at a café on the Boulevard. If you could remove all memories past the arrival of our coffees, that would be perfect."

"Very good." Dr Cask turned a page. "And what of the child?"

The child was unsuccessfully attempting to climb on to one of the chairs.

"Oh," said Georgie. "How about breakfast, the same day?"

"Certainly," said Dr Cask, closing his clipboard. "If you would all be seated."

Simone helped the child into the centre seat, and made her comfortable, but his mind was whirring. "Now, then," said Georgie to the child, in her most comforting voice. "This won't take very long at all. It's a bit like taking a bath, but for your mind. It will wash all the filth out. All you need to do is sit back and relax."

"R'lax," said the child, still clutching tightly on to her tube of lipstick.

"I'll be right here, and so will Simone."

"S'mone," said the child.

Simone settled into his own seat, but then immediately leapt up. "I can't!" he cried.

"Simone? Darling?"

"I can't do it! I don't want to forget prison. I don't want to forget how wonderful it feels to make clothes. I don't want to forget how wonderful it was to be reunited with you. Doctor?"

"Yes, Simone?"

"I don't want to forget."

"The procedure," said Dr Cask carefully, "is voluntary. However, studies have shown that retaining traumatic memories can result in aesthetic impairment. Symptoms include excessive frowning, weeping and sighing, and long-term effects may include depression and anxiety, all of which puts you at increased risk of ugliness. As your family beautician, I strongly recommend undergoing the treatment."

"I don't want to," said Simone, defiantly folding his arms. "I refuse."

Dr Cask exhaled slowly through his nose, making his mask flutter. "Very well."

"Georgie?" Simone knelt before her. "Will you remember these weeks with me?"

Gently placing her hands atop his, Georgie looked into Simone's eyes. "Did you really learn how to make clothes?"

"I did, dearest heart. Didn't you?"

"I'm afraid not. I only learned how to do plumbing."

"Like the fruit?"

"No, darling. It's a thing ugly people do with pipes."

"That doesn't sound very pleasant."

"It wasn't. And I wish to forget all about it."

Simone nodded, slowly. "I understand, darling. And when you wake up, I will be here."

Cupping his chin in her hands, Georgie smiled at him. "And I understand as well, dearest Simone. If I learned how to make clothes, I would want to remember it."

"And the child?" asked Dr Cask.

"Let the child forget," said Georgie, gently. "She's been through enough."

Simone nodded, and stepped back. "You may proceed, Doctor."

"Very well."

Simone huddled back against the wall, his mind in turmoil.

"You each may feel a slight burning sensation," said Dr Cask, who was operating a set of controls embedded into the wall. The helmets above the chairs began to gently ascend over Georgie and the child, fitting over their heads as neatly as motorcycle helmets. The child gripped Georgie's hand tightly. Then, there was a chromatic screech, and their bodies began to convulse.

* * *

It was wonderful watching Georgie wake.

Interior design fashions had changed considerably in the last three months, and the master bedroom was no longer fishy. Instead, the fashion was floral, and every surface in the room was vivid with flowers. The wallpapers had a silky, shimmering texture, depicting petals of a particularly luxurious quality – a quality Simone was able to confirm, by way of being wrapped up in sheets of the same material. The carpets were made of petals, and so were the drapes of the four-poster, and even the lampshades looked like flowers. Light gushed in from the window, making Georgie glow as she sat up.

"Oh, darling!" she exclaimed. "It's all flowers!" Taking a deep breath, as if she might catch the scent of it all (and indeed, a bouquet was apparent – not so pervasive as to be overwhelming, but of a richness that suggested flowers were being arranged elsewhere in the house), Georgie stretched indulgently, as if she had just awoken from a most delightful dream. Manoeuvring herself to the edge of the bed, she pressed her toes into the carpet, which was an ultrasoft hypergrass variant featuring countless tiny silken buttercups.

"It is," said Simone, and he could see not a single trace of prison in Georgie. It really was as if she had fallen asleep at that café on the Boulevard, and woken three months later at home. Rolling the doors of her walk-in wardrobe aside, she wandered in and turned on the spot, eyes wide as she beheld the shelves. Simone was glad to see her wonder as she rifled through the railings, admiring each new article she came across. The fashions had developed considerably since their arrest, and the unfashionable housekeepers must have taken pains to offer a few choice outfits to ease Georgie's transition. Holding some against herself, she twirled, and Simone felt aglow in her happiness, as if he were a flower and she was the sun.

Simone had been too exhausted upon arriving home last night for any exploration, so he now wandered through the corridors of his apartment, admiring each new fashion he came across. There were so many – the guest bedroom was pearlescent, the living room was plastic, and the bathroom now had reflective tiles, arranged to make the user feel as if they were defecating inside a mirrorball – that by the time Simone reached the kitchen, he was quite overwhelmed. Thankfully, the kitchen remained much as he remembered it (with a few exceptions – there were rather more sprigs of things decoratively placed here and there). There was a tower of magazines piled up on the counter, but Simone first went to the veranda doors, to look out at his garden. The garden, too, was familiar, and the silver skyscrapers reflected it back at itself in their myriad windows, so that it looked as if there were a thousand gardens brightening in the dawn light. And out there, in the soft bed of a planter filled with giant daisies, lay the child, fast asleep – apparently having found a floral bed of her own.

Satisfied, Simone returned to the magazines. It was time to see what had changed.

It quickly became apparent that both the fashion for nosebleeds and the fashion for vintage clothes had passed. Simone saw familiar faces among the pages, and everyone was wearing something different. There was a fashion for flowy, loose kaftans on Tuesdays, which he rather liked, and aviators had made a comeback, which he was a little uncertain about. Purple was out, and orange was in. Feathers were out, and scales were in. Neon was out, and khaki was in. Simone took each of these revelations in stride, and it was a delight to see some of his friends among the pages, looking so beautiful and self-satisfied. There was only one face he was not pleased to see. She was even on the covers of some. Yet as Simone beheld her, he realised that his feelings about Justine had changed. He no longer cared that she had stolen his looks, and stolen his lemon, and upstaged him at every opportunity. It didn't matter because, in the end, she didn't matter; the tides of fashion had moved inexorably on despite her.

The tides of fashion had moved on without Simone, as well, but he found that it didn't bother him very much; he was rather enjoying being an observer instead of a participant.

The magazines were all gushing about Justine's forthcoming wedding to Trevor Tremptor, and Simone realised he hadn't been to work for months. He idly wondered if he still had a job.

There was the sound of laughter from outside, and Simone looked up to see Georgie on the decking with the child. Georgie had brought a pair of ruby-red heels from her wardrobe, and the child was trying to walk in them. The heels were far too big, and the child kept slipping, but Georgie held her up by her arms and helped her clatter unsteadily across the planks. And all at once, Simone was furious. Not at the child and Georgie, whom he loved so much, but at Justine, who had almost successfully managed to separate the three of them as petty revenge for being upstaged. Justine had tried to destroy Simone's family, and now that they were free to return to fashionable society, Simone had no doubt she would try and do the same again. Her immaculate face pouted up at him from the covers of the magazines.

Simone knew what he had to do.

The only way to protect Georgie and the child from Justine was to destroy her so completely that she would have no means of retaliating against him. Flicking through the nearest magazine, Simone found an article that detailed the particulars of Justine's wedding, and saw that it was happening tomorrow. There would be no greater opportunity. She had sashayed so confidently into court, delivering lies to try and remove him from fashionable society for good. Well – Simone would not be so crude. His plan would be elegant, and beautiful, and destroy her utterly. Only… Simone realised he would not be able to pull it off by himself. He needed help from a person even more fabulous than himself. Pausing only briefly to admire the child's shaky progress across the decking, Simone rushed to get dressed. He didn't have much time.

* * *

Karpa Fishh lived in the legendary House of All Seasons, nestled in among the mountains. The peaks were as sharp as scalpels, cutting the clouds that dared to pass too close, and Simone shivered at the sight of the snow at their heights.

Of course, he had come dressed to impress. Nothing less than Simone's very best would do.

The magazines said that it was essential to wear lace on Saturdays, so Simone wore a white lace ensemble, including a long ruff, flowing blouse, tiered skirt, and socks that rose all the way to his knees. There were lengths of white lace arranged through his hair, and small measures clung to his lips and lashes. Simone had decided to go a step further with his look, however, and had plundered his garden (and bedroom) for its ample supply of buttercups. The tiny yellow flowers were interlaced across his outfit, so that he resembled a snowfall upon a meadow; there were petals clinging to the fringes of his socks, ruff, collars and hems, and an intertwined bib of them encrusted his throat and chest. As Simone navigated the forest path towards the House of All Seasons, he left a trail of yellow petals in his wake.

The forest to the left of the path bathed in the heat of summer, lush and vibrant. The forest to the right of the path, however, was deep in the grip of winter, cold and lifeless. Grasses swished tall and green to Simone's left, and frost crackled the roots and branches of the leafless trees to Simone's right, and he tried his best to keep as close to the summer forest as possible without spoiling his outfit. Obviously, the hard ground, and lack of insects and foliage, of the winter forest was friendlier to fashionistas (except for the low branches of the trees, which threatened to snag at Simone's delicate clothes), but the sheer chill of it was enough to make his knees tremble if he drew too close. The heat of the summer forest was a kind comfort, but Simone dared not leave the path; shadowy animal shapes moved among the trees, and bulbous insects bobbed and hummed, and those same snagging branches as the winter forest were still there, just better disguised beneath layers of leaves. Only the path was without peril, a meandering river of red bricks. It was wide enough for a person to walk along, but far too thin for any sort of vehicle (except for a motorbike, perhaps, but motorbikes were not currently in fashion), and Simone wondered how Karpa Fishh managed to get to and from his property.

At last, the rooftops of the House of All Seasons came into view ahead, and Simone admired them. The house was very tall, and had all manner of towers and turrets, each one seeming to exist in a different season. There was a summer tower, so encrusted with vines that it was completely green, and birds wheeled around it. A rooftop conservatory gleamed as if in the warmth of spring, its panes splintered by all the tiny flowers emerging from its overfilled interior. A set of small trees were planted up on a turret, their leaves all the colours of autumn, dancing in a cooler breeze. And there was a long set of cold tiles heaped with snow, sharp icicles hanging from the lip. The colour in all the spring, summer and autumn sections of the house was in stark contrast to the winter sections, which sent a chill down the back of Simone's neck; they were colourless, frosty and dead.

Only the suggestion of warm firelight in some of the windows offered any comfort.

When Simone reached the front gates of the house, they were shut tight. The right gate was slick with ice and looked impassable, but the left gate was so thick with vines that Simone considered the possibility of trying to climb it. Only the deadly-looking spikes atop the gate, and running all the way across the tall wall surrounding the house, discouraged him. There were no buttons, or levers, or pulleys; these gates were designed to keep anyone but the designer himself at bay, affording him the luxury of privacy (which made sense – he would no doubt be fending off an endless supply of sycophants were he to leave his gates ajar).

Simone had to find another way in.

The summertime forest still felt like the most plausible route. Simone imagined a back gate somewhere in its depths, leading to a small cottage with a little garden. Yet, as Simone took his first few tentative steps among the trees, he knew he would not get very far. The grasses were too tall, and the bushes too robust, and the air too replete with insects, which wove unpredictable dances and offered no easy way through. Resigned to having to navigate the winter forest, it was then that Simone noticed a dragonfly perched upon a toadstool. The dragonfly was so lovely that he crouched down to see it better, and it really was wonderful – its wings shimmered ethereally, and Simone could see himself reflected in its mirrored eyes – but it was also quite obviously mechanical; its wings were joined to its body with tiny hinges. Turning about, Simone began to examine the rest of the summer forest, and was delighted to see that it was all synthetic. The grasses waved not in the breeze, but to the rhythm of an algorithm delivered to the miniature engines at their roots, and a mechanical fox peered curiously from between the branches, glass eyes agleam, and the wings of the butterflies were made of a lace even more delicate than Simone's dress. Most interesting of all were the leaves in the trees, the mechanical designs of which were so intricate that Simone could not immediately guess at their purpose. It was only when he had returned to the path, and could see the summer forest laid out before him, that he realised the leaves were designed for every season. In summer they were fully unfurled, but in autumn they could be flushed with changing colours, and in winter they could be withdrawn into their branches, and in spring they could be made to bud and unfurl.

The myriad seasons of the House of All Seasons were not fixed. They could be changed.

This was a dazzling revelation. Of course, the very idea of the House of All Seasons was extraordinary; that a designer could live in any season he chose, to better predict coming fashions. But the sheer grandiosity of being able to alter those seasons at will – to speed them up, or reverse them, or stop them altogether – spoke to the brilliance of its designer. This was fashion technology far beyond anything available to mere fashionites. This was fashion at its most cutting edge. In effect, Karpa Fishh had invented a kind of aesthetic time travel, allowing him to cycle through seasons on command, and exist in a place where multiple seasons could unfold at once, each at a different pace. Simone was in awe. No wonder Karpa Fishh's gates were closed to visitors; he could barely imagine what other wonders and secrets were installed on the other side.

Having deemed the summer forest impassable, Simone hugged himself close and ventured into the winter forest. The ground crackled frostily beneath his shoes, his breath steamed into the chill air, and his teeth chattered so hard that he worried he might break a tooth. Still he persevered, ducking and weaving among the barren branches of the trees, and skirting the snowdrifts piled up against the wall. Dark shapes moved in this measure of forest as well, but Simone was not afraid of them; he knew now that it was all aesthetic; there was no real danger to him here. Already, the petals woven into his lace outfit were crisping and crumbling away, leaving frozen yellow flakes in his wake. Simone stumbled hastily on, hoping that an autumn or spring forest awaited him ahead.

Just as Simone felt as if his bones might shiver out of his skin, the trees parted to reveal a lake. The far side of the lake was indeed in autumn, and the reds and oranges of its leaves were a comfort to poor, freezing Simone. The house rose up to his left, revealed fully for the first time, and it was such a resplendent mixture of seasons that it thrilled Simone to behold it. The wall ended at the edge of the lake, making way for a springtime jetty engulfed in reeds, and it was there that Simone saw a way onto the grounds. The lake itself was partially frozen all the way up to the jutting edge of that jetty, and if the ice held, it might be possible for Simone to simply walk across.

Simone toed the frozen edge of the lake. This close to the winter forest, the ice was thick and solid, and did not so much as crackle. Placing the full weight of one shoe upon it, Simone was pleased to find that the coating of snow made it sticky enough that he did not slip. Quickly, before he became too discouraged, Simone crunched out onto the lake, all too aware of the freezing-cold water sloshing around beneath the ice. The jetty was not too far away; it would only take a few moments to rush across and mount the welcoming wood.

There was a cracking sound as Simone's foot crunched down on a thin piece of ice.

Windmilling his arms to retain his balance, Simone slid forwards onto a slick section of ice, narrowly avoiding the cracks he was causing with his every movement. The closer he got to the springtime jetty, the less snow there was, and the thinner the ice became. A little water was spilling out from the cracks, so he rushed quicker, dancing to keep his balance. The jetty was so close now – only a few more steps away.

The ice lurched perilously beneath him, and great chunks started to separate. Water splashed at Simone's ankles, but there was no going back. Using his momentum to drive him forward, Simone leapt from chunk to chunk, feeling each one wobble beneath his slippery feet. Silvery things slid around in the waters – fishes, no doubt – and Simone held his breath as he hurtled unsteadily forward. With one last tremendous leap, Simone soared over the water and landed heavily upon the jetty, sending yellow petals flying in a gust.

Breathless, he turned to see the thin ice break up completely, floes bobbing away in every direction. A trail of yellow petals clung to their surfaces. Simone's heart pounded against his ribs, sending a fierce heat through him that banished the cold, and he clung hold of the wood so tightly that it was a wonder splinters did not break his skin. Only when his heart slowed at last did he dare to breathe and celebrate his victory. There was no way he would have dared such a crossing before his time in prison – the likelihood of negatively affecting one's attire by performing such physical exertion was extremely pronounced – but here he was, safely within the grounds of the House of All Seasons. And it was time to find Karpa Fishh.

Wobbling on newborn foal legs, Simone made his way through the spring garden, wading carefully through beds of daffodils. This close, the house loomed as tall as the mountains surrounding the valley, and its many turrets and towers dwarfed Simone. At last, he came to the hard gravel path that led to the front doors, passing between a warm summer fountain, its wavering depths filled with shimmering carp, and a chill winter fountain, its frosted depths filled with gleaming frozen carp. One of the doors was in summer, and the other was in winter, just like the gates, and the doors were shut tight, just like the gates.

Taking a few steps back, Simone beheld the heights of the house, hoping he might be able to spot Karpa Fishh and draw his esteemed attention with a wave. The sills of the winter windows were heavy with snow, and the summer windows were open wide, curtains billowing, and the spring windows were running with rain exclusive to their panes, and the autumn windows were each cracked slightly ajar, wafting a comforting warmth, and Karpa Fishh was in none of them. Stepping back further (and taking care to not trip into one of the fountains), Simone peered at the tips of the towers and turrets, and it was there that he spotted the designer. There was a glass observatory built into the side of a tower, its edges bursting with fresh green growth. The panes of the observatory were hexagonal, refracting Karpa Fishh's handsome silhouette and making it look as if he were trapped in the eye of an insect. Some of the windows were levered open, and all manner of colourful birds dipped and whirled around it, calling prettily, and Simone knew his voice would never carry that far.

He would have to find a way up to the crystal observatory.

Thankfully, there were no more forests to trip through, only lawns and flower beds. Venturing past orchards in every season, their fruits engorged or rotting or budding, Simone came to a winter conservatory, snow heaped up against its thick glass panes. Frost crackled all the way across it, distorting the statues inside, and Simone was pleased to find one of the outer doors was slightly ajar. No amount of delicate tugging was making it move, however, leaving him with limited space to squeeze inside. As such, Simone slowly slipped through the gap, taking care not to snag his lace on the door. Inside, melancholy statues posed over crisp, dead trees with icicles hanging from their noses, and Simone rushed through to prevent any icicles from forming on his own nose. Luckily, the door inside was unlocked.

Simone stepped into a summer kitchen, so abruptly warm that it made him shiver, a shower of yellow petals falling from his outfit. Every window was open, and upon every windowsill was a hot fruit pie, cooling in the warm air. The counter-tops and tables were bursting with all kinds of sorbets and trifles and blancmanges, and pastries dripping with berries so richly glazed that they glistened in the bright sunshine. Simone briefly wondered how long it had been since he last ate, but he supposed it didn't matter so much; he would eat later. He didn't want to insult Karpa Fishh by disturbing the aesthetic sensuousness of his food.

Emerging into the central hallway, Simone was confronted by the staircase. The staircase was beautiful – there was no denying it – but it also presented a challenge to anyone hoping to climb. The problem was that there was a river running down it, its banks (the bannisters) richly green, its silvery flow so silken. The river was in summer, which did not make the climb entirely unappealing (at least the waters would be warm), but Simone knew his delicate shoes and socks would be ruined by the ascent. Approaching Karpa Fishh with sodden garments was questionable. Still, there was nothing for it. Simone was running out of time if his plan was going to be successful. The wedding was less than a day away.

Tiny green growths wavered in the current, emerging from the drenched carpet, and Simone squelched through the river. Each step was slightly slick, and he was fighting against the flow, so the going was slow, but eventually – one sodden step at a time – Simone managed to ascend all the way up to the first floor. There, he waded out of the river (sending frogs tumbling from their perches) and paused on the landing to survey the next flight.

Socks dripping, Simone saw the steps leading up to the second floor, and knew he was stuck.

The next flight of steps still had a river running down them, but this river was in winter, and was frozen solid. No snow or sticky frost clung to these icy surfaces – each step was a solid, slippery mess of ice, and so many clusters of sharp icicles hung from the bannisters that Simone knew his outfit would be shredded by any attempted ascent. Still, he had made it this far, and his progress had filled him with determination. There must be another way up, somewhere.

As he went to search for alternative routes, Simone considered how Karpa Fishh must navigate his own home. He imagined the designer changing a staircase season with the wave of a hand; carpeting it with the dying leaves of autumn, perhaps, and crunching from floor to floor.

The first door Simone tried led into a noisy autumnal aviary, brimming with cages and warm with the smell of cinnamon. Birds of every colour flicked their feathers and sang their songs proudly, and Simone quickly closed the door; there were no visible stairs or ladders in the room. Through the next door was a large ballroom, filled with trees on the cusp of spring, their branches budding in the bright light gushing through the enormous glass windows, and it was there that Simone saw a way up. Some of the trees were so tall that they were built into the ceiling, and there were gaps large enough for someone to pass through if they were to climb the branches.

But first, there was the problem of his ruined footwear.

Simone sat at the grand piano (the trunk of a tree passing through its body) and unlaced his sodden shoes. The laces were very complicated, and freeing his feet took a lot of wiggling, but it felt good to slide his sodden socks from his soles. Wriggling his toes (which were immaculate – he had treated himself to a comprehensive pedicure earlier in the day) in the sunlight, he admired the prawn tattoo. The tattoo was crude, and did not match his outfit at all, but Simone found that he did not mind it being on show; in fact, he quite liked being able to see it, because it reminded him of his love for Georgie, and how beautiful she was.

Leaving his socks and shoes on the piano lid, and locating the most likely tree, Simone began to climb.

The branches were rough against his palms and soles, and Simone was careful to make sure each could hold his weight. So determined was he to reach Karpa Fishh that he almost made it all the way to the distant ceiling before glancing down. Tiny yellow petals tumbled from his clothes, spiralling to the hardwood floor, but Simone swallowed against his dizziness and pushed on, through the gap in the ceiling and into the room beyond.

Simone emerged into a tall autumn library, where the leaves of the trees were flushed orange and yellow, and a faint, chill breeze rustled the pages of the books laid out on the tables. Pausing to catch his breath upon a rich leather-bound chair, Simone observed the titles of the books, and realised they were catalogues for fabrics and materials of every description conceivable. Flicking through a nearby tome, Simone saw detailed descriptions for the treatment of various velvets, and was thrilled. Here, in these walls, was such a wealth of designer knowledge that Simone desperately wanted to stay and enrich his mind with all the fabulous secrets of fabrics. Yet, he knew he must press on. The safety of Georgie and the child were at stake.

Reluctantly, Simone made his way to the second-floor landing. This time, the staircase leading upwards was in spring, but it was equally as impassable as the winter stairs. The river frothed and splashed fiercely down the steps, infused with snow-melt and tiny shards of ice. Again, Simone would have to find another way around. Feeling the ache in his arms and legs from his climb, Simone hoped there would be an easier way up, but room after room revealed nothing but fascinating curiosities: an autumnal chamber devoted to harvesting spider silk; a winter bedroom with a roaring fireplace; an enormous springtime bathroom, with a steady haze of rain falling from the ceiling. It was only at the very rear of a summer study, beyond its wide balcony windows, that Simone found a means of ascending further.

A veil of thick summer vines clung to the exterior stonework of the tower, leading two floors up, all the way to the base of the glass observatory. The problem was that Simone was already two floors up, and even grabbing hold of the vines meant leaning out over the balcony. Still – at this point, Simone was so buzzing with momentum that he felt as if he could do anything, and the vines looked gentle enough that they would not affect his outfit. All it would take was a little more climbing, he reasoned, and he would reach his goal.

Mounting the stone railing, Simone leaned over and took two great handfuls of vines. Then, he swung out and let them take his weight. It was only as he was dangling over the drop – the summer and winter forests sweeping out dramatically behind him – that he realised his arms were barely strong enough to hold him. Scrabbling with his feet, his toes managed to find purchase on the stone, and there Simone paused, knuckles white, eyes wide, attempting to determine whether he might be able to swing back to the balcony. But it was too late: there was no way back; he was too far out. The only means of saving himself from plummeting to the gardens below was to climb the rest of the way up the tower.

Grabbing bunches of vines, and curling his toes tightly into the stones, Simone heaved. Arms trembling with the effort, he ascended. Yellow petals tumbled from his outfit, and the vines creaked warningly, but they held, and so did he – arm over arm, pulling himself towards his distant goal, two floors up. Ahead, he could see the lip of another balcony.

There was a tearing sound as a handful of vines came loose, sending Simone swinging. Screaming and flailing, he let the torn vines go and grabbed for anything, finding yet more vines. His second handful held, and he clung hold with all his might, shaking with the effort. Then, before his arms gave out altogether, he continued his climb.

The rest of the ascent felt as though it took years – as if the vines might wither into autumn if he took much longer (which, he supposed, they might). Yet eventually his fingers scraped against the far balcony, and with several more hoisting heaves, he tumbled onto the safety of its flagstones and there lay in the baking sun, breathing heavily, arms numb. Simone was suddenly so grateful for every moment he had spent out in the prison yard, pumping the tiny weights that were so fashionable to the prisoners.

Birds circled overhead, their colours brilliant in the bright sky.

When Simone's vision no longer wheeled, he pulled himself, wobbling, up to his feet, and took his bearings. The observatory was nearby, with a shallow set of stone steps leading up to it, and this close he could see some of the telescopes bristling at its edges: silver and copper and brass. Among them wandered the handsome silhouette of Karpa Fishh. Taking a deep breath,

Simone approached the nearest windowpane (made reflective in the bright sunlight) to survey his outfit.

Of course, it was ruined.

There were a thousand tiny tears in the lace, and patches of it had been stained green. Loose leaves clung to Simone's hair, and what few tiny petals were still interlaced in the fabrics of his outfit were drooping and ripped. There were beads of sweat across his brow, cracking his powder, and his mascara had run slightly. And yet… Simone found that he did not mind the mess he had made of himself. There was something pleasing about it – as if his outfit now represented his perilous journey through the house instead of the fashion it had been designed for. It was a new kind of beauty – one he was unfamiliar with.

Removing the tiny leaf that had become tangled in his lashes, Simone advanced.

The doors into the observatory were open, and he stepped into a scene of spring freshness. Birds flitted beyond the hexagonal windows, and telescopes were arranged to observe every angle of the sky and the city beyond. This far from the city, the darkness of its depths was obscured by shining towers, and the spiderweb of vibro-rail tracks across it. And among the telescopes strolled Karpa Fishh, taking leisurely glances through lenses.

Karpa Fishh was wearing only a luxurious green lace robe, exposing his chest, and there was a wreath of leaves entwined through his hair, shifting from season to season so quickly that the crown was hypnotising to behold. The leaves of the wreath budded a bright green, and then bloomed a deep green, and then flushed orange and yellow, before shrivelling into a dark, crinkled mass that budded bright green again, in an endless loop of passing seasons.

Simone cleared his throat.

Startled, Karpa Fishh turned from his telescopes. "Simone? Is that you?"

Simone smiled as sweetly as he could. "Karpa."

Karpa Fishh's immaculate features curled into a frown. "How did you get in?"

"Across the lake. I hope you don't mind."

"Of course not. But how did you get all the way up here?"

"I climbed." Simone turned on the spot, presenting his outfit in full.

Shaking his head, Karpa Fishh laughed and made his way over to a table, upon which stood a crystal decanter filled with a rich green liquid. Pouring two glasses, he offered one across.

"Why didn't you just use the elevator?" he asked, gesturing at the corner of the room.

Simone turned to see that there was indeed an elevator embedded in the tower.

Taking the glass, Simone sipped. The liquid, whatever it was, tasted of spring, and he could feel the single sip immediately fill him with an awakening chill, spreading out from his chest.

"Thank you," he said.

"You are full of surprises," said Karpa Fishh. "Now. Why are you here? And where have you been? I haven't seen you in months!"

Taking another long sip of the green substance, Simone felt the breeze of it gust through him, strengthening him after his perilous journey. Then, he began to explain everything. He told

Karpa Fishh about his petty rivalry with Justine, and the child he had so recently found affection for. He told Karpa Fishh about his transformative time in prison, and the trial. And last of all, he told Karpa Fishh his plan. His plan to protect his beloved family from Justine by destroying her once and for all.

When he was done, Karpa Fishh turned back to his view of the city, eyes distant.

"Will you help me?" asked Simone.

Karpa Fishh sipped at his drink. "Yes," he said softly. "I think I will."

* * *

The city was resplendent.

There was something about fashionable weddings that roused the unfashionables. They hid their crude homes behind streams of bunting, and dressed in what Simone assumed were their finest clothes, and a few of them even wore cosmetics. They stood beyond the white velvet cordons lining the streets, waving little flags and cheering as the glitterati passed them by, and from the rear of his carriage Simone admired them. Today, he saw them in a new light; it was their sweat and labour that made his beauty (and the beauty of all the glitterati) possible. The sun was bright in the sky, the pigeons puffed their pretty chests, enormous flags billowed in the breeze, suspended from the silver vibro-rail tracks above, and Simone felt electric.

The only thing that could ruin his plan now was the horses.

There was no denying that the proud beasts pulling his

carriage along were aesthetically pleasing – each was a tall white specimen with a flowing mane, and they snickered to each other, as if sharing little morsels of gossip. Indeed, he rather enjoyed the way their powerful muscles moved beneath their shining coats – it reminded him of watching Darlington at the gym. They just made him nervous in the same way that fish made him nervous; because as beautiful as they were, they were unpredictable, and prone to acts of ugliness, and Simone's plan would only work if he maintained absolute decorum. The last thing he needed was for one of the horses to shower the road with dung. Back at the stables, he had specifically requested two starved horses, and was glad to see the jutting ribs of the two attached to his carriage. He glared at their swishing tails, willing them to remain constipated.

The carriage rounded a corner, and the cathedral came into view.

Of course, the cathedral had been transformed for the wedding. A blizzard of white confetti whirled around it like summertime snow, and organ music played out for the demi-fashionables amassed at its base. There were endlessly more demi-fashionables than usual, and every single one of them was wearing a past-season wedding dress. The crowds heaved tightly against the velvet barriers, their enormous dresses competing for space, and they raised their veils as Simone's carriage approached. Today, Simone was glad to see so many of them, and he raised his hand slightly, in a gesture of acknowledgement. The demi-fashionables roared at this generous admission – it was rare for the glitterati to profess having noticed any of them – and a hundred beautiful bouquets were flung into the air simultaneously, filling the sky with stray petals.

The carriage itself was made of coral, intricately dried and woven into an orchid curl, and its driver – a straight-backed, gaunt gentleman whose suit was so black and hat so tall that he looked like a beautiful dead person exhumed for the express purpose of serving the glitterati – stepped down from the forward bench and neatly unlatched the back door. There were no other carriages on the street, which was all to plan – Simone was arriving late to the wedding.

Photographers rushed from the open doors of the cathedral, cameras pointed at the carriage, hoping to snap pictures of the latecomers, and Simone took a deep breath; he was ready to face them. Leaning forward, he took Georgie's and the child's hands, and squeezed them gently. "No matter what happens," he said, "know that you are both so beautiful."

"I love you, darling," said Georgie.

"And I love you, Georgie."

"Bootiful!" cried the child.

Simone was the first to step from the coral carriage, and his wedding dress flowed prettily around him. It was composed exclusively of veils from head to toe, and each veil was so silken and thin that it shifted at the slightest breath of air so that the cheering of the demi-fashionables made it wave across his body. Veils poured across his face, so that only his eyes were unveiled, and they were painted pale and sharp to give the appearance of delicate nudity.

Karpa Fishh had meandered for hours between the summer rooms of the House of All Seasons, poaching the best billowing curtains from the open windows, and Simone had worked long into the night at the designer's dusty sewing machine, ushering them all into shape.

Photographers swarmed, lenses reflecting Simone back at himself, and he moved as if through water for them, exaggerating the shifting of his dress.

The cheers increased in volume as Georgie emerged, her wedding dress shining like a field of stars upon a white sky. It was composed of hundreds of tiny glass bottles ribboned together, each of which contained a bright firefly, painstakingly collected from the winter rooms of the House of All Seasons. Simone and Karpa Fishh had spent ages capturing them with delicate spider-silk nets, bottling each tiny body one by one, until there were enough to construct a dress out of. Then, Simone had strung them together by hand, pricking his toughened fingers repeatedly with the needle.

The bottles rolled and gently clinked as Georgie posed at the foot of the carriage, making the insects glow brighter as they tumbled to and fro, and there were further bottles dangling from her ears, and carefully ribboned into her hair, as if she were wearing all the stars in the sky. She showed the demi-fashionables and reporters and unfashionable onlookers every angle of her dress, and they responded fervently.

Last to step from the carriage was the child.

The crowds went silent. The photographers were still. All eyes beheld her.

The child wore a dress made of white petals, plucked from the spring gardens of the House of All Seasons. There were rose petals, and orchid petals, and snowdrop petals, and they were a silken mass, moving prettily as she skipped down the steps. Karpa Fishh had expressed surprise at how little material it took to make a dress for a child, and she had been wonderfully patient as Simone gently sewed the petals together across her in the first light of morning. She had continued to be patient as Georgie painted her face with cosmetics: dabbing pale lipstick across her tiny lips, drawing out her tiny lashes with a small amount of white mascara, and delicately gluing miniature petals to her face to draw out her cheekbones. Indeed, she had been positively bursting with her own beauty as she beheld herself in the mirrors of the House of All Seasons, twirling around to make her petal dress shimmer.

The child stepped out onto the white carpet between Simone and Georgie, and there struck a pose: hands on her hips, lips pouted, tiny basket at her elbow, petals falling across her tiny fingers.

"Fablus!" she exclaimed.

The crowds erupted into noise. The fingers of the photographers blurred as they vied with each other to take as many pictures as possible. Simone held his pose, and felt an unfamiliar sensation filling him up. It was the same sort of warmth he had felt when he had seen Georgie for the first time after three months in prison, but different, as if the child were awakening emotions in him he was not aware he could feel. Pride, Simone thought; it was pride. He was proud of her.

When the frenzy of photography began to abate, Simone returned to the rear of the coral carriage, and retrieved the package hidden beneath his seat. The wedding gift was large and heavy enough that he had to carry it in both arms. It was wrapped up in a pristine box sealed with a white ribbon, and as Simone advanced down the white carpet, the photographers focused on the unusually bulky present, the flashing of their cameras illuminating the mystery of its contents. At the foot of the steps, he turned, and posed with the gift, and Georgie and the child stood to either side of him, emphasising his apparent generosity.

Then, they ascended into the cathedral.

It was time to execute his plan.

The vestibule was tall, and bright, and as the noise of the crowds outside dulled down, the sound of the wedding ceremony became apparent, echoing through the alcoves. It sounded as if the vows were still being exchanged. The wedding gift was heavy in Simone's arms, but he clung to it and turned to Georgie. "You go on ahead."

"Good luck, darling." Georgie squeezed his wrist, and the child gave him a little curtsy, and then the two of them stepped into the main body of the cathedral, their footsteps fading as they found seating among the pews at the back.

Taking a deep breath to still his nerves, Simone reminded himself of his purpose. What he was about to do was for Georgie and the child. To save them from the consequences of his petty rivalry with Justine.

In the cool quiet of the vestibule, Simone set his wedding gift upon a table and pulled at the ribbon. It came free with silken smoothness, and he raised the lid of the box. In the light of the vestibule chandelier, the contents glittered ethereally.

Running his fingers across the heavy fabric, Simone savoured the feeling of it. Karpa Fishh had led Simone deep into the fabric archives of the House of All Seasons to retrieve this material.

They had descended into the very heart of the house, where cool, dark winter rooms were kept in perpetual night, to keep the fabrics stored there as immaculate as possible. And it was there, in a forgotten closet, that Karpa Fishh had shown Simone his roll of midnight denim.

All the denims Simone had ever known had been ugly, hard-wearing, tough fabrics, designed for practicality over any aesthetic appeal, but this denim – the midnight denim – was remarkable. It was dyed a deep, rich navy blue so dark it might be mistaken for black, and its threading was interwoven with subtle strands of silver, to give the observer the impression that they were looking into the sky at night.

Reaching into the box, Simone hauled the heavy denim free, and unfolded it.

The dress was Simone's finest work. He had made a long gown, composed exclusively of midnight denim, last of all. Lengths of the mystical material shrouded its shoulders like a cloak made of night. It had a closed collar, and a cinched waist, and came with a length of midnight denim ribbon for one's hair. And of all the dresses Simone had made in the House of All Seasons, this one had taken him the longest. The material was inflexible and tough, and Simone knew just how uncomfortable it would be to wear. But with perseverance, and the encouragement of the legendary designer, it had come together magnificently.

The ultimate denim wedding dress.

It was so easy to remove his dress of veils. It came free smoothly and silkily, and Simone carefully folded it away into the white box. Then, he stepped into the denim dress. There were all manner of catches and zippers and buttons hidden in the intricate design, and Simone had not had much time to practise with them, making it something of a struggle to slip into. At last, when the collar was sealed around his throat, and the cuffs were tight around his wrists, he tied the ribbon into his hair. After lengthy consideration, he had decided against any more cosmetics, leaving his face tastefully nude. This gave him the aesthetic effect of making his face look like the moon in a night sky. Only, not the ugly real moon (which Simone still hated) – a beautiful moon, devoid of defects.

The vows were underway. It was time.

Simone took a deep breath and entered the cathedral proper.

Every alcove and aisle was filled with twisted acacia trees, bursting with tiny white flowers. A gentle breeze rushed around the cathedral, tugging petals loose from branches and sending them tumbling, so that they filled the air like living confetti. Yet, while the acacia trees were beautiful, it wasn't the kinetic movement of their petals keeping the room in rapture. For beneath those petals were endless rows of thorns, gleaming deadly and white in the pale light of the chandeliers. Between the trees the glitterati huddled, doing their best to remain beautiful despite the effect the trees were having on them. For they recognised, just as well as Simone did, how deadly those thorns were.

A designer by the name of Horatio Haart had been the one to develop the fashion for deadly clothes. There had indeed been something thrilling about wearing an outfit that could kill you at any moment, and during that time Simone had worn a set of Horatio Haart glass earrings filled with a potent acid that threatened to spill across his shoulders should their delicate vessels crack. The fashion had been short-lived, however, after a significant number of prominent fashionites had been killed by their outfits. But a few of Horatio Haart's more extraordinary designs still existed, among which were his fabulous acacias. It was said that Horatio Haart had spliced his trees with snakes, so that the thorns bristled with deadly venom. Simone had never seen so many in one place before, and the collective threat of them made his breath catch in his throat.

Between the trees, he could see the bride and groom.

Trevor Tremptor wore a dress made of the inert leaves of the acacias, each tiny oval painted white so that he looked as if he was wearing a flowing gown of scale mail, and both his eyelids and cheekbones fluttered with the same. Yet it was the sight of Justine that drew the eye. Her dress was made of acacia branches intricately woven together, and thorns bristled from every angle of her. Tiny white flowers were in bloom across her shoulders, and hips, and around her neck, but all else was thorns; she wore a wreathed crown of them, and each of her fingers bore a ring of them, and tiny spikes poked out from between the flowers at her throat, revealing her deadly choker. It seemed as if she would prickle herself at any moment, yet she did not, her fingers and arms flowing elegantly around her thorns. Her mastery of the deadly dress was stunning.

Simone slowly sauntered down the centre of the aisle.

The first to notice him were the glitterati at the rearmost pews. They turned their heads to glance at the latecomer, and then glanced again when they noticed what that latecomer was wearing. After that second glance, they focused completely upon him, soaking in the sight. As he advanced, Simone drew the attention of row after row.

Murmuring began. It was only a soft murmur – the gentlest ripple of aesthetic appreciation – barely disturbing the solemn ceremony, but it gradually grew in intensity as Simone approached the altar. Then, at last, it was enough to draw the attention of the bride and groom themselves.

Justine's eyes grew wide. Trevor Tremptor's brows rose.

There was a spare seat at the foremost pew, and Simone took his time lowering himself into it, giving everyone in the cathedral the chance to see his denim dress. The murmuring of the glitterati continued unabated, and the bride and groom stared openly at Simone, who was pretending to be perfectly innocent of the disturbance. Then, the officiant cleared his throat, and the murmuring ceased. The bride and groom tore their gaze from Simone's dress and resumed their vows.

Photographers stepped carefully around the trees in the aisles, converging on Simone, and it was then he knew he had been successful. All eyes in the room had turned from the fiercely deadly acacia dress to the denim dress. He had successfully upstaged Justine at her own wedding.

Simone felt… satisfied. But it was a different kind of satisfaction than the one he was used to. It wasn't a self-indulgent satisfaction in his own beauty – it was a simpler thing, born of the fact that he had done his very best to protect Georgie and the child from Justine.

There was no doubt that Simone would be on the cover of all the magazines tomorrow, but the thought gave him no pleasure.

As photographers circled, and Justine recited the remainder of her vows between clenched teeth, he realised he was weary of fashion.

Turning in his seat, he sought the sight of Georgie. There she was, at the rear of the cathedral, every bit as beautiful as the first time he had set eyes on her. And it was then that Simone realised that his life as a fashionite was over. All he wanted in the world was to go home, and be with his family and make more beautiful things. He had enjoyed making the denim dress far more than wearing it.

Simone leaned forward, so that he would be able to see the child, but to either side of Georgie the pew was empty. In fact – glancing about – Simone could not see her anywhere.

A giggle echoed through the cathedral.

The bride and groom paused, rings mid-air.

There was another bright giggle.

All eyes in the room turned to an alcove, where one of the acacia trees was moving. At the base of it was the child, all petals, tugging at a branch. With each tug, the tree swayed precariously, its bounty of needling thorns shaking.

A shriek ripped through the solemn air. It was Justine.

"Darling!" cried Trevor Tremptor, but it was too late.

Sweeping down the aisle, Justine snapped a branch from a tree.

The child continued tugging at the acacia, giggling to itself.

Brandishing her deadly sprig, Justine advanced through the pews. Glitterati scattered before her. "Is that…" she breathed, outraged, "…a *child*? Who has brought such a horrible creature to my wedding? Which one of you would *dare* ruin my special day?"

Photographers tumbled over each other, taking snap after snap.

At last, Justine reached the child, towering over her. The child continued to play, so consumed by her joy that she did not notice the shadow shading her. Raising the deadly sprig, Justine emitted another keening screech of outrage. Then, she swung.

Simone was almost too late. His own sprig was hardly as elegant as Justine's. A few flowers encrusted the end, and its thorns were meagre things. Yet it was enough to push Justine's branch aside. The two sprigs met, bouncing off each other.

"*You!*" cried Justine, incensed.

The child, noticing the furore at last, wandered over to Simone and took his free hand.

"Of course the child belongs to you!" snarled Justine, thorns trembling with her rage. She brandished her sprig. "You horrible, unfashionable little man! Look at you – wearing denim! You and your child are both… so… *ugly*."

Nobody had ever called Simone ugly before. It was as if Justine had pricked Simone with one of her deadly thorns. Even though Simone had fallen out with fashion, he still loved beauty. He could feel the insult bleeding into him like a poison.

"No, darling!" said a voice. "Don't listen to her! Remember that you are beautiful!" It was Georgie, advancing between the pews, the lanterns of her dress swinging.

"Quite!" cried another voice. It was Darlington, up by the altar. "You are beautiful!"

The poisonous insult was losing its potency. Simone focused on his denim wedding dress, using it like a coat of armour against the insult.

The child squeezed Simone's hand. "Bootiful," she insisted, sincerely.

Puffing out his chest, and gripping the stem of his acacia branch, Simone raised his chin defiantly. "You are wrong," he said to Justine. "We are both beautiful."

"*Ugly!*" shrieked Justine, swinging her sprig.

Dodging just in time, Simone almost stumbled into the acacia tree at his back. Retaining his balance, he let go of the child and gripped his own sprig in both hands, taking care to avoid its thorns.

Justine advanced, striking with her sprig again and again.

It was all Simone could do to simply bat it aside, gradually stepping backwards to avoid each needling blow. It would take no effort at all for a single thorn to slip through the folds of his dress, and he was almost out of room to manoeuvre.

At last, Simone felt the brush of the tree's leaves against his back. Bracing himself, he raised his sprig defensively.

"Enough!" cried a voice, so authoritative that the leaves in the trees rustled.

Justine paused, mid-swing.

All eyes turned to see Trevor Tremptor, trembling with outrage, still up on the altar.

"Enough," he repeated. "Justine, look. Look at the child."

The child was holding on to Georgie's hand, eyes wide in the light. Her dress, made of the soft white petals of spring, was in such contrast to the rest of the room. There was no deadliness to her beauty, only a gentleness; all the youth of spring.

"It's horrible," said Justine, but with less conviction than before.

"The child is clearly fabulous," said Trevor Tremptor.

"But…"

"No, Justine. The child is fabulous, and so is Simone. You are wrong."

"But…" Justine turned to the glitterati for reassurance, but was met only with hard gazes. It was true. The child was inarguably fabulous. "But it's a *child*," she insisted, "and Simone is wearing *denim*. Only unfashionables wear denim!"

"The only ugliness here," said Trevor, trembling so furiously that the leaves of his dress shivered, "is your attempt at murder."

The glitterati murmured their collective agreement. Murder was both very impolite and highly unfashionable.

"But, darling…" keened Justine.

Trevor Tremptor cast his ring aside. "I will not marry you, Justine."

"Trevor! Please!"

"Furthermore," he said with finality, "you're fired."

Justine's mouth opened and closed several times. "No," she said. Then, with more insistence, "*No*." Shaking with such outrage that petals tumbled from her shoulders, she turned on Simone. "This is your fault," she said. "This is all your fault! You and your horrible child!"

Raising her sprig, Justine lunged forward.

This time, Simone was ready. He simply stepped aside.

When Justine fell into the acacia tree, it was as if she became a part of it. The wreathed branches of her dress became the branches of the tree, and the thorns of it sank into her flesh as if they belonged there. Petals rushed down her form, impaling themselves on her as she twitched, the last of her life fleeing her.

Then, after a few brief moments, it was over, and Justine was still.

"Bootiful," said the child again, her bright eyes gleaming.

* * *

Days passed, and Simone began to do a bit of gardening.

He started small, by relocating a patch of posies from one flower bed to another. There were altogether too many leaves, and the dirt kept clinging to his knees, and no matter which material his gloves were made of (leather, latex, fur – he tried them all) his fingers always ended up filthy, but there was something deeply satisfying about untangling the roots from the earth and arranging them in a slightly more aesthetically pleasing way. There was a shed in the garden, which Simone had never before entered, inside of which were all manner of bladed instruments that he did not understand. Selecting a pair of gigantic scissors, he set to work trimming things. At first, he trimmed the hedgerows, and then he moved on to the trees, slicing off leaves and branches until they looked prettier (and given no clear instruction on how to dispose of the severed remains, he simply threw them over the balcony). Then, on a day when he was feeling particularly brave, he mounted the machine that looked like a quadbike had been equipped with several sets of eyelash curlers, and with much trial and error discovered that it was for trimming the grass, which Simone proceeded to do with much enthusiasm. Emboldened by his gardening adventures, Simone even began to explore the greenhouse. It was swelteringly hot, but full of all kinds of vegetables, and using a smaller set of scissors (which a gardening magazine had informed him were called "secateurs"), he pruned a selection, brought them into the kitchen, and proceeded to make a salad. The salad tasted mostly of chemicals, but Simone was still certain it was the most delicious salad he had ever eaten.

Sometimes the child would come outside and garden with him. She mostly just tore at things – ripping up handfuls of grass and leaves – but she would also watch Simone, wide-eyed, and attempt to copy him.

"This," Simone told her, "is what your daddy used to do."

On sunny days, Simone let her ride the lawnmower with him, and they would do a slow tour of the lawns, cutting pleasingly parallel lines through the green together.

In the end, Simone's denim dress had only made page three of the magazines. A few months ago, Justine had been the darling of the fashion world with her faux-corpse look, and Simone liked to think she would have been pleased by her actual corpse making the front page as well. For all that Justine had disgraced herself by attempting murder, the fashionable press seemed to agree that her death was fabulous. Furthermore, it was the child who had made page two of the magazines, and while it looked as if the fashion for deadly clothes was back, so too was there a new fashion for children, and yet another for denim. For a while, Georgie wore jeans. Then, fashion moved on, and so did she. Only the child remained; a new constant in their lives.

As days turned into weeks, Simone's interest in fashion magazines waned, and he began to wear kaftans even when it wasn't Tuesday. Of course he sometimes missed his corsets and suits, and occasionally dressed up for company or for Georgie, but mostly he preferred being comfortable. Georgie continued to be a bright fashionite, and Simone loved her for it. Every morning he enjoyed fashion vicariously through her – in the way she would spend so much time delighting in selecting just the right outfit for the day, and making herself so beautiful. And there were more layers to Georgie's beauty that Simone began to appreciate. It was the small things: the way she would always order tiny pastries for her friends, and took the time to flick through the magazines with the child each evening, and spent just a little longer than necessary painting her nails, luxuriating in the gentle brushing. For all her grand gestures, Simone found that it was her smallest everyday habits that made him love her the most. Thankfully, Georgie was entirely unperturbed by Simone's sudden interest in gardening (and disinterest in fashion), and even encouraged him, taking trips down to the Boulevard in search of aesthetically pleasing gardening clothes for him.

Then, one day, Simone woke to find a new room in the apartment.

There was a door in the hallway that had never been there before, and behind it was a bright space composed of empty shelves, and at the very centre of it was a table with a sewing machine. There were spools of thread, and a selection of needles, and several different kinds of scissors, and Simone gasped at the sight of it. For most of the morning, he rushed from room to room, thanking the walls in the hope that the unfashionables who maintained the apartment would be able to hear him. Then – because it was the only place he knew for certain an unfashionable would be – he ventured down to the garage with armfuls of designer shoes and left them as an offering at the driver's door of the limousine.

At first, Simone was too overwhelmed by the idea of having his very own sewing machine and did not know what to make. There were not yet any fabrics for him to work with, either.

"Lulu!" he cried, and within moments the child appeared, summoned by her new name.

Simone and Georgie had spent ever so much time considering what to call the child. Part of the problem was that she already had a (decidedly unfabulous) name, given to her by her unfashionable parents, and neither of them could bring themselves to continue burdening her with it. In the end, they had settled on a significantly more fabulous version of the child's unfashionable name, and she had taken to it immediately.

"Lulu, darling," said Simone. "Would you like me to make you a coat?"

"Coat," said Lulu.

"Very well. Go and look through my wardrobes and find some fabrics you like."

The child toddled away, and within minutes had returned with a mismatched stack of clothes. Some of the clothes were fashionable, and some of them were not, but it did not matter. Simone carefully began to dissect each suit and dress and accessory, until he had a vivid selection of fabrics with which to work.

Then, he began to sew.

Lulu clambered onto his lap, and Simone showed her what he was doing. She watched with patient fascination – the way his scissors slid through silk; the rise and fall of the sewing machine's needle; the gentle application of buttons – and Simone explained each thing as he did it, slowly teaching her everything he knew about making clothes.

The patchwork coat would never make the front of any fashion magazines, but Simone thought that it was fabulous, and Lulu appeared to think so as well. She twirled in it, making its hem whirl, and together they laughed at the mismatched colours.

The chiming of the doorbell interrupted their merriment.

Dusting off scraps and threads, Simone opened the front of the apartment to reveal Mr Vivian, his gold-leaf tie shining. "Simone," he said, with a formal smile.

"Mr Vivian! How wonderful to see you. Would you like to come inside?"

"I'm afraid that we have some rather pressing business to attend to."

Lulu wandered over and peered up at Mr Vivian from behind Simone's trouser leg.

Mr Vivian crouched and addressed her. "Hello there, Louise."

"Her name is Lulu now," said Simone.

"Ah. Lulu. Yes, of course. Hello, Lulu. I'm Mr Vivian – your guardian's lawyer."

Lulu hid behind Simone's legs.

Standing tall, Mr Vivian straightened his tie. "I have a car waiting downstairs. Would you and Lulu join me, please? This shouldn't take long."

"Of course." Taking Lulu by the hand, Simone led her into the elevator.

Soft music played through hidden speakers, and Mr Vivian

hummed along with it. “How have you been?” he asked. “Since the trial?”

“Very well, thank you. Justine is no longer an issue.”

“So I saw.”

The elevator doors pinged open and there beyond the lobby was, indeed, Mr Vivian’s town car, idling in the street. The lawyer was kind enough to open the back door for them both, and Simone shuffled inside, helping Lulu to clamber across. When Mr Vivian was also inside and sitting comfortably, the car pulled away and into the city.

“What’s this about, Mr Vivian?”

Mr Vivian, who was sitting opposite, settled one of his hands atop the other. “It has come to my attention that you refused to have your memory erased after the trial.”

“Yes,” said Simone. “I didn’t want to forget.”

“I have received further reports that you are no longer attending fashionable functions. That you appear to be losing interest in fashion altogether.”

“I have been doing some gardening,” he enthused.

Mr Vivian nodded. “Unfortunately, this cannot be allowed to continue. Thus, we are going to hospital, where your memories of the past three months will be erased.”

Simone blinked. “Pardon?”

“Please understand, Simone. You are part of a delicate system. Hundreds of people rely on your continued placidity. The contract is thus: you get to live a life of absolute luxury, your every whim catered to, and in return you remain ignorant of your overwhelming financial power.”

"You are… forcing me to have my memories erased?"

"I'm not forcing you, Simone. The choice continues to be yours. But please understand: as part of my employment I am in control of your house staff, and I have it in my power to remove many of the luxuries you and Georgie are accustomed to."

"But…" Simone was aghast. "You're my lawyer."

"My job is to work in your best interest, and trust me when I tell you that this is in your best interest. You will return to a state of blissful ignorance. You will be happy."

"I wasn't happy. Not really."

This made Mr Vivian frown. For a few moments he was quiet, and then he said, "Do you know what a tax return is, Simone?"

Simone considered the question. "Is it a kind of vehicle?"

"What about a mortgage? Do you know what a mortgage is?"

"It sounds rather unpleasant, whatever it is."

"You're right. It is unpleasant. And it's my job to oversee all the trusts, accounts and debts your family's estate owns. It is your privilege to remain ignorant of them. I can't emphasise this enough – you do not know what true unhappiness is. If you continue learning about money, you will find it overwhelming you, just like it overwhelms every unfashionable person in the city. Your whole life will become about money – the accumulation of it, the distribution of it, the endless expenditure of it. It will corrupt every part of your life."

"I don't understand."

Mr Vivian's frown deepened. "Of course you don't. How could you?" He glanced around the car's interior until his eyes settled on Lulu. "Let me try explaining the situation to you in a way you might understand, then. You love your family, yes?"

"Of course."

"And it's your job to look after them? To help them when they need it?"

"Absolutely!"

"What if I told you that all the people who work for you – all the people who decorate your house, and cook your food, and pay your taxes on your behalf – are just an extension of your family? They look after you, and in return you provide them with nice homes to live in, and nice clothes to wear, and nice food to eat."

"But how do I do that?"

Mr Vivian smiled. "It's part of a complex process that I oversee. Because, you see, I am like family to you as well. I look after your legal interests, and in return you provide me with a house, and a car, and all the nice clothes I wear."

Simone's eyes settled on Mr Vivian's tie.

"Yes. You see this tie?" Mr Vivian raised it, so that it glittered in the sunlight. "My son picked it for me. I bet you didn't know that I have a son. His name is Jason, and he is eight years old, and he is learning how to play the piano. And do you know why he is learning to play the piano? Because in return for all the work I do for you, you have given me the means to afford a piano. Thank you for my piano, Simone."

"You are quite welcome," said Simone, who did not entirely understand how he had given Mr Vivian and his son a piano, but was glad he had.

"So you see? Your family is not just you and Georgie and Lulu. Your family is the hundreds of people who work for you, and their families as well. You provide for all of us."

"And if I forget the past three months… they will be safe? You will be safe?"

"Yes, Simone." Mr Vivian breathed a sigh of relief, his golden tie shimmering in flecks of sunshine. "We will no longer have to worry about you and any potentially ruinous financial whims you might have. One quick trip to the hospital, and all will continue just as it did before."

Lulu huddled in closer to Simone, fingers clutching at his waist.

"What about Lulu?"

"Lulu is going to school." Mr Vivian smiled at her. "She will learn everything she needs to join fashionable society. Then, sixteen years from now, she will be returned to you, with her memories of her upbringing completely erased. And when you die, she will inherit your fortune, and all those who rely on your family's wealth – all those who are like an extended family to you – will continue to live well."

Lulu's little fists bunched, and her lower lip trembled.

"I don't think she wants to go," said Simone, and the truth was that he didn't want her to go either. Not for sixteen years.

"Trust me," said Mr Vivian, his eyes tracing the streets beyond the windows of the town car. "This is in her best interest."

* * *

Reluctantly, Simone removed his clothes.

The hospital changing room was smooth and bright, and on the walls were racks of gowns. Simone took his time, folding his nice comfortable clothes into a pile and selecting the best among the identical white gowns to wear. Mr Vivian was gone now – escorting Lulu to school – and Georgie was elsewhere in the city, blissfully unaware of what was happening. The only consolation Simone had was that he was continuing to protect Georgie. By allowing Mr Vivian to take Lulu to school, and by erasing all of his memories of the arrest, and prison, and the trial, Simone would be allowing her to continue living the life she loved so much. And Simone would join her in living that life, returning to the state of anxious vanity he had been so accustomed to. Then, sixteen years from now, Lulu would return, a fully-fledged fashionite, and they would all be glitterati together, glorious and beautiful.

Gown successfully draped over his weary form, Simone slumped. It was, so far as he could remember, the first slump he had ever done in his life. He lowered himself into one of the plush white chairs at the centre of the changing room, and let his every limb relax, until he felt as if he were made of liquid. It was a wonder he didn't slide from the chair.

The door slid open, and there was…

Nobody.

Simone blinked. He had been expecting Dr Cask, clipboard in hand, ready to lead him through to the room with the chrome motorbike helmets. Instead, the door remained open for a few moments, and then swished shut again.

With a sigh, Simone returned to his slump.

There was a sound like somebody crushing glass, and part of the air in the room began to shift. Simone stared in awe as plates slid apart, revealing a figure beneath what appeared to be a lengthy cloak composed of misaligned mirror panes. Except the mirror panes were not reflective; instead, they rendered the wearer absolutely invisible. It was the same fashion technology as Justine's mansion except, instead of hiding a house, this technology hid a designer.

"Karpa Fishh!" cried Simone.

His hair was frosted silver, and he wore a great many glittering silver rings, and he pressed a single finger to his lips, which were, just like his brows and lashes, encrusted with tiny pieces of mirrored glass. "Hush, now," he said. "I'm not meant to be here."

"Dearest Karpa – it's ever so good to see you!"

"I came as soon as I heard. You're lucky I have friends on staff here." Karpa Fishh advanced to crouch before Simone, the mirror-pane cloak rendering most of him invisible. "We don't have much time. I'm here to rescue you."

"Rescue me?"

"Yes. You don't want to forget everything, do you?"

"Of course not. But Mr Vivian said…"

Karpa Fishh shook his head, making his lips glitter. "Don't worry about whatever it was Mr Vivian told you. He would have said anything to get you here. Mr Vivian's job is to make sure you never make any real decisions, so that he and the rest of your legal and financial team can continue profiting from you. This, now – this is your chance to make an actual decision. What do you want, Simone? Do you want to go back to living as a fashionite?"

"No," said Simone softly.

"I didn't think so."

"But it's too late. They've already taken Lulu."

"Lulu." Karpa Fishh smiled. "What a pretty name." The designer drew his cloak closer around himself, so that only his face was visible. "I have a modest yacht waiting at the quay. If you want to retain your memories and continue growing in the way you are, you may. But it comes at a price. You cannot stay in the city. You will have to leave."

"What about Georgie? And Lulu?"

"I can have them both delivered to you at the yacht. But understand, Simone – there's no going back from this. You only have two options. Either stay here and return to your fashionable life, or leave and try to find a new life for yourself."

"Why can't I stay?"

"As much influence as I have," said Karpa Fishh, "I can't protect you from those who profit from you. They will destroy you to preserve their income." He glanced up at the ceiling with a wistful expression, as if he were appraising the city beyond it. "You represent real change, and this city abhors change."

One last time, Simone considered allowing himself to be glitterati again. Day after day of nothing but fashion. Georgie would be happy, and so would he, in a way. But everything about that life felt so distant now. "Karpa, darling. Why are you doing this?"

One hand emerged from beneath the mirrored cloak, silver nails glinting. "For a while, I thought you might be a new designer," he said. "This city loves designers. We imagine beautiful things for people to wear, and they are made manifest. But you're not a designer. You're something else altogether."

"What am I?"

"You're an artist, darling."

"An artist?"

"Yes. I didn't see it at first, because you express your art through fashion. A nosebleed at a party. A beautiful lemon, brought to the beach. A vintage dress made of spider silk. I thought you were designing these things, but you weren't. You were *feeling* them. The nosebleed was a gorgeous accident. The lemon was an appreciation of a perfect specimen. The vintage dress was defiance – defiance of your rival, in the face of fashion convention. I only realised what you were doing when you explained your denim wedding dress to me. You didn't make it because it would be a beautiful piece of clothing – you made it out of love, to protect your family. Design is a type of art, yes – a functional and commodifiable art – but you don't create for function. You don't create to start new fashions. You create because you feel, and you want to express those feelings."

Simone looked down at his hands, still calloused from his time in prison. "I'm not sure I quite understand."

"That's all right. Maybe one day you will." Standing tall, Karpa Fishh parted his mirrored cloak, revealing enough room for two. "I have furnished my yacht with staff I trust. They will keep you safe, and make sure you arrive wherever you want to go."

"Thank you, Karpa," said Simone, ducking under the designer's arm. "You are easily the most fabulous person I have ever met."

The mirrored cloak enveloped them both.

* * *

In reality, Karpa Fishh's yacht was far from modest.

It was about the length of an aircraft carrier, and featured three tiered floors above the deck, each bursting with greenery. From the quay, Simone could see at least two tennis courts, a swimming pool the size of a small lake, and the faux-ruins of a castle. A small waterfall sparkled prettily as it ran from the edge, splashing into the ocean below, and the whole thing looked as if someone had crammed the contents of several picturesque landscape portraits into a boat. There were other yachts moored at the quay, of course, but they were dwarfed by Karpa Fishh's floating island, which was not so much an island as a small continent. There was a very real threat that, when the yacht moved, the waves it would create would smash every other boat in the quay to pieces.

"I designed it myself," said Karpa Fishh, his mirrored cloak sparkling like the ocean.

And there was Lulu, running down the gangplank, her patchwork coat whirling around her, tears still streaming from her eyes. Behind her strode two figures dressed from head to toe in what looked like a cross between medieval armour and Karpa Fishh's mirror cloak. The plates of their armour made them difficult to see, and Simone imagined that, much like Justine's house, they could become completely invisible if they wished to. Each also held a rifle that looked as if it were made of pieces of shattered glass. "Dearest Karpa," said Simone, "you simply must tell me how to get hold of a suit of that armour. It's fabulous."

"My private security," said Karpa Fishh.

Lulu ran all the way up to Simone and hugged his leg.

"There, there." Simone crouched, and took her in his arms. "No more school for you. We're going on a trip. A wonderful trip away from the city."

"Boat," said Lulu, pointing at the yacht.

"Yes, darling. Big boat." Simone turned back to Karpa Fishh. "What about Georgie?"

As if on cue, there were a series of shimmering crackles nearby, and three more glassy figures appeared, as if the air were crystallising. Two of them were members of Karpa Fishh's private security, also clad in mirrored armour, but the third was dressed in the same shimmering cloak as the designer, and emerged from beneath it.

The fashion was for scales, and Georgie was dressed in a pale yellow snakeskin suit. There was a certain oily quality to the way it moved, and there were wisps of white threaded across the pattern of it, so that the beholder might mistake it for a laminated map of a desert. She wore a matching pair of oversized yellow sunglasses, which she lowered at the sight of Simone and Lulu. "Simone? What's going on? These gentlemen told me I was to be meeting Karpa Fishh!"

The designer advanced, glittering hands emerging from beneath his glittering cloak.

"Georgie. It's good to see you again."

"Karpa!" Georgie air-kissed him.

"Georgie," said Simone. "We don't have much time."

"Much time for what, dearest heart?"

Simone took a deep breath. "I'm afraid that Lulu and I must leave the city."

"Whyever so?"

"Because if I stay, I will have some of my favourite memories taken from me, and Lulu will be sent to school for sixteen years."

Georgie slid her sunglasses into her breast pocket. "How utterly dreadful!"

"Thankfully, Karpa has offered us a yacht upon which to make our escape."

At last, Georgie noticed the yacht. "That is an enormous yacht."

"It is," Simone agreed. "Would you like to come with us?"

Georgie frowned. "Come with you?"

"Yes, darling. You would have to leave everything behind. But we can have a new life, out there, beyond the horizon, and make new memories that no one can take from us."

Georgie glanced at the yacht, and at Simone and Lulu, and at Karpa Fishh, and then at the city beyond them all. In the bright summer sun, the silver towers of the city gleamed, and the vibro-rail tracks were looped silver threads running through and around them.

"But… what about fashion?"

"We can make our own fashions," said Simone. "Together."

"Oh." Georgie instantly brightened. "That sounds pleasant."

Taking Georgie's hand, Simone kissed her firmly on the cheek. "I love you, darling."

"And I love you. But we simply must find you something a little less revealing to wear."

Glancing down, Simone noticed that he was still dressed in his hospital gown. Thankfully, it was a hot day, and the slow breeze gusted warmly around his nethers.

"I think we're ready now, Karpa."

The designer nodded. "Sergeant," he said, to one of the four identical mirror-armoured men. "You are dismissed." And at that simple command, all four of them shimmered into invisibility, leaving Karpa alone on the quay. "The yacht is yours," he said, to Simone and Georgie and Lulu. "I do hope you'll send letters. I look forward to hearing all about your new life."

"Thank you for everything," said Simone.

Karpa Fishh smiled. "You are most welcome."

At Lulu's insistent tugging, Simone and Georgie mounted the gangplank and ascended onto the deck of the yacht. There was a garden immediately on deck, and nearby was what looked like a small spa, staffed with stiff unfashionables. From here, Simone could see bottles of champagne bubbling. The gangplank automatically withdrew behind them, and with the slightest of shudders the yacht began to move.

At the railing, Simone called: "Goodbye, Karpa Fishh!"

The designer waved a handkerchief that looked as if it were made of crushed glass. "Farewell!" he cried. Then, with the shimmering of his mirror-pane cloak, he was gone.

THE END

ACKNOWLEDGEMENTS

There are many people to blame for this book.

Chiefly responsible is George Sandison, who first commissioned *Glitterati* as a short story in 2017, and then decided to pick it up as a full-length novel for Titan. This book would also not have been possible without Tam Moules' continued enthusiasm and good advice. Davi Lancett helped me to untangle the last act, and Lydia Gittins delivered some encouragement at a critical moment. Julia Lloyd is the reason why this book looks as fabulous as it does. And Hayley Shepherd and Kev Eddy worked hard to make sure that Simone's world is as consistently glamorous as it is.

Without Ross Weryk, this book would never have been written.

ABOUT THE AUTHOR

Oliver K. Langmead lives and writes in Glasgow. His long-form poem, *Dark Star*, featured in the *Guardian*'s Best Books of 2015, and he is currently a doctoral candidate at the University of Glasgow, where he is researching terraforming and ecological philosophy. In late 2018 he was the writer in residence at the European Space Agency's Astronaut Centre in Cologne.

ALSO AVAILABLE FROM TITAN BOOKS

THE SHADOW GLASS

Josh Winning

***Dark Crystal* meets *About a Boy* in a race against the clock to save the world in this nostalgia-infused adventure!**

Jack Corman is failing at life. Jobless, jaded and on the "wrong" side of thirty, he's facing the threat of eviction from his London flat while reeling from the sudden death of his father, one-time film director Bob Corman. Back in the eighties, Bob poured his heart and soul into the creation of his 1986 puppet fantasy *The Shadow Glass*, a film Jack loved as a child, idolising its fox-like hero Dune.

But *The Shadow Glass* flopped on release, deemed too scary for kids and too weird for adults, and Bob became a laughing stock, losing himself to booze and self-pity. Now, the film represents everything Jack hated about his father, and he lives with the fear that he'll end up a failure just like him.

In the wake of Bob's death, Jack returns to his decaying home, a place creaking with movie memorabilia and painful memories. Then, during a freak thunderstorm, the puppets in the attic start talking. Tipped into a desperate real-world quest to save London from the more nefarious of his father's creations, Jack teams up with excitable fanboy Toby and spiky studio executive Amelia to navigate the labyrinth of his father's legacy while conjuring the hero within—and igniting a Shadow Glass resurgence that could, finally, do his father proud.